"22 DAYS HATH NOVEMBER"

A Novel By

ROBERT DORFF

Copyright 2006 – by Robert Dorff
PaU3-024-391 – PaU3-045-098 – PaU3-096-415
PaU3-107-842 ISBN 978-1-4243-3827-6
R-5C

FOR MARY ELIZABETH FERRELL

The author Bob Dorff
with Mary Elizabeth
at JFK Conference,
Dallas 1991

"We live lives based upon selected fictions.
Our view of reality is conditioned by our
position in space and time -- not by our
personalities as we like to think. Thus every
interpretation of reality is based upon a
unique position.
Two paces to the east or west and the whole
picture is changed. In the end everything will
be found out to be true of everybody."

--Lawrence Durrell

TABLE OF CONTENTS:

PREAMBLE:

The early sixties began with a lie -- and ended with a lie.

In May 1960 President Eisenhower went on television to "explain" that a high altitude American U-2 aircraft shot down over the Soviet Union had strayed off course while collecting weather data.

When irrefutable evidence presented by Russian Premier Nikita Khruschev revealed the downed craft's sophisticated camera equipment and its advanced espionage technology, Eisenhower went back on television and admitted he'd lied.

It was a costly one. Not only was Eisenhower's integrity tarnished, an indignant Khruschev promptly canceled a summit meeting scheduled for June.

Eisenhower's lie is long forgotten.

For those of us who were around in November 1963, lies our government told us about the murder of President Kennedy will never be forgotten.

There was far more to the early sixties than government dissembling.

An ever increasing number of women took "the pill"; husbands slept with their wife's friends; an increasing number of men let their hair grow as long as "Prince Valiant"; women donned bright colored formless dresses worn above the knees, put flowers in their hair and went to civil rights rallies.

Chubby Checker gyrated and wailed:

"Come on baby, let's do the twist!"

Jackie Kennedy demonstrated to friends how to do
this new dance: "Pretend you're using a towel to dry
your back."
Filmmaker's Otto Preminger and Kirk Douglas defied
Hollywood's "Blacklist" by placing writer Dalton
Trumbo's name on the screen as the author of
"Exodus" and "Spartacus" -- because he was.

In the South segregation was under relentless
assault by "freedom riders" and organizations
dedicated to the proposition that black people
were just as entitled to sit at the same lunch
counters and use the same tax supported facilities
as whites.

A twenty-two year old from Hibbing, Minnesota wrote
"protest songs" which resonated around the country
and around the world.

Bob Dylan's powerful and poetic observations about
life in America was an invitation to stop
listening to "Doggie In The Window" and tune into
someone with something to say.

In August 1963 singers Joan Baez, Peter, Paul
and Mary and Dylan marched on Washington with
Martin Luther King and an army of peaceful
protesters. They inspired the crowd with Dylan's
"Blowing In The Wind," "The Hour That The Ship
Comes In", and Pete Seeger's hopeful and
enduring ballad, "We Shall Overcome."

They sang to a constituency that would no longer
tolerate tyranny, demanded justice and listened to
Doctor King talk about his "dream."

In that moment, the crowd and the people watching
on television heard and saw "the chimes of freedom
flashing."

There were those who hated President Kennedy -- and
those who loved him. As one who loved him I later
realized that love blinded me. Years later Dylan
observed, "you can't be wise and in love at the

same time. Yes, the young man from Hibbing had
lots to say about the early sixties. He summed them
up in six words:

"Oh,the times they are a'changin'."

Robert Dorff March 18th 2006

CHAPTER 1

SECRET SERVICE HEADQUARTERS - CHICAGO FRIDAY NOVEMBER 1ST 1963 - 7:15 a.m.

Yesterday the FBI informed the Secret Service that a four man hit team planned to kill President Kennedy during a motorcade to Soldier's Field, Saturday. Pressure on the Agents has been intense. The Chicago office has pictures of the suspects who allegedly came over the border from Canada.

The landlady of a North side rooming house told police she had observed rifles with telescopic sights in a room occupied by four of her renters. The Chicago police immediately alerted Maurice G. Martineau, Acting Chief of the local office of the Secret Service. Martineau assigned two of his meager eight man staff to survey the run down brick structure where the four are staying. Thirty hours have passed without any sign of them.

Another concern is a man named Thomas Arthur Vallee.

Of French and American extraction, Vallee recently threatened to kill Kennedy. He has a history of selling guns to fellow anti-Castroites. A former Marine, he's trained Cuban exiles in guerrilla tactics and the use of weapons.

Among the agents under Chief Martinau's command are two black men, including Abraham Bolden. He and the only other black Agent are sent to handle investigations on Chicago's *south side*. The lily white *north side* is reserved for white Agents only.

Chief Maurice Martinau's expression is grave.

"Chief Rowley called me from Washington again this morning. There will be no written reports on this case. Any information is to be given to me orally. Nothing is to be sent by telex. I am to report to Chief Rowley . . . *personally*. No file numbers are to be used. Here are pictures of the four suspects in the plot and a list of their names . . . all of which are probably alias's. FBI believes the suspects entered the country together. Even if these are their real names the likelihood of them appearing on Chicago police records or other records of their presence here is very remote. If the mob is behind this --and we don't know that they are -- using hit men from out of town who don't have local arrest records is standard procedure. The President is due to land in twenty eight hours. We've got to arrest Thomas Vallee and the four man hit team before Kennedy gets here."

WASHINGTON D.C. – SATURDAY NOVEMBER 2ND – 6:47 A.M.

The sun tried vainly to break through dark clouds that threatened rain but delivered thunder. Even for a Saturday morning Pennsylvania Avenue was sparsely traveled, a condition exacerbating a feeling of gloom hovering over the White House.

THE PRESIDENT'S BEDROOM

In the throes of a disturbing dream, forty six year old John F. Kennedy thrashes around his bed.

THE DREAM: Jack (fifteen) and Joe Jr.(seventeen) are competing in a sailing race with their Wianno Junior Class sixteen foot sloop. Joe is at the helm; Jack crews. The wind is ferocious. Their Egyptian white cotton sail races across the skyline. At the moment their boat is neck and neck with their nearest competitor. The buoy denoting the finish line looms up. It's going to be close. Joe yells instructions to Jack: "Shift ballast and harden the sheet!" Jack can't hear him. They lose by a few feet. Joe jumps on Jack, begins pummeling him. Jack fights back with all he's got. It isn't enough. Joe is thirty pounds heavier and much stronger. Often confined to his bed with scarlet fever, asthma and Addison's disease, Jack is frail, no match for his older brother.

The President awakens with a start -- shaken from the effects of the dream -- and now, beyond that, the sight of brother Joe standing at the foot of the bed, wearing his Navy bomber pilot's combat gear, complete with helmet, goggles and the insignia of a Lieutenant J.G. He's extremely handsome, blue eyes, an appealing smile revealing straight teeth. Beneath his flight helmet there's a liberal supply of light brown hair.

At the moment he's enjoying Jack's abject amazement, combined with fear. (When Joe speaks, his tone is natural, revealing no trace of the supernatural.)

JOE: Good morning --*Mister President.*

JACK: (panic combined with awe) Joe! Joe!

JOE: It's okay.

The President is sure he's still dreaming.

The grief he experienced when he got the news of Joe's death abruptly re-invades his consciousness. Tears flood down his ruddy cheeks. When finally able to speak he barely gets the words out.

JACK: "Why did you volunteer for that mission?"

JOE: "I've volunteered for a new mission - to save you."

JACK: (mystified) "From what?"

JOE: Yourself.

Joe's image abruptly vanishes.

Jack raises up, looks around the room and calls out: "Joe!" "Joe!" . . . "Joe", come back! . . . "Joe?"

Satisfied now that Joe's "appearance" was part of his dream, JFK settles back on his pillow, takes a few deep breaths.

"I was still half asleep -- imagining all kinds of things while I listened to the thunder.

After Caroline was born I never slept well again. Always going into the nursery to make sure she was breathing. Jackie slept better than she ever had. Since I moved into the White House sleeping has become even more difficult.

During the election I told voters things were a real mess in Washington. When I took over from Ike I found out they were even worse.

I'll never forget what he told me driving through the snow to the inauguration:

'Jack, leaving this job is the second happiest day of my life. The first was the day after Normandy.'

Just can't understand why Ike felt that way. I love being President -- can barely wait to get to the office every morning.

I'd been restless for hours ruminating over a host of problems: My father was Ambassador to Britain in the thirties. Before his stroke last December, I

could always get his counsel. Now he can't speak.
We still call him "the Ambassador" -- a term of
respect and affection.

Yesterday's coup in Saigon ousted President Diem
and resulted in his murder. I approved the coup but
I assumed Big Min and the rest of his gang of
generals would put Diem on a plane for Paris.
Instead, they murdered him.

Problems in next year's election keep nagging me.
My approval rating hit a new low -- fifty-three
percent. Presidential advisors tell me it's
because of my stand on Civil Rights. Screw 'em.
I'd rather lose on that one than changes in the
tax law, or problems in Vietnam, or Social
Security. Advising the President is a great job.
When their advice pans out they take a bow. When
it doesn't, they move on to *new* advice.

I'm the first President in forever to balance the
budget. But the Republican's call me 'a big
spending liberal' because I authorized ten billion
for defense and millions for the Peace Corps.

The telephone startled me. At this hour it had to
be my mother or Bobby. I grabbed the phone.
"Hello?"

"Yeah Jack," Bobby said.

"So who are you trying to put in prison today?"

"Everyone I can," Bobby chuckled. "Listen, I just
wanted you to know that Lyndon is in really big
trouble. I think the Rules Committee is going to
refer him to us for prosecution."

"If you indict him he'll have to resign and
goodbye Texas."

"What can I do?"

"Why can't they stall till after the election?

"Do you really think Senator Williams and the
Republican's counsel . . . Burkett . . .what's his
face . . . would go along with that?"
"For Chrisakes we're the majority on that' Committee
of snoops'. Let them do something *to help me* for me
for a change."

"Kerry was up half the night with whooping cough,
I'm running late. See you in the Cabinet room at
eight."

"Sure," I sighed and hung up.

I wonder what my brother Joe would have done if he'd
lived to become President like Dad expected him to?
Outside of the Ambassador, he was the smartest,
toughest, most competitive and responsible person I
ever knew. Joe was everybody's hero, especially
mine. He was healthy; I was sickly -- always coming
down with something. He was powerfully built with
big bones, really smart and very outgoing; I was
frail, light boned and introverted. He used to
muscle me and tease me, but if anyone else tried it
they'd better be able to outrun Joe.

In August of forty-three, having completed two tours
of duty as a Navy bomber pilot trying to locate and
exterminate German U-Boats, Joe was waiting for
orders to go home. His Flight Commander asked for
volunteers to knock out one of Hitler's secret V-3
rocket bases. Crews from four, Army Air Force B-17's
had already died trying. So they decided to give
Navy pilots a chance.

Joe was the first to volunteer. His fellow pilots
begged him not to go. He went anyway. On their way
to the target his plane loaded with eleven tons of
dynamite, blew up over an area known as Blytheburg,
reducing the plane, my brother and his co-pilot,
"Bud" Willey to pieces so small they couldn't be
identified. The news was delivered in

Hyannis on a Sunday just as the whole family sat down to dinner. Dad came back from answering the front door and told us Joe was dead. Without another word he went up to his room and shut the door.

A while later I went to see him.

He was lying face down on the bed, sobbing. I hovered over him shaking with grief - barely able to talk.

"With Joe gone, it's up to you to become President.

"I'm a writer, Dad, not a politician. I'm not qualified."

"You have plenty of qualifications. The first three are my money, my money -- and my money. With my money, plus your charm and good looks --and one other thing -- you can't miss.

What "other thing?"

You're a Kennedy. You've learned how important it is to win. Besides you're a war hero.

Dad, I barely escaped being court marshaled.

All I remember is what everyone remembers. You saved your crew and got a medal."

So Dad's ambition for Joe to become President was passed on to me. In forty-six I was elected to Congress in a landslide.

I began thinking about my conversation with Bobby, eight and a half years younger than me.

Bobby's great at his job but I wish I'd made him the head of the CIA instead of Attorney General.

Even with Lyndon on the ticket in 1960, I only carried Texas by forty-six thousand votes --some of which I'm sure Johnson pulled out of his desk drawer. I better ask Chairman Bailey to draw up a list of possible candidates to replace him.

I'd been trying to get to Texas for over a year, but Governor Connally and Johnson kept stalling me. Now, finally, I'm going there later this month.

I'll be in Chicago at eleven for a motorcade then on to Soldier's Field to watch the Army-Air Force football game.

Jackie and the kids are staying in Virginia. She hates crowds and hullabaloo and photographers. An invitation to ride with me in an eleven mile motorcade from O'Hare airport to Soldier's Field received a "No -- No -- and *No!*" She won't even let me take John-John. A golden photo opportunity squandered. I already directed the event in my mind. I'd hold John-John on my knee while the little guy munched a hot dog and the shutters clicked away. Votes, votes and more votes. But Jackie won't have it. Says, I'm 'exploiting' him. "It's all about politics, Jack."

"That's the business I'm in honey," I said.

So my only company will be Mayor Daley. Through his good offices and an assist from Sam Giancana awakening dead people in the Cook County cemetery, we squeaked by in Illinois. Plenty of cash had to be handed out. My father was right about politics: "It takes lots of money." His money helped 'smooth over rough spots' in Illinois which was crucial. Without Illinois and Texas, Nixon would have won.

When rumors went around that my father bought the election I answered them with a joke: 'Dad told me he wouldn't pay for a landslide.' I hope

I won't have to drop Johnson from the ticket. He's
clumsy, talks like a hillbilly and's really very
crude. He's also the smartest politician I've
ever known.

He got elected to the Senate by a margin of
eight-nine votes, all of which his opponent
claimed were stolen.

When The Federal Election Committee sequestered the
ballot boxes from a crucial county where all the
votes except one were for Johnson they discovered
the boxes were empty. But Lyndon wiggled his way
into the Senate and became the youngest Majority
Leader in history. His genius for passing
legislation made him a legend. When I got to the
Senate four years later, I used to call him,
"landslide Lyndon", a term he didn't appreciate,
especially from a freshman Senator.

After the Convention in Los Angeles lots of his
friends were surprised when he gave up 'The
Leadership' to run for Vice President. I was kind
of alarmed by what he told them: 'One out of every
four President's dies in office . . . and I'm a
gambler.'

My valet, George Thomas came quietly into the
room. "Good morning, Mister President." "Good
morning, George." He always came armed with a load
of newspapers which ordinarily I devoured. "No
time for the papers this morning. I have a meeting
in fifteen minutes." George helped me struggle out
of bed and get my back brace on.

I heard a knock at the door. "Come on in, Doc, "I
said and Doctor Max Jacobson appeared with his
black medical bag. He always wore a peculiar smile.
I could never decide whether he was amused or
confused. "Hi! Give me my morning cocktail will ya
doc, I'm late." Jacobson put that smile on again.
"Yes, mister President. How do you feel this
morning? "Lower than a lizard in Death Valley. Will
you fix that, doc?"

"Doctor Feelgood", as Jackie called Jacobson, withdrew an already prepared syringe from his bag, and plunged it into my thigh. Some of it was cortisone for my back and Addison's disease, the rest was Procaine to help blunt the pain of my osteoporosis.

He produced another syringe filled with Amphetamines which greatly increased my energy level.

"My regular doctor, Admiral Burkley doesn't know about 'Doctor Feelgood.' It's all part of my philosophy . . . *have at least two of everything*: *Two* doctors, *two* women . . . more if opportunity knocked, *two* Cuba policies --*one* using back channels to negotiate a rapprochement with Castro . . . *another* to have the CIA murder him. Living on the edge is part of the excitement that makes life more interesting."

(It never occurred to Kennedy that his duplicity would lead to the grave.)

THE NORTH SIDE OF CHICAGO - 6:15 A.M.

Last night's storm dumped a foot of snow on the ground. A chilling twenty mile an hour wind sent the barometer into the low teens.

Two men emerge from an older brick rooming house begin walking toward a gray sedan parked at the curb. One, in his mid-thirties, over six feet, has dark complexion and thick black hair. Probably a Latino.

The second is older, dark complexion, has a receding hairline, looks a bit on the frail side. He goes to the driver's door and gets

behind the wheel. His companion plops into the
passenger seat. The car begins moving slowly
down the mostly deserted residential street
spewing mud in its wake.

An unmarked Secret Service vehicle carrying two
Agents trails the gray sedan at a safe distance.
Inside we hear radio transmissions from Secret
Service headquarters to field units.

Agent J.L. Stocks is seated in the passenger seat.
He shuffles through photographs seen earlier. "Yeah,
Pete that's two of them for sure." He picks up the
mike: "Stocks to headquarters . . . over." A Voice
on the radio: "Go ahead Stocks . . . over." "We're
following two of the suspects driving south in an
older gray Ford Fairlane, Illinois license plates,
number 3MGR492. Any luck locating the other two?"
"Negative. Will keep your advised, over."

Agent McPheters keeps their quarry in sight. "Wonder
if the Police located Vallee", he mutters. "Must be
getting real short of help if the Chief had to hand
the Vallee surveillance over to them.

"Maybe he should call 'Manpower' Stocks
chuckles.

**WASHINGTON D.C. — 7:25 A.M. SATURDAY — NOVEMBER
2nd.**

Robert Francis Kennedy gripped the wheel of his
Cadillac with hands that were covered with grease
and dirt. He cursed several times. "Goddam, flat
tire in the rain and mud and I'm going to be late."
As he was leaving his house, the lead prosecutor in
the deportation case against Carlos Marcello called
to say things were going well. This was welcome
news. The Attorney General had been trying to put
Marcello away for two and a half years.

Later some of the same group will join other officials to decide the substance of policy discussions with coup leaders who have taken power in Saigon.
Bobby can't forget the look on his brother's face when he learned Diem had been murdered.

Jack's was one of the loudest voices in the U.S. Senate backing the little Vietnamese Catholic --a religion representing barely four percent of the population. Now he had okayed the coup which resulted in Diem's demise.

When the meeting at the White House adjourns, Bobby will have to rush back to "Hickory Hill", his home in McLean, Virginia for a luncheon meeting with *"The President's Special Group, Augmented"*. This includes several high officials from Defense, State and CIA, plus Bobby's select list of Cuban exile leaders --all veterans of Brigade 2506 whom he ransomed out of Castro's prisons by raising almost fifty-five million dollars in medical supplies and spare parts. The thirty-seven year old Attorney General solicited the money from large corporations who received special tax breaks for their donations.

From his home, the Attorney General directs the most secret plan in the U.S. government --
"Operation Second Naval Guerilla", *another invasion of Cuba.* (Its name was changed many times, usually prefixed by the letters "OPLAN", followed by a number. To avoid confusion we will continue to refer to it by its original name.)Hopefully Fidel Castro will have been disposed of prior to the invasion. If not, doing away with him will be the first order of business for the insurgents. Seven previous attempts on the Cuban leader's life

ordered by Bobby and his brother, failed. "SECOND NAVAL GUERILLA" is known to less than two dozen people in America. "Guerilla's" success would be the answer to the Kennedy's most cherished dream -- evening up the score with Fidel for the debacle at The Bay of Pigs.

At the top of the group's agenda this afternoon: choosing a date for the invasion plus the exact wording the President will include in his speech when he gets to Miami on the eighteenth. The coup leader in Cuba insists on hearing assurances directly from the President guaranteeing that the U.S. will back them as soon as Castro is "out."

CHICAGO — 7:21 A.M.

In a nearby neighborhood, similar to the first, two Chicago policemen, Benson and Andrews are ransacking a dingy apartment. The floor and shelves are burgeoning with various extremist literature, especially from the *JOHN BIRCH SOCIETY* and *THE FREE CUBA COMMITTEE*. The former is perhaps the leading right wing organization in America, more popular at the moment than *"The Minutemen", or the KKK.*

Benson yanks cupboards open: Andrews throws items out of a closet. "Thought you said the Secret Service interviewed this joker a few days ago." "Did. He had an M-1 rifle and lots of ammo," Benson replies. "That's what they said, anyway. It's in their report." "So, what happened to the stuff", Andrews asks. "And what happened to Vallee?"

Benson scratches his head. "Let's go talk with the landlady again."

8:29 A.M.

Stocks and McPheters are still trailing the
suspects.

Up front, the Fairlane suddenly hangs a U, moves
back toward the Agent's car rapidly gaining speed.
"Must'a forgot something" Stocks says. The radio
abruptly blares again. "Base to Stocks -- base to
Stocks over." Before Agent Stocks can turn down the
volume, the Fairlane moves past them. The suspects
hear the Agent's radio as they pass. Wisely, they do
not make a run for it. "Shit", McPheters exclaims.
"They made us!" "Hang a U and we'll pull them
mover," Stocks replies.

ROBERT KENNEDY

The younger Kennedy glances at his watch, then slams
the pedal to the metal. The Cadillac surges forward,
soon is traveling at seventy-five miles per hour. If
he gets a ticket what the hell, he's the Attorney
General, certainly he can find a way to fix it.
Remembering one of his brother's favorite
expressions he laughs out loud. "You never realize
how little influence you have until you try and use
it."

CHICAGO - 8:35 A.M.

Benson and Andrews stand at the open door to an
apartment on the first floor. Mrs. Johansson, the
Manager, has makeup caked all over her face. She
uses a hand mirror as she applies another coat of
powder and talks with the two policemen at the same
time.

"Always goes to work on Saturday's. Said he had
something else to do today and might not be home
till dark. Asked me to feed his cat."

"Does he own a car?" "Yes, little foreign one .. .
with one of those . . . what do you call them . . .
hunchbacks." "Hatchback, huh?"

"When you called the Secret Service this morning, was Vallee still here?" "No, he'd just left. I got real scared . . . so I called Chief Martinau." "Scared of what?" "He works half day's on Saturdays. So with the President coming and all -- you know he just hates that man." "Has he said that to you?" "Yes, that's why I called them --the Secret Service I mean. They were here a few days ago questioning Thomas and all. He was a Marine you know." Officer Andrews pushes his hat back from his forehead, studies notes he's been making on a small notepad. "And this printing company where Vallee works, you're sure it's located on Jackson Street?" "Yes -- right where you get off the Expressway to take the road to Soldier's Field."

CHURCHILL FARMS – CIRCA NEW ORLEANS – 9:00 A.M.

Here the sun shines brightly, illuminating the grounds surrounding a spacious well appointed country home situated on the outskirts of "the jazz capital of the world."

The six hundred plus acres is the property of mob boss Carlos Marcello. Isolated from the bustle of humanity in the city and prying eyes, Carlos uses Churchill Farms for private meetings to hatch all kinds of plans including how to defend himself in his court battle with Bobby Kennedy's prosecutors.

Marcello revels in telling the story which brought about the court case. His two brothers, Pete and Joe plus a third, strange looking man, David Ferrie, listen to a story they've heard countless times but are resigned to hearing again.

Ferrie suffers from Alopecia Praecox, a disease which leaves one completely hairless. To compensate, Ferrie wears a red toupee and eyebrows which he's painted on. This combines to give him a sinister yet comical look.

Carlos continues: "When I come here from Tunisia I hadda fill in this form like all da other aliens. I didn't wanna put down where I was born cause I had some problems there, ya know? So I put down Guatemala City, cause I know there ain't nuttin' der on me. After I been here long enough, I don't apply for a citizen, cause I know if they gonna do one dem 'background checks' der gonna find out I wasn't born in Guatemala an make me say where I *was born.* I couldn' do dat because what they gonna find out gonna make dem deport me. Bein' an alien I hadda go down to da INS office at City Hall to report, *every week.* Everybody der --de knew me and we get along real good.

Back in fifty-seven, doz Kennedy brothers were on what de called 'da Senate Rackets Committee'. Dat Bobby sonofabtich give me a real hard time -make me look bad . . . but I give it right back to 'em.

Nineteen sixty come along and I'm backin' Lyndon-- an Bobby sonofabitch is sore cause I won't give dem my support with da Louisiana delegation. Da brother gets nominated anyway, wins da da election and puts Bobby sonofabitch inder as Attorney General. Right den, I know I'm in for it."

CHICAGO

In the parking lot behind Letterman's Printing Company, Thomas Arthur Vallee, blond, blue eyes, studies the off-ramp which is easily observed from where his Renault hatchback is parked. He glances at his watch, -- focuses on the off-ramp again. A hunting knife in a leather sheath lies on the seat beside him.

Born and raised in Chicago, the thirty-year old
Vallee was in the Marine Corps from 1949 to 1952
and saw combat during Korea where he was awarded
the Purple Heart with Oak Leaf Cluster for injuries
sustained at "Pork Chop Hill." He was honorably
discharged, re-enlisted in the Marine Corps Reserve
a few years later; went on active duty again in
late 1955. The following September he was honorably
discharged after doctors diagnosed him as
"schizophrenic, paranoid type, manifested by pre-
occupations with homosexuality and femininity."
To the Corps, Vallee was a sick puppy, but as a perk
for being wounded in combat they awarded him
disability. Earlier this year he used his Marine
experience to train anti-Castro exiles in
Hicksville, Long Island, New York.

Glancing at his watch again, Vallee becomes
visibly agitated. He starts the engine of his
hatchback and zooms out of the parking lot.

Officers Benson and Andrews have their unmarked
police car parked on Jackson Street just beyond the
printing company. It's many stories with large
windows afford an unobstructed view of the
Expressway and Jackson Street. (Years later,
researchers would note its similarity to The Texas
School Book Depository in Dallas.)

Vallee races past the police car ignoring a stop
sign. "That's him! Benson shouts. Andrews gets their
car in gear and gives chase. Vallee is preoccupied,
unaware he's being followed. The police car suddenly
moves alongside his car. Benson gestures to him to
pull over. Confused, the ex-Marine keeps driving.
Executing a quick maneuver, Andrews angles his car
across Vallee's, path, almost causing a crash. Their
cars skid simultaneously to a halt on the wet
pavement. In a couple of seconds Benson and Andrews
are out of their car flanking both sides of the
Renault. Vallee is frightened and confused. "What's
the matter, officer?" "You ran a stop sign back
there by the printing company. Let's see your

license and registration." Vallee reaches into the glove compartment, fumbles with some papers, extracts his registration, hands it to Andrews. "How about your driver's license?"

"I guess I left it at home." Noticing the knife, Benson yells to his partner. "Knife on the seat! "Okay" Andrews shouts, "out of the car." Even more frightened now, Vallee disembarks.

Benson comes around the hood and joins them. "Get your keys and open the back. Vallee flinches at this request, then freezes. "Well" Benson demands. "Are you going to open the back or do we have to do it for you? Vallee removes the keys from the ignition, goes to the rear of the car and opens the hatchback. A section of canvas covers some bulky items. "What's underneath the canvas?" Vallee is paralyzed. "Take that cover off," Andrews barks. Vallee slowly lifts the canvas cover, revealing an M-1 rifle, hundreds of rounds of ammunition and an automatic handgun.

Andrews stares at Vallee. "Going duck hunting, huh?" Vallee begins trembling -- doesn't reply.

"You're under arrest. We're impounding this car and taking you to the station", Benson says. Andrews snaps a pair of handcuffs on the ex-Marine.

CHURCHILL FARMS

"First week of April my driver takes me down ta INS. Upstairs I get da 'cold shoulder' from people in da office. Nobody talkin' ta me, yasee. Before I know it, two INS officers came from a back room, put da cuffs on me! Den, de take me out da back way and da next thing I know I'm at the airport and de tellin' me I gotta get in da plane! I keep sayin' 'hey, what's dis about --come on, what's dis about? Finally one of dem says: 'You lied about where you were born on da application for citizenship and dats a felony and da Attorney General sent us here to deport you to Guatamala City, 'cause dats where ya said ya was born.' "I say 'Widout no trial or hearin' or nuttin'?" 'Dats right,' he say,'and I say ain't dis America? Dey start ta drag me on da plane! I say wait a minute -- I gotta call my wife and tell her what's happenin'. De don't say nuttin' --just drag me in da plane. We get ta some mountain aroun' Guatemala City, dey put da plane down and throw me out! Dats dat Bobby sonofabitch!"

SECRET SERVICE HEADQUARTERS - CHICAGO 8:55 A.M.

Chief Martinau, Stocks and McPheters circle a table at which the two suspects from the rooming house are seated. One of them, "Rodriguez" chain smokes; Gonzales chews bubble gum, occasionally blows a bubble.

Agent Stocks glances at his notebook. "So you decided to come down here from Montreal just to see the football game?"

Both suspects nod. "Yeah", Gonzales says, "we're real fans."

"And you expect us to believe you crossed the border without passports" the Chief asks.

"Just asked us where we were born and waved us through."

"That's right, Chief," Gonzales chimes in. "We had the passports with some other papers and someone stole 'em out of our car when we went to the market."

McPheters places a hand on Gonzales' shoulder. "How'd they get in?" Gonzales shrugs. "We don't know -- just opened the door, I guess." "Yeah", Rodriguez adds, "lucky we keep our money in our pants, or that'd be gone, too."
Stocks bangs his hand on the table. "Wanta know something?" "What," Rodriguez grins?" "I don't believe you! "Why would we lie" Gonzales grunts. "We haven't done anything *wrong*."

CHURCHILL FARMS – 9:11 A.M.

Marcello's recitation is still in progress.

"Just had da clothes on my back, and some money in my wallet. I walked for miles looking for a telephone. Couldn't speak da language so no way I could ask where anything was.

Finally I find a phone and make a collect call to an attorney friend of mine in Shreveport. He's one smart guy. Few weeks later, Dave flies down der and takes me back to da Texas border and I give myself up at da INS. Dat attorney, he gets dis Federal Judge in Brownsville, to give me a hearing and da Judge says I gotta a right at a trial.

"Believe me, Carlos" brother Joe opines, "these jerks from Washington don't have a case."

"Doesn't matter," Carlos replies. His remark confuses his brothers, but not Ferrie.

"Whatta ya mean" Pete asks. "I mean dey can't win," Carlos grunts. "I got ta two of da jurors before the trial started. So, we just go through da motions -- da jury comes back hung, or not guilty."

Pete chuckles. Joe isn't so sanguine. "I still say we should have someone kill that little Bobby sonofabitch! "No" Carlos replies. "Cut off da tail and da dog still lives. Cut off the head, da tail's gonna stop wagging and Bobby sonofabitch he gonna be just another lawyer. I put out da money to have his brother killed and der ain't gonna be nuttin' done about it."

The brothers exchange puzzled looks. Ferrie stares at Marcello, knowingly. "Tell 'em why nuttin will happen Dave."

"Santos has this guy at CIA in Miami who told him about a plan the Kennedy's have for another invasion of Cuba. Might cause a nuclear war. They'd do anything to keep it secret. They know, *we know* and if we see to it word leaks out before it goes da Kennedy's would be finished."

"Bobby would still be Attorney General," Joe interjects.

"Not after my friend Lyndon is President. For da money I paid him over da years and da chance I'm givin' him to be President, he'll look da other way"

Carlos watches for reactions. "Whadda ya think Dave?" "Someone should have shot Kennedy a long time ago."

"It's in da works. What time ya got?"

Ferrie consults his watch. "Nine thirty."

"Okay den," Carlos says to Ferrie. "Go inside and put on one of my Connie Francis records and turn da volume all the way up. Den phone Banister. Let him know we're here all day working on da case and want to hear some good news from Giancana."

9:40 A.M. SECRET SERVICE HEADQUARTERS –CHICAGO

By now, the ashtray has another half dozen
cigarette butts in it.

'Let's try it again" Chief Martinau barks. He bends
close to Gonzales' face. "Where were you born?"
"Nova Scotia." "Where in Nova Scotia?" "Halifax."
"And where is that?" "In Canada." "And where did
you cross the border to get here?" A buzzer on the
wall sounds. Stocks lifts receiver on a phone
attached to the wall.

"Yeah". "Pierre" who? Waits. Repeats, "Salinger".
Cradles the phone. "Some guy named Salinger is" --
"Oh yeah," Martinau interrupts, "Kennedy's Press
Secretary. I called him earlier. Gotta go out there
and talk to him. Keep on 'em. I'll find out if
Interpol responded yet."

The Chief moves from the interrogation room into
the reception area, where a portly man nearing
forty, with a shock of dark brown hair is waiting.
Salinger puts out his hand, the Chief shakes it.

Pierre looks at his watch. "Getting pretty late
Chief. Where does it stand?" "Still in the dark and
no sightings of Vallee or the other two suspects
out of Montreal." The one's we've got inside for
questioning are pretty cute. Can't hold them much
longer." The phone on a nearby desk rings. One of
the other agents answers it. "Secret Service,
Sanderson. Almost immediately he extends the
receiver to Martinau. "Sorry, Chief. Chicago Police
for you." "Tell them I'll call back."

"The Chief says he'll have to . . ." (pauses as he
listens, studies Martinau again). "They arrested
Vallee near the Jackson Street off ramp from the
expressway. He had a knife, an M-1 rifle, three
thousand rounds of ammo and a hand gun in the

trunk." Salinger grimaces. "What's next, Chief?"
"We have to find the other two before the President
gets here."

CHICAGO — 9:30 A.M.

At a hastily convened news conference, Salinger
briefs reporters:

"Because of the extraordinary events in South
Vietnam, a special communications center has
been established underneath the bleachers at
Soldiers Field. This facility will allow
President Kennedy to keep informed about the
aftermath of the coup in which President Diem
and his brother lost their lives.

"Then the President is still coming to Chicago?" a
reporter shouts.

"Absolutely," Salinger replies. The President has
no intention of canceling his visit."

THE OVAL OFFICE — 11:15 *Eastern Time*

Assistants Dave Powers and Kenny O'Donnell watch
JFK expectantly as he winds up a telephone call
from Secret Service Chief, James Rowley.

"I appreciate your concern Chief, but this trip is
extremely important, politically." He listens. "I
realize that but they're threats on my life every
day. If we arranged my schedule according to
threats, I might as well move to Hyannis and stay
there." He pauses to listen a moment. "Thanks,
Chief"

President Kennedy puts the receiver down.

"Chief Rowley insists it's too dangerous for me to
go to Chicago. I'm going anyway. Kenny --see if
you can get Pierre again."
Joe,Jr appears next to his brother. Jack is
aghast, takes a couple steps backward. Kenny and

   Dave don't react. They can't see Joe.

On the intercom, Missus Lincoln says: "Your mother
is on line five, Mister President."
Still trying to recover, he hesitates a moment:
"I'll take it in the prayer room."

*("The prayer room" is a metaphor for a small
cubicle located next door to his secretary's
office, where he takes personal calls, mostly
from family and girlfriends).* Jack signals to
Powers:

"Call Colonel Swindal at 'Andrews' and tell him the
trip to Chicago is still on." Joe Jr's image
disappears.

The "prayer room" has only a couch, a chair, a
small writing table and a bank of telephones. As
Kennedy reaches for the receiver, Joe, Jr.
reappears. Jack hesitates.

"Listen to Chief Rowley, Jack. Don't go to
Chicago."

"I have to go. Illinois is one of the two states
that put me here. I only won by eighty-eight
hundred votes. If I don't go I could lose it next
year.

"If you go, you might not be around next year.
Listen to me, Jack *--don't go."*

After a stare down, Jack reluctantly presses the
intercom button.

"Missus Lincoln -- have Kenny O'Donnell tell
Colonel Swindal we're canceling the trip to Chicago
-- and see if you can get Pierre for me.

Two minutes later, Salinger is on the line.
"I'm sorry to make you look bad Pierre, but after
what Rowley told me, I have to cancel." He listens
awhile. Look --it's vital everyone gives out the
same story. I think you should just say something
like . . . 'due to the precipitous actions by people
involved in the coup in Saigon the President deemed
it advisable to hold an emergency meeting of the
National Security Council and members of his
Cabinet. He deeply regrets having to cancel his
visit and apologizes to Mayor Daley, the Army and
Air Force football teams --and the people of
Chicago." Also, *and hear me well, Pierre* -there will
be no dissemination about 'a hit team', threats on
my life or any other information of that kind *given
to anyone*, press people, networks, local
politicians, or otherwise. 'Deepening problems in
Saigon' is the only reason for the cancellation of
the President's trip. I'll tell Bobby to have the
others clamp the lid down, **tight**. With names like
Rodriguez and Gonzales they may well be Cubans."

What none of them would know until many days later
was that at the same time the CIA was quietly
trying to locate *another suspected assassin*, Miguel
Casas Saez, a Cuban national whom they tracked to
Chicago -- then lost. Saez, they are sure is under
the direct control of Raul Castro.

CHICAGO 10:50 a.m.

On Jackson Street, crowds were assembling along the
motorcade route. Armed with cameras and banners
proclaiming, **"WELCOME MR. PRESIDENT,"** they could
not subdue their excitement. The women hoped Jackie
would be with him . . . so did the men.

At the airport, Mayor Daley and other city officials were on hand to greet the President. So was Chief Maurice Martinau, who was still unaware that Kennedy already canceled his appearance in "the windy city."

CHURCHILL FARMS - 11:00 A.M.

Carlos and his brothers are still seated around the glass table, drinking beer. In the background they can hear Connie Francis singing the last stanza of "Where The Boys Are".

"The little man", closes his eyes and swoons." Dat Connie looks like an angel - sings like a canary. Gonna have a new picture out soon. I'll be der first matinee opening day."

"Yeah", Pete chimes in," she's a good one, alright." "Good hell!" Carlos replies "She's da best!"

Ferrie takes his seat again -- a look of consternation spread over his bizarre features.

"Guy called. He just heard from Cain in Chicago. Kennedy canceled his visit.

The brothers unleash a stream of invectives.

"The good news," Ferrie continued, is the secret service turned two of Giancana's guy's over to the Chicago Sheriff's Department. They didn't have anything on them so Cain got them released. Didn't even take mug shots or print them. They got the patsy in custody. Nailed him near the printing company with an arsenal in his car."

"He don't know nuttin" anyway", Carlos exclaims." I'm pissed . . . but I'm not worried. We struck out in Chicago, but Santos will nail smiling Jack when he gets at Tampa. And if dat don't work, our people will be waiting for the prick in Dallas."

"We shouldn't be talking like this", Pete says. "The FBI might be listening." "No dey ain't -- no telephone taps either. J.Edgar leaves me alone, cause I got a certain arrest record Meyer gave me from da twenties with J.Edgar's name on it, for molesting a minor. Everyone in D.C. knows he's a queer."
Except for Ferrie, they all laugh. "Ya know what the FBI's local guy here says about me?' Marcello's not involved in crime he's just a tomato salesman!' Now, Ferrie joins the other's in raucous laughter.

"Hey, Dave, turn dat record on again, and make da volume louder!"

MCLEAN, VIRGINIA - 1 p.m.

Bobby Kennedy's home is called "Hickory Hill." He's conducting a meeting of the 'President's Special Group—*Augmented.*' This ultra-secret group was created by the President to deal with" the Castro problem."

Membership is limited to fifteen individuals, The Attorney General, Joe Califano from Defense, Richard Helms, Ted Shackley and Desmond Fitzgerald from CIA, Cuban exiles Harry Williams, Manuel Hernandez, Tony Varona, Mira Cardona, Roberto and Pepe San Roman, and Joint Chief's Chairman, Maxwell Taylor and Cyrus Vance. President Kennedy rarely attends.

They lunched on tuna fish sandwiches and cokes. In his shirt sleeves, his tie askew, Bobby Kennedy bangs a knife against a coke bottle to get some quiet.

He withdraws a wrinkled piece of newsprint from his pants pocket.

"For the benefit of those who haven't read this Miami Herald article from last week:

'Nicaragua Denies Cuban Exile Force. Luis
Somoza, eldest of the two heirs who boss this
country, is supporting a Cuban liberation group
whose members include Carlos Prio Soccares, Ex-
President of Cuba, and Manuel Artime, political
leader of the 1961 invasion. The group's intention
is to mount another invasion of Cuba.' End quote.

"I want to know how this got into the Miami
Herald!"

After a protracted silence Harry Williams gets up
and faces Bobby. "You know Bobby, we have a saying
in my country: (Holds up one finger)."Tell one
Cuban and one knows." (Holds up two fingers).
"Tell two Cubans and eleven know",(Holds up three
fingers). "Tell three Cubans and a hundred and
eleven know."

"Do you have any idea which of the *hundred and
eleven* flapped his mouth to the Herald", Bobby
asks.

"No," Williams replies and sits down.

Tony Varona stands up and addresses the group. "I
hate to say this about my countrymen but they take
great pleasure in being the one to reveal secrets -
- makes them feel important. I'm afraid it's a
genetic trait."

"Great", Bobby responds. "The next thing we know
one of them will write and Op-ed piece for the New
York Times." The Attorney General releases a sigh
of frustration.

"So much for the hundred and eleven. I want
suggestions accompanied by reasons for a target
date for the landing in Cuba."

Desmond Fitzgerald (William Harvey's replacement at
ZR RIFLE) clears his throat. "I think it should be
the last part of October, *next* year. An *'October
Surprise'*, if you will, timed for the election.

There are murmurs of approval and disapproval. Ted
Shackley breaks in: "I think it should be as soon
as possible. Christmas eve would be my choice. My
reasoning is security. This so called secret is
leaking like a sprinkler can."

Chapter 2

HAVANA— NOVEMBER 3rd. 5:45 P.M.

In his inner office at the Palicio, Premier Fidel

Castro put the phone back on it's cradle, withdrew a

Monte Cristo cigar from his breast pocket and lit

it. Feeling restless, he walked onto a balcony

overlooking downtown Havana. Castro, who was thirty-

seven in August, took a piece of yellow foolscap

from his jacket pocket, studied it, then put it in a

different pocket.

The sheet of yellow paper contained the text of a
decoded message from Rolando Cubela, a member of his
inner circle who was in Paris on official government
business.

Kennedy's creatures were still making plans with
Cubela to assassinate Fidel. The Americans were so
naive, Castro mused. Cuban Intelligence was always
way ahead of them. Dozens of double agents had
infiltrated the exile community in America, also the
CIA, the INS and other agencies of the U.S.
government. The ranks of American gangsters had also
been penetrated. Santos Trafficante for instance
warned Fidel of every plot against him since the
Mafia was first recruited by the CIA to destroy him.
Formerly a casino owner in Havana, Trafficante was
hoping for favored treatment if Fidel repealed the
ban on gambling.

Castro gazed at the last rays of sunlight bouncing off the waters in Havana Harbor and stroked his beard. The whole thing with Kennedy puzzled him. Cuban Intelligence had been aware of exiles training in Nicaragua for months. The beginnings of another force had just been established in Guatemala.

As recently as yesterday, Ambassador Attwood had phoned Fidel's go-between, Doctor Rene Vallejo. They talked for over an hour about setting a date for a meeting in Havana to discuss an agenda to normalize relations between the U.S. and Cuba. Fidel sat next to Vallejo, monitoring every word. Without authorization from Kennedy, Fidel knew Attwood would never make these kinds of representations.

The contact between him and Vallejo had been going on since September. The idea of initiating a rapprochement with Kennedy was Fidel's, relayed by his Ambassador to the UN, Carlos Lechuga, to Ambassador Attwood, a member of the U.S. delegation.

Their discussion took place in New York.

There followed some feelers from Kennedy through an ABC reporter, Lisa Howard with whom Fidel was having an affair. She had met with Kennedy who authorized her to talk with Castro about normalizing relations between the two countries. Rapprochement was a bold initiative by the Cuban Premier to extricate himself from total dependence on the Soviets.

This new message from Cubela was indeed Noticia Mala -- bad news.

Castro had survived countless attempts on his life since the revolution triumphed and he would continue surviving them -- of that he had no doubt. Still, this recent duplicity by Kennedy left a bitter taste on his tongue.

For many months Fidel had been under extreme pressure from his younger brother, Raul, to authorize Cuban G-2 to put together a plan to *kill Kennedy*. Next to the Israeli's Mosaad, Cuban Intelligence was the best in the world.

Surely, Fidel reasoned, they could find a better way to handle this. Nothing would make the CIA happier than proving a Cuban sponsored attack on Kennedy. Such an action would trigger a massive retaliation by the United States. "That's if they found out we did it" Raul argued. "Leave it to us -- they'll never know." As head of The Revolutionary Armed Forces, Raul exercised considerable influence over his brother. Still Fidel resisted. Now Cubela's message cast a pall on the veracity of Kennedy's response to the Cuban leader's overtures for a rapprochement.

On September seventh, Castro had attended a reception at the Brazilian embassy in Havana. In an impromptu interview with Associated Press journalist, Daniel Harker, the Cuban leader launched into a tirade against Kennedy: "He's a cretin, the Batista of his times. The most opportunistic President of *all time*." He went on excoriating Kennedy for allowing exile raids against Cuba. Then he added:

"We are prepared to fight them and answer in kind. The United States leaders should think that if they are aiding terrorist's plans to eliminate Cuban leaders, they themselves will not be safe."

These statements provoked instant reaction in the U.S. media, especially in South Florida. For the embittered exiles hoping to return to Cuba, Castro's intemperate remarks was manna from heaven. If Castro had Kennedy killed, the U.S. would mount a retaliatory attack -- and El Comandante un Jefe would be history.

What they didn't know -- and along with the

Americans wouldn't know until 1989, was that the removal of Soviet medium range missiles **did not include _tactical_ nuclear weapons,** which Castro would not hesitate to use in event of an attack.

Fidel remained motionless on the balcony considering what to do. Presently, he went back into the office, dialed a four digit number and waited.

"Raul . . . come over tonight at twelve. I want to talk to you about our friend in Washington."

MIAMI, FLORIDA NOVEMBER 3rd. 6:10 p.m.

In a spacious apartment at the Scott Bryant Hotel, two men had been conferring for hours. The meeting was arranged by their mutual friend, Macho Gener. Jose Aleman came from a wealthy Cuban family that had amassed a fortune in real estate. Prior to the triumph of the revolution, their holdings numbered in the many millions. After world war two, "the boss of bosses", Charles "Lucky" Luciano ran gambling in Havana. While doing a long stretch in a New York prison for running prostitution rings, "Lucky" earned a get out of jail free card from the Office of Naval Intelligence (ONI) by using his enormous influence with corrupt New York dock worker's to stamp out German agents targeting departing ships for destruction by Nazi U-boats. After this success "Lucky" worked with American intelligence officers helping to get friendly Sicilians in operations against the Fascists. When Castro came to power, he outlawed gambling and chased the gangsters out of Cuba. Without gambling, the once lucrative tourist trade vanished. Under the "guidance" of the new head of the Cuban National Bank, Ernesto "Che" Guevara, the Cuban peso plummeted to a tenth of its value. Guevara, an Argentine doctor highly experienced in guerrilla warfare, had no experience in economics and Cuba's economy soon lay in ruins.

For the Aleman's there remained just a few holdings in Miami, among them, Miami Stadium and the Scott Bryant Hotel. Jose sold the stadium to raise cash for other investments. In his early forties now, the Cuban exile is desperate for anther infusion of cash. The other man, is considerably taller and wears thick horn-rimmed glasses. This is Santos Trafficante, Jr. -- forty nine.

His father, a leading figure in the Mafia, ran the show in Tampa for years. During the war, he teamed up with Lucky Luciano, then in prison, Frank Costello and Meyer Lansky, operating illegal gambling casinos in Havana. For looking the other way, Cuban dictator Flugencio Batista was generously rewarded.

When Santos Senior died, his son took over. Not satisfied with meager pickings in Tampa, he moved to Havana, hoping to make it big with his father's casinos. When Castro came to power, the younger Trafficante owned significant interests in gambling establishments like the San Souci, the Deauville and the Commodore. The coming of Comandante un Jefe spelled disaster for Trafficante and other American Mafioso's with enormous investments in Cuban casino's. By then Luciano had already been exiled to Italy.

Before he even arrived in Havana, Fidel Castro declared gambling would be outlawed. The loss of revenue was such a blow to the economy, Fidel temporarily reinstated gambling. But the tourist trade had already evaporated so the casinos remained empty and were soon outlawed again. Trafficante and others were arrested and jailed in Trescorina prison.

While incarcerated, Santos' daughter's wedding was scheduled to take place in Havana. Santos' mother appealed directly to Fidel to allow her son to be present at the wedding. Fidel put his imprimatur on

her request. Santos -- and a corps of policemen,
attended the wedding. When it was over, he was
returned to Trescorina, which was more like an army
camp than a prison. Everyone had their own room,
the "detainee's" were allowed to bring in all the
food they could pay for. Visitors could come and go
as they pleased. One of Santos' visitors was Dallas
nightclub owner, "Jake Rubenstein", later known to
the world as Jack Ruby.

When in August 1959, Santos was released, he went
to see Raul Gonzales, a friend whom he suspected of
being instrumental in arranging his freedom.
Gonzales was running the Hilton Hotel. There,
Gonzales told him, "Don't thank me, Santos, thank
Raul Castro." "How can I do that" Santos replied.
"He's at the upstairs bar right now. Go up there
and talk to him." Trafficante bounded up the stairs
and introduced himself to the younger Castro. He
thanked him profusely for arranging his release.

"It's okay", Raul replied. "We thought you were
involved with narcotics, but Gonzales vouched for
you and I trust him." Trafficante's further thanks
was met by a thoughtful stare.

"Maybe, one day" Raul said, "you'll have a
chance to do something for the revolution."

Trafficante's main purpose in visiting Aleman was
to see if the young exile could arrange a meeting
with Dominican Republic President, Juan Bosch.
Through Macho Gener, Santos learned the Dominican
leader was a friend of the Aleman family. Jose had
a standing invitation to visit the island and bring
American businessmen with him.

For Santos, the lure of a new gambling empire is
irresistible.

Also, there is the issue of a large real estate
loan Aleman is seeking from the Teamster's union,
a transaction which had so far not been looked

upon with favor. Trafficante arranged many such transactions for business associates during the past, always collecting a fee for doing do. Santos and Aleman spoke in Spanish:

ALEMAN: "If I could get the loan, Senor Trafficante, I could pay off some debts and retire the second mortgage my mother in-law has on this hotel."

SANTOS: "I'm glad my mother-in-law doesn't have a mortgage on my property. She'd foreclose if I was an hour late."

ALEMAN: "Our friend, Macho Gener, told me you have a great deal of influence with Mister Hoffa."

SANTOS: "I know Jimmy." And I'll talk to him for you, but now isn't the time."

ALEMAN: "Why is that?"

SANTOS: "Have you seen how this man Kennedy has treated Hoffa? A friend of the blue collars --a hard working individual trying to advance conditions for the workers. Don't worry it won't take long before Kennedy is out of the picture."

ALEMAN: "But the election isn't for a year. I can't wait that long. Besides, Kennedy is certain to be reelected."

SANTOS: "Mark my words, this man Kennedy is in a lot of trouble. He's not going to make it to the election, Jose, he's going to be hit."

Aleman realized Santos' remark wasn't idle speculation. Two days later he went to the Miami office of the FBI and reported what Trafficante told him. The Miami Agents sent their report to Washington and to the Secret Service. Neither organization forwarded an account of this threat to Dallas.

SUNDAY – 8:15 P.M. THE PRESIDENT'S HOME IN MIDDLEBURGH, VIRGINIA

"I awakened with a start from a late afternoon nap, relieved that I was in our bedroom in Virginia.

I dreamt I was picking up bits and pieces of Joe's body from the sand at the water's edge, putting them into a gunny sack then counting the pieces over and over again -- fifteen. When I counted them another time there were only eleven. Beyond me, I saw the tide wash more body parts onto the sand. By the time I got to there the tide dragged them back into the breakers. I waded in, holding the gunny sack over my head but I was too late. The tide had already swept them out to sea. The sand broke from underneath me. The current grabbed my gunny sack and sucked it away, too. My mouth formed words to vent my frustration, but no sound came out."

Jackie and I spent Sunday entertaining several of Bobby's kids, watching Caroline ride her pony, "Macaroni" -- and giggling at John-John's futile attempts to put salt on the tails of birds hopping around the patio. A phalanx of them swooped over the picnic table trying to make off with crumbs and bits of food. Salting birds-tails was an old gag Jackie learned from her stepfather. "If you want to catch a bird," he told her, "you have to put salt on his tail."

In August we lost our third child, a few days after his premature birth. At four pounds, ten ounces little Patrick Bouvier Kennedy was "an emergency c-section" -- as they say in the maternity wards. Attempts to sustain his life failed.

With my encouragement, Jackie accepted an offer
from Aristotle Onasis for a long Mediterranean
cruise aboard his sumptuous yacht. Would anyone
have dreamed that four years later, they would
marry, --- after Ari paid Jackie over twenty
million dollars for the privilege!

Since coming home on October 17th, we've been
getting along much better than at earlier times
during our marriage. My liaison's with other women
has been kept secret from the public. Some of them
weren't secrets to Jackie. She was on the verge of
leaving me once when my dad put a million dollars
in her bank account. That settled the matter."

The President was reading "The Three Pigs",
John-John's favorite story.

'If you don't come out, I'll huff and I'll puff- -
-' Jack signaled to his son - - - The boy
responded: 'and I'll blow your house down!"

In Caroline's room, Jackie read her something a
little more sophisticated . . . Whittier's,
'Barbara Fritchie'.

"Oh shoot if you must this old grey head --- but
spare your country's flag she said."

Caroline was wide eyed. "Did they shoot her,
mom?"

"Listen," Jackie replied, "and you'll see."

At John-John's bedside, Kennedy was winding it up:
'And the three little pigs lived happily ever
after.' "Now put your head on the pillow and go to
sleep." "Will you be here when I wake up" John-John
asked. "No, pal, I've got lots of work to do at the
office. Maybe your mother will bring you and your
sister up to spend the night tomorrow." In
Caroline's room, Jackie was reading the final part
of Barbara Fritchie: 'And ever again the stars look
down, On thy stars below in Frederick town.'

Caroline released a sigh of relief. "I'm glad they didn't shoot her, mom."

In the den, Agents Ed Morey and Kenneth Wiesman looked forward to midnight, when their shift ended. They were gabbing with Agent Clint Hill who guarded Jackie and the kids. "Lotta travel coming up" Morey observed. "Yep, we leave for Florida on the sixteenth and don't get back till the nineteenth" Wiesman sighed. "You'll have to be extra sharp", Hill observed. "Those Cuban exiles are probably planning some kind of demonstration." It could be worse in Dallas . . . the home of the real crazies - - The Hunt's, General Walker and the rest of that bunch of right wing fanatics. "I wonder if the boss can talk Jackie into going" Hill mused.

In an unmarked car Agents William Straughn and John McCarthy Wells played gin rummy while they waited. It was against regulations but so were many other things they enjoyed, like drinking on duty -- grounds for immediate dismissal if they were caught.

In the living room John and Jackie sat close to one another on a love seat underneath the beautiful Tiffany lamp Jackie purchased during a recent trip to New York.

Kennedy was constantly chiding her for spending too much money, especially on clothes. "Remember, honey, you married a Kennedy not a Rockefeller." "I do remember" she murmured," every time I see Nels Rockefeller."

"He's an old man!" Kennedy laughed. "Oh that doesn't bother me, I like older men -- that's why I married you."

She leaned forward and gave her husband an affectionate kiss. Kennedy responded then began pulling himself up off the love seat, a process which took a while because of his back brace.

"Where are you going? Jackie asked. "Back to the White House. I've got a lot of work piled up on my desk. I'm already falling asleep just thinking about it."

Driving to D.C. Kennedy rode in the back seat of the second Secret Service limousine tailing Roberts and Wells in their unmarked car. I want to stop in Georgetown, Kennedy advised. Okay, Mister President. Where would that be?"

"Don't be coy, Morey, we're going to Mary's house."

"On 'Q' Street isn't it?"

"What a memory" Kennedy chided. "We were just there three days ago."

Ken Wiesman spoke into the mike. "Orion to Juneau." "Go ahead Juneau." "We're going to Mary Meyer's house." "Roger" came the reply.

Cursing to himself, Wiesman knew he probably wouldn't get off shift till one or two o'clock. The boss's appetite for this kind of thing was insatiable.

10:15 P.M. NOVEMBER 3rd.

At the Plantation Yacht Harbor Motel, forty miles south of the CIA station known as JM WAVE, a meeting was in progress between three men; William King Harvey, Johnny Roselli and David Sanchez Morales (aka "the Big Indian").

   From being no more than a common assassin for
the Agency in 1951, Morales had worked his way up
to Chief Of Operations at "the Wave." (*As a former
colleague of the "Big Indian" told the author:
"Morales was not a candidate for Mensa. But if you
needed someone to take a couple of guys over the
fence and murder someone, Morales was your man."*)

"The Big Indian" is in a drunken rage. "Shackley
got the word from someone way up at NSA who heard
it on taps they got in the oval office and a
conversation between some diplomat at the UN -- and
Castro's doctor. That sonofabitch in the White
House is trying to make a deal with the sonofabitch
in Havana! Santos has to get the job done in Tampa
for sure," he yells.

Harvey was a legendary figure at the CIA. Weighing
three hundred pounds he was nonetheless the
prototype for Ian Fleming's James Bond. Born in
Indiana in 1916, Harvey was first an FBI Agent,
then switched to "the Agency" after repeated run-
ins with Director Hoover.

His greatest "accomplishment" was digging a
tunnel under the Berlin Wall and tapping East
German telephone lines.

*(KGB Colonel Oleg Nechiporenko told the author they
were aware of this, so constantly fed
disinformation into Harvey's listening devices)*.

President Kennedy was so taken with Harvey's
accomplishments and "can do" attitude he invited
him to the White House. The President was appalled
by his size and the fact that he had a silver
plated 355 Magnum in a shoulder holster underneath
his coat. How he got past Security remains a
mystery.

Having created the CIA'S infamous ZR RIFLE (an
assassination's program), Harvey ran afoul of
Bobby Kennedy for sending raiding parties to

Cuba during "the missile crisis", posing the risk
of upsetting negotiations between Khruschev and
President Kennedy. Infuriated, Bobby relieved
Harvey of his post and exiled him to the their
station in Rome.

"These guys don't have any sophistication in
assassinations, Johnny", Harvey observed. "They
just hire someone to walk up to a guy, blast him
and leave."

This ruffled the feathers of the nattily dressed
Roselli but he didn't let on. He had come a long
way since his days as a street thug for Capone and
was now known in Mob circles as "Mister Cool."
Suave and well spoken, Roselli was Sam Giancana's
representative on the West coast, specializing in
"settling" labor disputes in the film industry.

"Someone ratted out the guys who were going to
'do' Kennedy in Chicago. They had plenty
sophistication, the right weapons and Sam had the
perfect patsy in place."

"How sophisticated could they be if they get
caught before anything went down", Morales
interjected.

"Probably because too many people were in on
it," Harvey said. "How many knew?"

It took a few moments for Roselli to count them in
his head. "Ten -- maybe -- eleven."

Harvey fixed Roselli with a cold stare. "With four
shooters, the number should have been five. The
four guy's, and the man who sent them there. A
patsy and two shooters were all you needed."

CHAPTER 3

12.40 a.m. NOVEMBER 4th.

At Mary Pinchot Meyer's townhouse in Georgetown, she and John Kennedy were making love in her bedroom. This, after the beautiful divorcee and talented painter shared a couple of LSD pills with her lover, a habit she turned the President onto when they began their affair the previous year. In a state of total ecstasy the pair had no notion of time or distance. For Kennedy these feeling are occasionally interrupted by visions of his mother chastising him for masturbating when he was nine. Mary's concentration is totally focused on the psychedelic pleasure of making love to her very special friend. She consulted Tim Leary about the use of LSD before experimenting with Kennedy. Later, Leary, too, became a "friend."

Pinchot had first been introduced to young Jack Kennedy by her date, Bill Attwood, while the couple were attending a dance at Choate, one of the best prep schools in America. Several years younger than they were she soon began dating Jack, but just as soon the pair went their separate ways.

In 1945 the tall, stunningly beautiful Mary, projected an intense look, softened by emerald green eyes and blonde hair. She married Marine lieutenant, Cord Meyer. At the time, Mary was working as a journalist for The North American Newspaper Alliance. They sent her to San Francisco for the opening of the United Nations. Another young reporter named Jack Kennedy was also sent to cover this event. Unfortunately for him, Mary was accompanied by her new husband.

By 1954 John and Jackie Kennedy were living in Georgetown, where they discovered new neighbors,

Mary and Cord. Jack had recently been elected to
the Senate. Jackie and Mary became close friends.
With three kids, Mary was a housewife, but still
found time to attend art classes. Her sister,
Antoinette, married a promising journalist named Ben
Bradlee. Cord, who was already working for the CIA
became an officer of that agency the following year.
The Meyer's had three beautiful children. In
December, 1956 their nine year old son, Michael, was
struck and killed by an automobile. Mary and Cord
divorced in 1958.

By 1961 Mary was a regular visitor at The White
House and soon found herself upstairs, in the
President's bed.

Kennedy looked at his watch and groaned. "Gotta go"
he whispered to Mary, whose body was pressed firmly
against his. "All you can do when you get there is
go to bed." "True" Kennedy responded, but it's
three o'clock and those guys out there need some
rest." "So tell them to go home . . . you'll see
them tomorrow . . . or see 'em later, or
something."

The President chuckled. "Mary, I'm crazy about
you." "Then take me with you," she smiled. Kennedy
laughed. "Okay, come on. Uh, while I think of it,
can this stuff cause hallucinations a long time
after taking it?" "Uh-huh, why?" "Oh, I just
wondered."

HAVANA -2:59 a.m. NOVEMBER 4TH

Contemporaneous with the activity in Georgetown,
Fidel Castro and brother Raul, were walking all
over Havana Viejas ("the old city.") With its night
life mostly outside, a sizable portion of the
populace didn't go to bed until dawn. So it was not
unusual for its inhabitants to see the Castro
brothers sporting beards and dressed in fatigues
walking in the streets. A three-man security detail
trailed them. As was their custom, both brothers

were armed. Raul had been Minister of Defense
since the revolution triumphed. If he resented his
older brother's pre-eminence, the younger Castro
kept it to himself.

Occasionally someone who knew them stopped the
pair for a word or two, but basically their
privacy was respected.

When prying ears got to close, they spoke in
French or used metaphors to convey their
thoughts, always in subdued tones.

Soon they reached Jose Marti Park. Located next to
the sea wall, it was a site favored by Fidel for
sensitive conversations like this one. With the
tide crashing against the wall others could not
hear what they were saying.

Raul gesticulated his position with gusto.

"Let me get Pinero alone so I can impress him
with the need to insulate both of us from the
plan being traced back."

"Without killing Pinero after he does his job,
there's no way to be certain of that; so that
kind of action is out of the question."

Unable to keep exasperation out of his tone, Raul
observed: "You have a difficulty for every
solution."

"Because this kind of solution is very
difficult."

They continued walking, each brother trying to
decide where to go next in the discussion.

Finally, Raul spoke again.

"There is one idea. I could use a *cutout* to
approach one of Santos Trafficante's friends
with a note for him in a sealed envelope.

Here's what it would say: "Someone in Havana says
you might do something important for the
revolution'. He wants you to put a plan
together to terminate an individual who is
coming to Florida soon.

You could get your casinos back if you're prepared
to do this for someone in a position to arrange
it." That way, we would have complete deniability.

"How will Santos know where this came from?"

"Four years ago, just after he got out of
Trescorina, he came to me at the bar at the Hilton,
effusive with thanks for authorizing his release.
He'll remember what I told him."

"Which was?"

"One day you might be in a position to do
something for the Revolution."

Fidel began walking again. Lost in thought he
mumbled: "Okay. But the message must contain this
caveat: Don't implement any plan without a signal
to proceed."

MONDAY – NOVEMBER 4TH – 9:45 A.M.

In the Oak Park suburb of Chicago, Sam Giancana
slouched on a bench behind the eleventh tee at Tam
O'Shanter country club.

Frustrated by the cancellation of Kennedy's visit
on Saturday, the fifty-five year old ironfisted
boss of the Chicago mafia, banged his driver
against the ground. Richard Cain, his man at the
Sheriff's department, allowed amateurs to flub
"the hit." Cain was "a made man" in the Chicago
mafia, a detail which would escape notice by law
enforcement for several more years. Leaks,
confusion and stupidity squandered a golden
opportunity to dispose of Sam's nemesis. Giancana
was being so closely watched by the FBI he

couldn't participate. If he had, he assured himself things would have been different. The pressure on the mafioso was intolerable. Even on the golf course the FBI tailed him relentlessly, never more than a couple of holes behind. They marched in lockstep everywhere Sam went. He'd fly to Vegas to see Phyliss McGuire, they'd have a seat right behind his. At the Cal Neva Lodge he'd catch pal Sinatra's act . . . they'd be at the next table. He'd go for a swim, they'd be there in swim trunks a few seconds later. He'd go to take a leak, they'd be in the next stall.

And it was all because of those "dirty-double-crossing, sons of bitches . . . the Kennedy's." Recalling all he did to get Jack elected - Sam wanted to puke. What a sucker he'd been.

At eighteen he'd been arrested for murder. "Luckily" the key witness died in "an accident." In the thirties he was a hood in Paul Ricca's gang. He excelled at brutal murders and armed robbery. These exploits earned him the nickname "Boom-Boom". By the late fifties Sam was at the top.

During Eisenhower's last year in office, "Moony" as many called him, was tapped by the CIA to participate with pals, Johnny Roselli and Santos Trafficante in schemes to eliminate Fidel Castro. When Kennedy moved into the White House, "the off Castro" programs continued.

By then Sam was sharing a knockout brunette named Judy Exner *with Kennedy*. So close were they that Exner served as a courier between the two, carrying a briefcase stuffed with cash for Giancana to "grease" county sheriffs during the West Virginia presidential Primary. Once, Judy recalled having to sit in the Sam's bathroom while he and the President discussed business in a hotel suite. When Jack named Bobby Attorney General, the fat was in the fire. From that moment the friendship between the Mafioso and the President was on the wane.

By 1963, they were mortal enemies. The new
Attorney General was putting Sam's friends in jail,
one after the other . . . and "Moony" was next.

"Sam you're up," his playing partner shouted.
"Oh, yeah," Giancana responded, then strode to
the tee box, teed his ball up and promptly hit
"a duck hook" into the adjoining fairway barely
missing another golfer. About to launch an
apology, Sam recognized "his shadow", Chicago
FBI agent Bill Roemer, doubled up in laughter.

"Too bad I didn't bean the s.o.b." Giancana
grumbled.

WASHINGTON D.C. — 11:00 a.m.

In his private office at teamster's headquarters,
James Riddle Hoffa, (50) crushed the subpoena he
held in his fist, banged it on top of his desk
and yelled at his lawyer Frank Ragano (41).

"This is going to end now, do ya hear me! These
Kennedy rats have to get poison."

"What should I do Jimmy, call a pest control
company?"

"It ain't funny, Ragano, they're already
sweeping out a cell for me at Sing-Sing."

"You're a long way from that Jimmy, they haven't
even set a date for a preliminary hearing. Besides,
a conviction for a Federal rap like this jury
tampering thing would get you into a Federal pen."

"I'm not waiting for that," Hoffa roared." Santos
is in New Orleans this week, visiting Carlos.
You'ré going down there and tell them Jimmy says
you gotta kill this bastard, now!"

Ragano stared at his client in disbelief. "I know you're upset but -- "Do like I'm tellin' ya! Buy a plane ticket to New Orleans and deliver my message to those dagos."

OVAL OFFICE - THE WHITE HOUSE 12:45 p.m.

President Kennedy listens to FBI Director, J. Edgar Hoover (69). Since 1924 that post is the only job Hoover's had. He's an ugly little bulldog of a man, -- in truth, a homosexual --who makes a practice of persecuting homosexuals. It is well known in D.C. society that Asst. FBI Director Clyde Tolson is Hoover's "main squeeze." They cavort all over Washington and New York, take annual vacations together at the Del Charro Hotel in La Jolla, a few miles south of their favorite west coast hangout, Del Mar Race Track.

It was at the Del Charro one summer that visiting gangsters were able to photograph the two crime fighters, inflagrante delicto --on the floor of their room. ('What comes around, goes around.')

As he listens to "the little bulldog" recite from one of his Agent's reports, Kennedy rocks back and forth in his wooden rocker, with an impassive expression.

"The Rometsch woman is a B-girl at Bobby Baker's Quorum Club in Maryland. Her job consists of encouraging customers to drink all they can. Special Agent Hesselschwerdt has documented sixteen different men whom Miss Rometsch has been intimate with during the past five months."

Hoover glares at Kennedy. "One of them is your friend, Bill Thompson, whom I'm alarmed to report brought Rometsch here for liaisons with you."

"Edgar, have you got this office bugged?" "That would be illegal, Mister President."

"Then how did your 'Agent Hesselschwerdt' come by this knowledge?"

"That *knowledge* concerns me because of its potential for blackmail, the risk of assassination and the probability she's an East German spy. She *is* East German, you know?"

"And how do you know she's a spy, Edgar?"

"A 'confidential source' confirmed Rometsch used to be Walter Ulbricht's secretary."

"I asked you a question and I want an answer, Edgar. Are you bugging me?"

"Certainly not, **certainly not!** The 'Rometsch episode' came to my attention when a correspondent for The Des Moines Register, was about to run a story detailing her involvement with quote: "Several prominent New Frontiersmen in the executive branch of government."

"Your brother Bob got wind of this impending disaster and came to me for help in blocking publication of the story."

Hoover gloated. He had the Kennedy's right where he wanted them. In exchange for seeing to it that the story was killed, he forced Bobby to authorize four wiretaps on the Director's most hated public figure, Martin Luther King.

The Senate Rules Committee, about to lower the boom on Lyndon Johnson, was also planning to investigate 'the Rometsch episode.' Again, Hoover rode to the rescue, convincing Majority Leader Mike Mansfield and Minority Leader Everett Dirksen that pursuing the investigation "would not be in the best interest of" those two magical words: 'National Security'. The Senators acquiesced. JFK dodged the bullet again. "You don't do anything for nothing,

Edgar. Why did you want to see me? To extract payment?"

"That would be blackmail, Mister President."

Kennedy knew Hoover would never go public with information acquired through electronic surveillance. It was illegal and would ruin the Bureau's image.

"What is it you want, Edgar?"

"That tenure of office act you and your brother pushed through the Congress at midnight last June, mandating retirement for all Federal appointees at age seventy . . . I'd appreciate a waiver from you, so I can continue serving my country as I have for over thirty-nine years, prosecuting criminals, ferreting out communists and serving six President's -- my life's work."

The Director did not reveal a letter he'd received from American Intelligence officer, Richard Case Nagell in September, warning that Kennedy would be assassinated by a man named Lee Harvey Oswald. He just hoped it was true.

THE INDOOR SWIMMING POOL AT THE WHITE HOUSE – 1:18 P.M.

This splendid facility was constructed with funds donated by Jack's father. At the moment it's being used by three naked persons: The President and two "staff secretaries" whom the Secret Service gave the code names: "Fiddle" (21) and "Faddle" (23). These "secretaries" are primarily employed to provide "in house" sexual services for the Commander in Chief. Having worked in close proximity to JFK during the presidential campaign, he promised them if elected they would have jobs in the White House.

Watching them from the other end of the pool was
Special Presidential Assistant, Dave Powers. The
older Bostonian has served Kennedy since he ran for
the congress in 1946. Seeing how much fun Jack was
having with the two young "secretaries" was
gratifying. It had already been a long day and
Powers knew Jack's back pain was intense. He could
always tell by the white pallor that supplanted the
President's normal ruddy complexion.
Kennedy never complained about the pain, just
looked forward to his next shot from "Doctor
Feelgood" and went on with his day. The Secret
Service's White House Detail (WHD) was banned from
the pool during these private "swimming parties".
It was a direct violation of their duty to shield
the chief executive and grounds for dismissal if
discovered.

The President's instructions were for them to
keep in touch with the Agents guarding Jackie and
make sure she did not show up without Kennedy
knowing when she'd arrive. The entire situation
was one the Agents found demeaning.

"Fiddle and Faddle" did not share these feelings.
Having "fun" with "the Prez" was the center of a
universe they loved.

(Only recently was the pair's real identities
revealed: "Fiddle", was in fact Patricia Wear --
"Faddle" was Jill Cowan. They came from good
families and had attended the best schools.)

It had already been a long day and there was still
lots to do. After an eight-forty-five breakfast
meeting with legislative leaders, the President
went to the Oval Office and reviewed bills and
other documents awaiting his signature.

But mostly he read a-half dozen newspapers,
especially the New York Times and The Washington
Post.

The Vietnam thing was still a hot topic and the papers were full of it.

Lingering doubts about U.S. complicity in Diem's overthrow and murder would not go away. The tabloids hammered away with the most lurid speculation, some of it true.

Instability in Saigon was rampant. Something had to be done or the South Vietnam's new government might collapse.

Kennedy buzzed for his private secretary, Evelyn Lincoln. A pleasant, highly efficient woman she appeared, promptly. Lincoln started with Kennedy when he entered the Senate in 1953. When he became President they used to joke about the fact that when Lincoln was President, his secretary's name was Kennedy.

"Uh, Missus Lincoln, please get me the following people: My brother, Bob, Mister McNamara and Mister Rusk and General Taylor."

"In that order Mister President?"

"Uh-huh, but if one's not available, try the next one."

During the next two hours, Kennedy discussed an idea he hoped would put the new regime in Saigon on their toes. The President instructed General Taylor (Chairman Of The Joint Chiefs) to create a National Security Memorandum, calling for the withdrawal of one-thousand U.S. troops from Vietnam by Christmas and the balance of all U.S. forces by the end of 1965.

While the first thousand soldiers would (and were) actually withdrawn, the thrust of his plan would be to frighten Big Minh and the other generals into resisting efforts by the North to consolidate

Vietnam. Also, to solve religious dissent and other unrest in Saigon and instill the resolve to fight in "the hearts and minds" of South Vietnamese soldiers.

If the new Saigon regime didn't get the job done, they'd face the prospect of a wholesale withdrawal of all U.S. forces.

Without American troops to protect them the Generals would soon be at the mercy of Ho Chi Min.

It was another one of JFK'S duplicitous maneuvers, I.E. a bluff. With the election a year away, to announce the withdrawal all American forces from Vietnam would put a sword in the hands of the Republicans they would use to hack the President to pieces.

National Security Memorandum 263 would have historical implications which Kennedy had no way of foreseeing.

Following his assassination worshiping "Camelot" was practiced by practically everyone. Kennedy became a martyr based on several premises -- especially "his plan to withdraw from Vietnam." As if by divine intervention *a cold warrior was transformed from a hawk, to a dove. For the Kennedy's, showing the myth was more important than showing the facts.*

In his oral history to the Kennedy Memorial Library, Bobby Kennedy was asked: "Was there ever any consideration to pulling out (of Vietnam?" *ANSWER: "No."*

CHAPTER 4

STONEWALL, TEXAS — 2:15 P.M.

At his 2700 hundred acre ranch near Johnson City, Vice President Lyndon Johnson and his ranch manager, Dale Malecheck, drove eighty miles an hour in Lyndon's huge Cadillac, over various sections of his property. Johnson was checking to see if jobs he ordered accomplished had been satisfactorily completed.

Located in West Texas' "Hill Country", it's mostly barren, unforgiving land. The only water for miles comes from the Pedernales River, which runs through the center of the LBJ Ranch. Four hundred head of Hereford cattle graze on various types of grass planted and irrigated on the sprawling property.

Johnson, a wily fifty-five year old veteran of national politics was contemplating how to extricate himself from a plethora of charges under investigation by the Senate Rules Committee. Except for a few hours in October the Vice President had not been seen in the capitol since Bobby Baker resigned on October 7th.

Known as "the 51st Senator", Baker (34), was the Secretary to the Senate, a post Johnson created for his 'protégé.'

The genesis of most of LBJ'S problems with The Rules Committee involved "services" Johnson rendered for Billy Sol Estes, a slick tycoon from Pecos, Texas.

Prior to his arrest in 1962, Estes amassed millions from fraudulent cotton allotments that Johnson helped arrange with the Department of Agriculture. It was all part of a popular government program to encourage growing cotton. To receive these generous allotments recipients had only to prove that they owned or leased the land on which the cotton would be grown.

In Billy Sol's case, this was mostly accomplished with false lease agreements on millions of acres of Texas farmland.

For his part in this arrangement Johnson received hundreds of thousands of dollars in cash payoffs from Estes funneled to him through Bobby Baker.

When the scheme began to be investigated by local Department Of Agriculture official, Henry Marshall, Johnson sent his long time associate Mack Wallace to "convince Henry to stop investigating."

When Marshall refused, Wallace shot him five times with a bolt action rifle. Through the good offices of the local coroner, a Johnson political ally, Marshall's death was ruled 'a suicide' and the case was forgotten, or so it seemed.

Marshall's 'demise' was not the end of Johnson's problems. An insurance salesman, Don Reynolds, was scheduled testify before The Rules Committee on November 22nd about kickbacks he'd paid to Johnson through the ubiquitous Bobby Baker; also a hundred thousand dollar bribe that went to the Vice President for his part in securing the award of the TFX fighter plane to General Dynamics in Fort Worth; a vending machine scheme Bobby Baker created for use in Defense Contractor's facilities. "Want favorable treatment? Install our machines."

Another item involved payoffs to Johnson from Sam Halfen, bagman for *Carlos Marcello*. Halfen, known as 'big fix' claimed he passed a hundred thousand dollars a year to Johnson for ten years for the powerful Democrat's support in defeating Federal Anti-Gambling legislation. Halfen's efforts were on behalf of Carlos Marcello.

Johnson's options were limited: Do nothing and receive a long prison term . . . or become President. Chances for achieving the second goal might soon become a reality. Discreet inquiries had been sent through intermediaries for 'the little man'. If JFK met with an untimely end, could the new President be counted on to deflect investigation from "The Big Easy?"

A not so discreet flier had been distributed in and around Miami.

It read:

"Only through one development will you Cuban patriots ever live again in your homeland as free men responsible as must be the most capable for the guidance and welfare of the Cuban people.

This blessing would come to pass if an inspired Act of God should place in the White House, within weeks, a Texan known to be a friend of all Latin Americans . . . though he must under current conditions bow to the Zionist's who since 1905 came into control of the United States, and for whom Jack Kennedy and Nelson Rockefeller and other members of the Council of Foreign Relations and allied agencies are only stooges and pawns.

Though Johnson must now bow to these crafty and cunning Communist-hatching Jews, yet did an Act Of God suddenly elevate him into the top position (he) would revert to what his beloved father and grandfather were, and to their values and principles and loyalties."

OAK CLIFF, TEXAS (suburb of Dallas)

Lee Harvey Oswald lay on his bed at a rooming house located at 1027 N. Beckley Avenue. Rent: $8.00 per week. Oswald was registered as "O. H. Lee."

He shuffled through the mail housekeeper Earlene Roberts handed him when he returned from the local library.

His wife Marina and 18 month old June lived in nearby Irving at the home of a Quaker couple named Paine. The Paine's weren't really a couple anymore because Michael and Ruth Paine were in the process of getting a divorce. There was plenty of room.

When he first arrived there from Mexico City Lee spent every day haplessly looking for a job.

A neighbor of the Paine's, Lillie Mae Randall, told Ruth and Marina her brother had recently gone to work for The Texas School Book Depository, a seven story brick building, located at Houston and Elm streets in downtown Dallas.

Ruth called the manager, Roy Truly, and got his okay for Lee to interview for a job. He was hired as an "order filler" at a wage of a dollar and twenty cents and hour. Two days later, a second daughter, Rachel, was born to the Oswald's -- the same day, Lee turned twenty-four.

His work at the Depository was easy. Lee collected orders from his Supervisor, wheeled a pushcart to various floors, "picked" the required books, took them downstairs, packed them and delivered the packages to the shipping department.

The FBI had been haunting Oswald ever since he returned to Texas following his defection to the

Soviet Union. While he was in Mexico City a Dallas based Agent, James Hosty waited for Marina outside the Paine residence, stepped out of his car and began questioning her as to Lee's whereabouts. The next week this happened again. Marina was frightened; she told Lee about Agent Hosty when he got back from Mexico. Oswald was furious.

Lee tore open a letter from the New Orleans Public Library. They claimed he still had four books out that were overdue. He would be charged five-cents a day for each succeeding day. They were mistaken. These titles had been returned on September 24th, prior to Lee's departure for Mexico City.

The pay phone in the hall rang three times before Earlene Roberts answered it. Seconds later, Lee heard her shuffle to his door. "Call for you, Mister Lee."

In the hallway, Oswald picked up the receiver. "Hello."

A cultured voice, tinged with the slightest hint of a Texas accent, said: "It's Maurice Bishop, Lee. I have some new titles for you." "Hang on", Lee replied, "I'll get something to write with." Returning with a pad and pencil, Lee gripped the receiver again. "Okay." 'Ryder's Principles of Flight' -- (a long pause) and 'Strategies For Breeding Foxes', by Henry Stovall." Then he heard a click, followed by the dial tone.

PLACE de REVOLUCION (15 miles from Havana) 10:45 P.M.

Fidel Castro wound up a four and a-half hour speech on the economy, with the revolution's most honored slogan: "Patria O Muerte --Venceramos!" (The Fatherland or death -- we will prevail).

During the speech Fidel exhorted his revolutionary
comrades to work harder in order to meet certain
quotas, especially those for sugar cane. That crop
amounted to eighty-three percent of Cuba's exports
and without the required production the country's
economy would sink even deeper into its economic
malaise. Cuba was receiving over a million dollars
a day from the Soviet Union, but it wasn't enough.
Riding back to Havana with brother, Raul, Fidel
spoke quietly concerning a growing problem with
"Comrade Che".

"He's going all over the world making speeches
against the Russians and praising the Chinese.

Can you imagine such audacity and lack of regard
for our relations with Khruschev? During one speech
in Algeria he called the Soviet's 'Imperialists',
no different than the United States!!'

"Mikoyan called me five times complaining about
Che." 'After all', he said, 'for a million dollars
a day we're entitled to better treatment.'

Raul offered Fidel a Monte Cristo cigar, then
lit one himself.

After a few puffs he said: "Maybe we should
convene a secret meeting of the party leaders
and confront Che about this."

Fidel puffed his cigar. "Too soon. In the minds of
most people Che and Camilo Cienfuegos are still
revolutionary heroes." "At least we don't have to
worry about Camilo anymore," Raul observed.

Fidel stared out the window at the lights of
Havana blinking on the horizon. "I know Che's
spent time in New York recently, talking with some
of Kennedy's people.

"Huh?" Raul grunted. "What was that about?"

"I don't know. I'm growing more suspicious of him every day. Before he left for Europe, we were talking in my office and he all but flatly accused me of responsibility for Camilo Cienfuegos' disappearance."

A knowing glance passed between the two. Raul looked his brother in the eye and spoke very softly. "That could lead to serious problems. We'd better start thinking about how to get Che out of the picture . . . permanently."

"I've already given that plenty of thought. And by the way, that matter we were discussing the other night in the park about your friend, in Florida?"

CHAPTER 5

DALLAS — WEDNESDAY NOVEMBER 6th — 12:15 p.m.

At the FBI'S Dallas office in the heart of downtown, Lee Harvey Oswald stepped off the elevator, went to the receptionist, Annie Fenner, and asked to see "Agent Hosty."

"Jim's out to lunch, Fenner smiled. "Can I say who called?" Hosty's absence exasperated Oswald. He thrust an envelope at her and growled: "Get this to him", then disappeared into the elevator.

The envelope was not sealed. Unable to contain her curiosity, Annie Fenner withdrew a single sheet of paper which read:

"Let this be a warning. I will blow up the FBI and the Dallas Police Department if you don't stop bothering my wife.

Lee H. Oswald"

After work, Oswald went directly to the Oak Cliff Library. He pulled the books off the shelf which

"Maurice Bishop" mentioned on the phone, "Ryder's Principles of Flight" and "Strategies For Breeding Fox."

Lee checked them out, took them to his rooming house and scanned the pages for micro dot encryptions that could only be identified by someone trained to do so. Using a Minox Camera he photographed each dot, then, with technology he stole while working at a map company he enlarged the images. Written in "Bishop's" bold handwriting were further instructions memorializing information the intelligence Agent would not discuss on the telephone. It involved specific action on how to further undermine the Fair Play for Cuba Committee.

NEW ORLEANS –1:35 p.m.

The Dining room at The Royal Orleans Hotel was all but deserted. A hard rain had been falling since ten, inhibiting patronage, especially from the hotel's regular luncheon clientele.

At a corner table, three middle aged men lunched on clam chowder and giant crawfish. The trio consisted of Carlos Marcello, Santos Trafficante and attorney Frank Ragano. The latter, a native of Tampa, also represented Trafficante. Despite the fact that the nearest patrons were at least twenty yards away, Ragano spoke in Italian, his tone, subdued. Translated, what he said was:

"You won't believe what Jimmy wants me to tell you. He wants you to kill President Kennedy. "The men's faces betrayed no sign they'd even heard Ragano's chilling recitation. They just continued consuming their meal. This confused the little lawyer. He looked from one to the other. Presently, he stirred his chowder then resumed eating. To a passing waiter, Trafficante said: "Another cup of coffee, and make it hotter this time, please."

Ragano knew Hoffa would interrogate him regarding

the mob bosses reaction. He had delivered
Jimmy's message. There was nothing else he could
do.

"Hurry up", Marcello urged his companions.
"Havt'a get back ta court."

Half a mile away at 544 Camp Street, two men on
Marcello's payroll were conferring in the office of
one time head of the FBI'S Chicago office, W. Guy
Banister. A legend during the Dillinger, Bonnie &
Clyde era, the tall sixty-one year old intense,
fanatic anti-communist and arch segregationist was
speaking with pilot and fellow investigator, David
Ferrie.

"Heard from Oswald?" "Yeah," Ferrie replied. "Called
him last night, in fact." Banister's stare bore into
Ferrie like an ice pick. "Where from?" he asked "A
phone booth outside the Wynn Dixie."

"Is he still on board?"

"Yep."

"Incredible that he got that job in Dealey
Plaza." Banister said shaking his head.

"You know the old saying, Guy, "better to be
lucky, than smart."

Banister did not smile, just muttered: "Hope our
luck holds till the twenty-second." Ferrie's thin
lips twisted into an ugly smile. "Gotta get going -
- I'll be late for court." Ferries scurried out of
the office and padded down the steps to the street.

Banister was contemplative. A native of Louisiana,
he ran for City Council in 1961. His platform was
segregation and uncovering communists. It failed.
Now he devotes all of his time to Guy Banister
Associates, a detective firm. One of his clients,
G. Wray Gill, is Carlos Marcello's regular
attorney. Guy's recent work for him has been

focused on "the little man's" deportation case.

His other interests involve investigating "subversives", particularly at Tulane University. He helps funnel funds "from anonymous donors to violent anti-Castro Cuban organizations like ALPHA 66 and the DRE. His office is littered with military equipment used to train the exiles. Rifles, ammunition, mortar shells, hand grenades, pistol belts, pup tents, everything for waging guerrilla warfare.

Guy is a key participant in planning what is scheduled to occur in Dallas on the twenty-second. Johnny Roselli, a prime mover in the conspiracy to murder Kennedy is due to visit soon. Banister has collected some vital intelligence including blue prints of Dallas' storm drain system and the Secret Service's manual for protecting the President.

The manual was sent to him by Chief James Rowley, a friend from their days together in the FBI. These items are of vital importance to the success of the impending assassination. They underscore Banister's thesis for success:
"There's never been a great man without a good espionage system."

MIDDLEBURG, VIRGINIA — 2:00 p.m.

At the Kennedy's "Atoka" estate, Jackie was reading Vogue magazine. Bright sunshine poured into her spacious living room enabling her to read without turning on the lights. The children's nanny, Maude Shaw came into the room. Jackie questioned her without looking up. "Are they down?". "Yes, Missus Kennedy. I think Caroline may have a fever. Her cheeks are flame red. And, oh, Mister Gilpatric is on the phone." Jackie smiled to herself put the magazine down and crossed the living room. "She might have Rosella Fever again. Gets it from the kids at school. I'll take Mister Gilpatric's call in my room."

Alone in her spacious bedroom, Jackie sat on the bed and picked up the phone.

"Ross", she said. An esoteric smile played on her lips as she listened. "No, I've been fine, thanks. Her tone became more intimate. "How about my favorite Assistant Secretary of Defense?" Listens. "You have? Well I've missed you too." She reclined and lay her head on a large white pillow. "Can't this week." Listens. "He's going to New York on the fourteenth. That's a Thursday. I could have Missus Shaw take the kids to the zoo." Listens. "How about a little tea and . . . recreation -- right here?" Listens. "Why not? Jack signs his girls in at the White House and takes them right upstairs. Last week I found a pair of women's panties tucked inside my pillow. I gave them to Jack and told him he'd better find out whose they were, 'They aren't my size.' Listens. *Men!* Always protecting each other. "Listens, then laughs again. "If you believe that I've got some gold mine stocks I'd like to sell you!"

THE WHITE HOUSE DINING ROOM - 2:15 p.m.

The President was hosting a luncheon for Ohio Editors and Publishers.

They had just been served sorbet and coffee.

One of them, an attractive younger woman, Pricilla Sanderson, sat on the President's right. "Tell me Mister President" she smiled, "what kind of music do you like?" Kennedy responded with a serious face: "I think "Hail to The Chief" has a nice melody, don't you?" Sanderson tried to suppress a laugh, but couldn't. Kennedy grinned, letting her know it was just a joke.

"What do you think of our chances for taking Ohio, next year", he continued. Feeling right at home now, she replied: "I think it's going to be close, don't you?"

"I was hoping you'd say I was a cinch," Kennedy smiled. Leaning closer she giggled: "That's what I said." She leaned even closer now. "Call me Pricilla." "Well Pricilla, I think you've missed your calling. You should have been a politician." "For you, Mister President, I'm liable to switch parties!" They both laughed.

DALLAS — 7:45 P.M.

At the Crestwood Apartments, a strikingly beautiful twenty-four year old brunette, Cuban-exile Silvia Odio, was putting the final touches on her coiffeur while her seventeen year old sister, Annie continued packing boxes for a move to another apartment.

The doorbell buzzed. "Oh, my god, he's early. Let him in Annie and tell him I'll be right there."

When she opened the door, Annie was confronted by three men standing in the dimly lit hallway. Two of them were Latino's, the third, much younger, was an Anglo. Alarmed, Annie put the chain lock in place and squinted at them questioningly.

The taller of the two Latino's, a man about forty, smiled and spoke to Annie in Spanish. "We'd like to talk with Sarita Odio", he said. "She doesn't live here anymore", Annie replied.

Silvia sidled up next to Annie and stared at their visitors. "Sarita's my sister. I'm Silvia, what do you want?" "We're from JURE. I'm Leopoldo, he's Angelo. "And I'm Leon Oswald", the Anglo said in halting Spanish." We're with "JURE", Leopoldo continued, "just like your sister. We know your father Amador, from Cuba. He and your mother are both in jail."

Their claim of being affiliated with JURE interested Silvia. Barely three months earlier, she and Sarita helped to organize the exile group *Junta Revolucionaria* (JURE). Leopoldo's information about her parents was correct. A prominent and well to do family, the Odio's were communists who originally supported Fidel, but turned on him when they realized he'd become a dictator. Opting instead for *"Castroism Without Castro"* was considered counter revolutionary.

To protect his daughters, Amador Odio sent them to America. Later, he and Silvia's mother were accused of harboring an individual plotting to murder Fidel. The Odio's were thrown into the infamous Isle Of Pines prison where they still languished.

Silvia glanced at her tiny wristwatch. "Someone is coming to pick me up at eight and I must finish dressing. What is it you wanted?"

"We're raising funds to help fight Castro. Our English is very poor, so we were hoping you'd help us write letters to people in the community asking for donations to JURE."

"Call me in a couple of days. I'll think about it." Before departing, "Leon" repeated his introduction: "I'm Leon Oswald." Leopoldo jotted down Silvia's number and left. Unbeknownst to Odio, the real Lee Oswald was miles away.

Two days later, Leopoldo phoned Silvia. "What", he asked "did you think of our friend, Leon Oswald?"

"I didn't think about it, why?" "Well you know he's kind of loco -- an ex-marine and a great marksman. He thinks Cubans don't have any guts. Says Kennedy should have been assassinated after the Bay Of Pigs."

Whether the Odio sisters' subsequent identification of the man accused of killing the President was

correct or not, men posing as *members of a*
communist organization, accompanied by someone
calling himself Leon Oswald, implicated the former
Marine and self proclaimed Marxist in the impending
assassination of JFK.

(In his recently released book, "JFK: The Cuba
Files", former head of Cuban Intelligence Fabian
Escalante theorizes that "Angelo" was **Isidro Borja
Simo** and "Leopoldo", **Rogelio Cisneros Diaz**. The
pair were in fact *members of the violently anti-
Castro, anti-communist DRE*, who had years earlier
been recruited by propagandist David Atlee
Phillips. Phillips "ran" this CIA funded
organization.)

NOON — THURSDAY — NOVEMBER 7th — TAMPA, FLORIDA

In the comfort of his den, Santos Trafficante
spoke Spanish with Macho Gener, a Cuban he'd
worked with since the early days in Havana. About
Santos' age, Macho is overweight, has flecks of
silver in his otherwise dark brown hair, heavy
lines in his face and deep circles under his
eyes.

Santos keeps fingering a small white envelope,
turning it over and over in his fingers.

"And this was yesterday", Santos asked.

"Yes", Macho replied. I wanted to come then, but
they said you wouldn't get back from New Orleans
till late last night."

"And the guy who gave you this — what did he
look like?"

"I only saw him for about ten seconds . . . on
Calle Ocho just after I left "Antonio's Bar." Cuban
guy . . . tall like you. Wore a white guyabera and
a Panama hat. Says to me: 'You're a friend of
Santos', give him this. If you open it — I'll cut
off both your arms.' And then he walked away —

    fast."

"So, did you open it?"

"No." This guy meant what he said. Besides, it's addressed to you."

"Okay, Macho. Thanks."

After Macho left, Santos reread the slip of paper in the envelope: "Remember what I said to you in the bar at the Hilton. Now is the time to '*do something for the Revolution*'. We know the man is coming to Tampa. If you receive no further contact, make sure he doesn't go home."

Typewritten on a plain sheet of paper it was not signed.

Didn't need to be. Santos knew it could only have come from one person -- Raul Castro.

The humor of the whole situation suddenly was too much. Santos put his head back and roared. Raul didn't know plans were already in place to make sure 'the man doesn't go home.' "This guy is number one on everybody's hit list," Santos chuckled.

"The way it's going we'll have to draw straws to see who gets to kill the sonofabitch!"

CHAPTER 6

MEXICO CITY - 12:45 P.M.

At the small El Encanto Hotel, located on a
street just off The Reforma, "Maurice Bishop"s
sat at the bar, alternately sipping a Pina-Colata
and inhaling a cigarette . . . his thirty-fifth
for the day. It was warm, very warm -- even for
November, a month that in Mexico beckoned the sun
closer.

"Maurice Bishop" was the name *David Atlee
Phillips* used in the field.

Six feet-two, two hundred pounds, he had light
brown hair and silvery blue eyes. Well tanned, his
appearance was marred by large dark sunspots under
both eyes. He always dressed impeccably.

During 1950, Phillips ran a small public relations
firm in Havana. At night, he pursued his real
passion . . . acting. The local little theater
group he belonged to did classic drama, which
Phillips thrived on.

Twenty-eight at the time, he spoke fluent Spanish. A
CIA recruiter from the U.S. embassy came calling.
Phillips, a combat veteran from WWII, was only too
happy to become an agent and later an officer of
"the company." Joseph Stalin still held sway in
Moscow. To the native of Fort Worth and graduate of
Texas Christian University, the dreaded Communist
dictator and Communism, was an aberration.

Now, as the Agency's Chief Of Anti-Castro Covert
Action for the Western Hemisphere, his duties
included fomenting anti-Castro propaganda and
directing the activities of two of the most violent
exile groups in America, Alpha 66 and the DRE.

Of special interest was countering the Fair Play
For Cuba Committee (FPCC) which CIA wanted
destroyed.

That summer, Phillips used Lee Harvey Oswald to
embarrass the group in New Orleans. After organizing
a fictitious chapter of "The Committee", signing the
name *Alec J. Hidel* as the organization's Secretary,
Oswald went to various locations around the city,
passing out FPCC literature. In a television debate
with an anti-Castro exile, Oswald admitted being a
former defector to the Soviets and acknowledged he
was "a Marxist."

Although inspired by Phillips, "Oswald's pro-Castro
sympathies" were all part of a charade, run covertly
from 544 Camp Street, the office of former FBI
Agent, W. Guy Banister. FPCC was also a target of
the FBI.

Phillips, a thirteen year veteran of the CIA works
out of Langley, Virginia, "JM WAVE", in Miami, and
the Mexico City CIA Station. During the "cold war",
Mexico City was the Berlin of Latin America. Spying
and intrigue abounded.

In Guatemala, Phillips had and his CIA associates
were instrumental in the overthrow of the Leftist
Arbenz government, organizing and transmitting fake
radio reports detailing how the "massive rebel
forces" were closing in on the capitol . . . all
lies. Arbenz fled and a regime friendly to the U.S.
was installed. The fact that Arbenz had been
elected by the people was of little consequence to
the Agency's "cold warriors."

The Guatemalan effort was directed by E. Howard Hunt
who many years later would be arrested with others
for conspiring to "bug" the Democratic National
Committee at the Watergate Hotel.

Another "action officer" behind the putsch was
David Sanchez Morales who specialized in
assassinating Arbenz followers and other dissidents.
"The Big Indian, or "El Indio" as he was sometimes
referred to, currently held the post of Operations
Chief at JM WAVE. "The Wave's" four hundred case
officers direct the activities of thousands of anti-
Castro exiles, who consider South Miami their
temporary home. The exile's most cherished dream:
overthrowing Castro so they can return to Cuba.
David Morales asked Phillips to "sheep dip"
Oswald for an operation the Texan wasn't privy
to. In another two weeks he would understand only
too well.

He spotted his "luncheon appointment" coming into
the bar --a twenty-three year old Mexican national
named Sylvia Duran. Short and rather plain, she
took a seat two stools from Phillips and pretended
not to notice him. Phillips lit his thirty-second
cigarette for the day, and surveyed the clientele,
trying to ascertain whether someone who knew him
might be watching. "Buy this woman a drink" he
muttered to the bartender, then got up and went to
the men's room.

A few moments later, there was a knock at the
men's room door. Phillips opened it, Duran
stepped inside and Phillips locked the door.

During the next three minutes Phillips discussed
several items with the young Mexican whom he had
arranged, through contacts inside *the Cuban
Embassy*, to be hired as the Consulate's secretary.
Sylvia was only one of many Embassy employee's on
"The Company's" payroll.

The previous secretary was killed by a hit-and run
driver. Two days later, Duran had her job.

Phillips showed her a black and white picture of a
man about her age. He had a receding hairline and a

chin, too small for his face. "Do you remember seeing him," Phillips asked. Duran stared at the picture and nodded. "Yes," she said but I don't remember where." Phillips smiled and stowed the photograph of Lee Harvey Oswald in his inside coat pocket.

Nearly two months earlier, Duran was at her desk when the ex-Marine appeared at the Consulate to apply for a transit visa to go to the Soviet Union --*via Havana.* His request was denied. Had the photograph been of the "Oswald" who returned to the embassy several times to plead with Duran for the transit visa she would have remembered *him. That "Oswald" was the "Leon Oswald", who visited Silvia Odio.* He had green eyes, blond hair, shorter with a weaker build than Lee. In *her* mind, *that was Lee Harvey Oswald.*

"How are things between you and Ambassador Lechuga," Phillips asked. Duran blushed, suppressed a smile, then replied: "About the same." "When did you see him last", Phillips wanted to know. "Yesterday," she replied.

In addition to his posting with the Cuban delegation to the United Nations, Lechuga was Cuba's Ambassador to Mexico. He and Ambassador Attwood were still pushing for the rapprochement between Castro and Kennedy -- an effort the CIA was determined to sabotage.

"Do you know when Lechuga's going back to New York?" "No," she said. "We don't spend much time talking." Phillips fought off the urge to smile. "Were you able to install that little device I gave you in his telephone?"

"I was only at his apartment for twenty minutes, wasn't any chance to do it. Besides, I was afraid."

A loud knock on the door interrupted them. Phillips motioned for Duran to go inside a stall and whispered "lock it." "Don't be upset. Whoever this is will only be here long enough to. . . you know, relieve himself. I'll be leaning against the door outside to make sure no one else comes in. Try and put the bug in Lechuga's phone next time."

With that, he unlocked the door and left.

After Duran "escaped," Phillips took his seat at the bar, sipped his Pina Colata and lit his thirty-third cigarette. Reflecting on what transpired, he decided "the little puta" (whore) was doing her best.

FRIDAY - NOVEMBER 8TH - THE OVAL OFFICE -11:58 A.M.

At the request of Presidential advisor Arthur Schlessinger, the President was meeting with Mr.Samuel Barber and Mr. Giancarlo Minotti, the creative force behind "Vanessa", an opera which was being presented by The Opera Society of Washington.

These kinds of amenities were a constant distraction. JFK found opera and ballet an unrelenting bore and used every excuse he could think of to avoid them. Jackie loved both. After two minutes, Kennedy bid Barber and Minotti goodbye.

He had to hurry with the balance of his appointment schedule in order to depart for a hastily organized "off the record" trip to New York where he planned to meet with Ambassador Attwood to discuss the Castro matter. Hopefully, he could squeeze in some time to be with movie star Angie Dickinson who was in New York promoting her latest movie.

From 12:15 to 1:15 Kennedy held an "off the record" meeting on wheat with Secretary Of

Agriculture, Orville Freeman and seven other
administration officials including Special
Assistant Ted Sorensen and National Security
Advisor McGeorge Bundy.

At 1:45 he instructed Dave Powers to scoop up
"Fiddle and Faddle" and bring them to the pool.

He only had time for "a quickie."

Later, while he was toweling himself off, his
eyes feasted on the young girls posteriors.

Powers herded them back to change and get
dressed.

Brother Joe appeared next to Jack, his gaze fixed
on the President.

Seeing Joe stops Jack cold.

"What is it, now?"

"Put an end to this Jack. Those two could ruin
you."

"If they talked -- which they won't. Been with me
since the campaign. We're pals -- I trust them --
and they trust me.

"They'd be all it would take to get booted out of
here."

"I can't put up with all this pressure without
some diversion."

"What about *Judy and Helen and Mary Pinchot, and
Pamela and Purdom's wife Alicia, and Angie, and
prostitutes . . . and Jackie, what about her?*"

"Jackie isn't going to do anything. After the
Ambassador put a million bucks in her bank
account she hasn't complained."

"Then why didn't she show up at Madison Square
Garden for your birthday party when Marilyn
Monroe sang 'happy birthday'?"
"Jackie was sick that night."

"Sick of being embarrassed, or sick of you?"

There eyes met for a moment, then Jack headed for
the exit.

Upstairs he gulped lunch then got "a booster
shot" from "Doctor Feelgood" which had to last
the weekend.

Returning to the Oval Office at 3:30, Mrs. Lincoln
advised there was "a call on hold from Miss Judith
Exner." Kennedy hesitated, then, told her: "Just
say the President hopes you're well but is unable
to take your calls anymore." Mrs. Lincoln nodded
and disappeared into her office.

Judy was Kennedy's favorite "outside mount", but
with so much heat from Edgar, he couldn't risk
continuing their relationship. Perpetuating her
association with gangsters like Giancana and
Roselli had finally made Judy persona non-grata.

Then too, avoiding Exner was due in part to the
Marilyn Monroe episode which occasionally still
occupies his thoughts. He and Bobby partook of
Marilyn's favors. She obsessed over both brothers.

On a Sunday in late July the previous year, Jack
and Bobby sat next to each other at Mass. Jack
whispered to Bobby to stay while the others filed
out. When the pews were empty and while the family
and the Secret Service waited outside, the brothers
held an impromptu meeting:

JACK: Peter called me this morning about Marilyn.
She's threatened to "tell all" about us at a
press conference next week.

BOBBY: She's tried to call me at the office a half-dozen times in the last few days. I don't take her calls anymore.

JACK: Some stories are making the rounds at the studios. She told that guy Bacon out there and a couple of others about us. Someone's got to shut her up and you're the one to do it.

BOBBY: I'm taking Ethel and the kids out to California this weekend. I'll see what can be done.

The look that passed between them could not be misunderstood.

Not long afterward Monroe was found dead in her small Brentwood bungalow. Even after Bobby "sanitized" the home, they overlooked a piece of paper in the folds of her bed sheets.

L.A. Homicide detectives didn't. Scrawled on the little piece of white paper was the phone number for the White House. Chief of Police William Parker was a good friend of Bobby's. The piece of white paper did not surface again for another twenty five years.

L.A. County Coroner Thomas Naguchi had problems with the DA'S finding of "suicide." When he performed an autopsy on Monroe's body, Naguchi could find no trace of the "yellow jackets" from the Nembutal found in her stomach. He maintained they could not have dissolved in such a short time.

Naguchi found numerous bruises on her buttocks which were never explained. Some theorized the Nembutals had been forced into her anus.

Mister Archie J. House, National Commander of the United Spanish War Veterans, accompanied by his wife and Mrs. Olive Bradley, and National President of the Women's Auxiliary of United Spanish War Veterans, were ushered into the office and introduced to the President.

He asked them to sit down, and reclined in his rocker, hoping he could get rid of them in ten minutes. This was not the case. Finally, Mrs. Lincoln rescued her boss, reminding him the Secret Service was in the hallway waiting to take him to the helicopter. It would shuttle him to Andrews Air Force base where Air Force One was waiting to fly him to New York.

KENNEDY ESTATE - MIDDLEBURGH, VA.

Contemporaneously, Jackie Kennedy sat on the couch holding the telephone as she spoke to her *other squeeze*, Rozwell Gilpatric. "No" she said, "it came up suddenly." (Listens) "Today would be better, but Saturday's okay as long as it's early." (Listens) "Good -- see you here tomorrow at noon."

She put the phone down, leaned against the back of the couch and chortled: "When the cat's away. . ." Then a sobering thought. What would she wear? After mulling this over Jackie giggled and rationalized that whatever she wore he wouldn't have very long to look at it.

NEW ORLEANS FEDERAL DISTRICT COURT - 4:45 p.m.

Hunched forward at the defense table, Carlos Marcello listened to his attorney, Jack Wasserman wind up the cross-examination of the government's witness. The venerable immigration lawyer was earning his enormous fee. But it was hard for "the little man" to remain focused on what was happening in the drafty courtroom, erected during Andrew Jackson's Presidency.

Marcello's thoughts were on information he received from Santos regarding their newest competitor in the race to kill Kennedy. The implications of a Castro sponsored "hit" were endless. To "the little man", the chance to pin the murder of Kennedy on Castro would go a long way toward deflecting suspicion from the mob, the CIA and the Cuban exiles, all of whom would rejoice if Castro got stuck with the check.

The triumvirate's hopes for ridding the world of Kennedy *and Fidel* looked promising.

MIAMI — SATURDAY — NOVEMBER 9TH. — 9:15 a.m.

William Sommerset was expecting company. In preparation for receiving his guest he strapped a recording device around his torso, put his shirt and jacket on -- and waited.

A veteran informant for the Dade County Police Intelligence Bureau, commanded by Captain Charles Sapp, he was sent to meetings of various extremist groups to monitor activities Sapp wanted to stay abreast of.

These groups included:

The National States Rights Party, The White Citizen's Council, The John Birch Society, The Minutemen and others.

Over the years, Sommerset formed friendships with men in these organizations. One of them, Joseph A. Milteer, was from Valdosta, Georgia, located in the extreme Southeast corner of the state a few miles from the Florida border.

Milteer, a wealthy retiree was an ardent racist and belonged to a pot puree of extreme rightwing organizations. His friends included Jack Brown, the main suspect in the bombing of a church in Birmingham that claimed the lives of four young black girls.

Florida's White Citizen's Council was having a meeting in Miami, Saturday night. Milteer telephoned Sommerset to confirm a visit earlier that day.

Milteer was an outspoken opponent of President Kennedy, most especially for his stance on civil rights. Sommerset soon steered the conversation to the Commander in Chief.

SOMMERSET: I think Kennedy is coming here the eighteenth, or something like that to make a speech."

MILTEER: You can bet your bottom dollar he's going to have something to say about the Cubans. There are so many of them here.

SOMMERSET: Yeah, well he will have about a thousand bodyguards, don't worry about that.

MILTEER: The more bodyguards he has, the easier it is to get him.

SOMMERSET: Well how in the hell do you figure would be the best way to get him?

MILTEER: From an office building, with a high-powered rifle . . . he knows he's a marked man.

SOMMERSET: They are really going to try and kill him?

MILTEER: Oh yeah, it is in the working . . .

SOMMERSET: Boy, if that Kennedy gets shot, we have got to know where we're at. Because you know it will be a real shake if they do that.

MILTEER: They wouldn't leave any stone unturned there . . . no way. They will pick up somebody within hours afterward if anything like that would happen. Just to throw the public off."

Later that day, Sommerset delivered the tape of their conversation to Captain Sapp.

When the information on it was transcribed, Sapp forwarded transcripts to the Secret Service and the FBI. Neither agency forwarded this information to their offices in Dallas.

IRVING TEXAS - 4:15 P.M.

At the IRVING SPORTS SHOP, Dial Ryder waited on a customer who wanted a telescopic sight mounted on his 6.5 Manlicher Carcano rifle. After the assassination Ryder would remember the customer, Lee Harvey Oswald. His 6.5 Manlicher Carcano rifle was found at the bottom of a stack of books on the sixth floor of the Texas School Book Depository. However, there was a problem. Ryder drilled *three* holes to mount the telescopic sight on the barrel. The weapon identified as being the one used to kill the President had only two holes drilled to mount the scope.

THE CARLYLE HOTEL - MANHATTAN - SATURDAY - 10:10 P.M.

The famed old-world hostelry with its chic modern décor, stood like a beacon on Madison Avenue and 76th Street since 1930.

Erected during the great depression there was nothing depressing about the Carlyle, which enjoyed an international clientele.

JFK maintained a penthouse at the swank hotel which Jackie used during frequent shopping sprees. Kennedy used it mostly for "social engagements" with movie stars like the late Marilyn Monroe and other ladies who caught his fancy.

The President's friend, movie distributor Arthur Krim, owned an apartment across the street from the Carlyle. Its location was a great convenience for

Kennedy. The apartment house basement had a series of tunnels through which one could reach the basement of the Carlyle.

With appropriate notice, Krim made his apartment available as a transit station for the President's girlfriends.

Kennedy wanted Angie Dickinson to come Friday night, but a heavy schedule connected with the premier of her latest movie, "Captain Newman, MD" made that impossible. She apologized and promised to visit him Saturday night.

So the President had to settle for a late dinner meeting with Ambassador William Attwood, whom he had known since their days at Choate. It was there Attwood introduced John Kennedy to Mary Pinchot.

As they supped on the hotel's finest cuisine, the pair hashed out some of the problems associated with effecting an accommodation with Cuba.

Their discussion lasted over three hours and covered a myriad of problems associated with initiating *official* talks with Castro about a rapprochement.

Having Attwood fly to meet Castro in a remote area near Havana was approved in theory, but could not go forward until the President gave the word. There were "other plans in the works" Kennedy said he could not discuss. (This involved efforts to have "AMLASH" kill the Cuban Premier.) Meetings on that issue were in progress in Paris and needed to be resolved before talks regarding normalization of relations could proceed.

Of paramount importance was for Fidel to address his ongoing relationship with the Soviet Union. Would for instance he terminate Cuba's relationship with the Soviet's if the U.S. picked up the tab for the stipend they were sending the beleaguered island?

Was Fidel now willing to allow American inspectors to determine whether or not *all* the nuclear missiles had been removed?

Until the President had a chance to discuss the situation with his top advisors, Attwood's instructions were to stall Castro long enough for Kennedy to make a final decision. In the meantime, the Ambassador should keep the door ajar.

One problem neither man was unaware of: The CIA had electronic surveillance inside the penthouse. Every word they said was monitored and recorded.

Attwood departed. Kennedy looked at his watch. Angie was due in fifteen minutes. In the bathroom he combed his hair and applied some underarm deodorant.

The actress, born in a small town in North Dakota, was riding the crest of a wave of success and nearing the pinnacle of her career.

Angie's relationship with Kennedy began prior to his election. In a wild plane ride aboard a small chartered aircraft they made out in the cabin during a round trip flight from Palm Springs to Phoenix.

The next time they met was in January 1961, the night before the inauguration. In an exercise of brinkmanship James Bond would envy, the new President slipped away from Jackie at the inaugural concert just long enough to be serviced by Angie and get back to his seat. About this incident Angie would later say:

"The best twenty seconds of my life."

Palm Springs was the setting for at least two
additional assignations: One, recounted to author
Anthony Summers by a respected photographer for a
national magazine, involved opening the wrong door
at Bing Crosby's house and finding Angie lying in
bed reading a magazine a few minutes before the
president's arrival by helicopter. The other was
reported by a former mayor of Palm Springs, who
claimed that while attending a party at Frank
Sinatra's old house, Kennedy abruptly went into the
garage and drove the singer's brown Impala a few
blocks to Dean Martin's residence where Angie
awaited. This episode occurred before the Secret
Service realized what happened.

The fifteen minutes expired. Then another fifteen,
and another. Kennedy called her hotel. No answer in
her room. After another forty-five minutes without
hearing from Angie, the President of the United
States came to the conclusion he'd been stood up.

"Actresses" he murmured. "They're all the same--
totally self absorbed."

CHAPTER 7

DALLAS — 5:05 P.M.

Albert Bogard, a used car salesman was worried. The man taking a demonstration ride in a five year old sedan had the car traveling at eighty miles an hour on the Stemmons Freeway. The young customer said he wasn't ready to buy just yet but was coming into a great deal of money in the next two weeks. "Or", he said, "I might have to go back to Russia where they treat workers like men."

The experience seemed odd to Bogard. It wasn't until Lee Harvey Oswald was identified as the prime suspect in the murder of President Kennedy that it became even more peculiar. *Lee Oswald* was the name his customer gave. It was later determined that the man accused of killing the President *didn't know how to drive a car.*

SUNDAY — November 10th 10:59 a.m.

In Atoka, Virginia, a twenty-five mile an hour winter wind slashed across the countryside like a scythe.

Robert Francis Kennedy, stood at the side entrance to St. Stephans Martyr Church waiting for his brother to emerge. Bobby's mission was urgent. What he needed to tell the President was something he didn't dare talk about on the telephone.

He blew warm air on his hands and stomped his shoes on the gravel trying to stimulate circulation.

There were only two bright spots in the thirty
seven year old Attorney General's weekend:

Encouraging news from his lead prosecutor in New
Orleans on the course of the Marcello prosecution --
and his daughter Kathleen's Report Card which
contained all A's. The rest of the news was bad.

The church doors swung open. Seconds later the
Priest emerged to greet his congregation. To avoid
the crowd and autograph hunters the President,
Jackie and Caroline exited the side door, where
brother, Bobby waited.

They were all surprised to see him. After saying
their "hello's", Bobby's ice blue eyes focused
on his older brother.

"Can we take a quick walk before you leave?"
"Sure." Bobby waited while the President helped
Jackie and Caroline into the limousine, then
motioned for him to follow.

JFK pulled up the flaps on his overcoat and closed
the distance between them. Four Secret Service
Agents trailed at a respectful distance. Two others
waited with Jackie and Caroline in the limousine.

"Before we get into whatever you came for - I
heard you're feeding The Senate Rules Committee
details about Lyndon's involvement with Baker and
the rest of that mess."

"It's my *job* to supply information in our files"

"As my brother it's your job to protect my
chances for re-election. Without Lyndon we can
kiss Texas goodbye and probably Georgia, too."

"With the right replacement on the ticket you can
make it up with states we lost last time."

"Like?"

"California. Only lost it by a hundred thousand. Our polling shows you way ahead out there."

"Unless you let up on Giancana we'll lose Illinois this time."

"If you didn't want me to do the job you shouldn't have appointed me."

The President had no rejoinder for this.

"Whatever you have in mind, I hope it won't take long -- my ears are about to fall off."

"You know those contingency plans we talked about relating to Second Naval Guerrilla?" Bobby asked.

"Sure. Did you see the New York Times article-- 'Khruschev says U.S. attack on Cuba will lead to war?'

"Yeah -- I read it." Bobby blew on his hands, then continued. "Dez Fitzgerald called me half an hour ago and said some of their security people were trying to locate a Cuban G-2 guy, named Miguel Casas Saez, one of State Security's stop hit-men. Jim Angelton's counterintelligence people had him in their sights in Chicago, but he slipped away."

"How does that affect us, now?"

Bobby sneezed, took out a handkerchief and blew his nose. "Counter Intelligence thinks Saez was in Chicago to assassinate you -- might be waiting to try again in Tampa."

"Aside from alerting Chief Rowley and the White House detail there isn't much we can do."

"The trip to Florida. If they can't locate this Saez fellow, you should cancel it and find another way to get your message through."

"No. That only promotes a lack of confidence. The OPLAN leader in Cuba expects a signal from me during my speech in Miami, confirming our support for the coup."

"What about these back channel negotiations with Castro?"

"I talked with Bill Attwood about it in New York Saturday night. He's keeping the door open, but until we make some decisions I can't give the final authorization for him to go forward."

"This Saez thing -- looks like Castro is double dealing us."

The President laughed. "Just like we're doing to him!"

Bobby saw no humor in this. The enormous danger confronting his brother and the country was too sobering for him to laugh.

Jack stopped and stared at the overcast sky. Presently he began walking again. A decision made, he turned to his brother.

"It's too big a risk to wait for a Christmas invasion. If Second Naval Guerrilla is compromised, we could face another "missile crisis." Push up the date for the invasion to the first week in December. You think the exiles could be ready to go then?"

"I can ask them, but I already know their answer will be *yes*."

"Then get them together with the others and say I think it's wise to go the first week in December. Either way, I'm going to Florida on the eighteenth and sending the signal."

DALLAS - EARLY AFTERNOON

At a local private firing range, three men taking target practice were firing indiscriminately. This irritated Mrs. Lovell Penn, who owned the property. She asked the troublemaker's to leave. One of them would be remembered. She retrieved an empty cartridge ejected from his rifle and put it away. Following the assassination she recognized Lee Harvey Oswald as one of the three men she asked to leave. Mrs. Penn gave Dallas Police the empty cartridge case "Oswald" left behind. Tests on the casing revealed it could not have been fired from the rifle found on the sixth floor of the Book Depository.

VERADERO BEACH - CUBA - NOVEMBER 10th.

The sun of noon looked down on swimmers and sun worshipers who came to Veradero Beach to socialize and "take some rays."

Located less than an hour from Havana, its sugar-white soft sands and turquoise blue water made Veradero very popular with Cubans and tourists. One can walk out to sea for a kilometer before the tide gets above your waist. And the water is still so clear you can see every wrinkle in your toes.

Before the revolution, only the wealthy or otherwise privileged were welcome here. Since then, it has been available to the workers, who make up the majority of today's crowd.

A notable exception is Fidel Castro and the beautiful ABC newswoman, Lisa Howard, who scored a coup when she interviewed the Cuban leader in April. A delicate blonde with fair complexion and brown eyes, she was a movie actress before becoming a reporter and could easily be mistaken for film

star, Audrey Totter. Whatever the attraction,
Fidel invited her to his Villa at Veradero and soon
made her his mistress.

The interview was promptly aired in the U.S.
Howard's report went against the tide of anti-
Castro sentiment and lifted a few eyebrows
"upstairs." Known as "a tough cookie", she does not
give Fidel any quarter on issues about the
Revolution, which she criticizes to his face.
Fidel keeps his cool, takes great interest in
her opinions of him and the revolution.

The ABC interview included many positive things
regarding the revolution, especially in healthcare
and education. (The illiteracy rate among Cubans
is the lowest in the America's).

It was Howard who in September gave a cocktail
party at her New York apartment inviting Bill
Attwood and Ambassador Carlos Lechuga both of
whom she knew personally.

Half an hour later the two diplomats went onto the
balcony to discuss the best way for them to
approach their respective government's interest in
Castro's overture for a rapprochement.

Later, Lisa met with President Kennedy for a
second time. He encouraged her to keep
communications on the subject open through
direct talks with Castro.

"Go see him again and let me know about your
progress when you get back. I've told Bill Attwood
we want to pursue this. Remember, secrecy is very
important. If this leaks it will cause a fire storm
and probably cost me the election." He smiled and
lowered his voice: "It's very nice for a President
to be courageous. It's also very nice to be
President."

He did not reveal that sources inside Cuba had
already reported that Lisa and Fidel were "an

item." It was the type of intrigue the President loved. In fact, he had designs on the attractive newswoman himself.

At Veradero, Fidel subtlety picked Lisa's brain,
all the while searching her face for clues to what
she really knew regarding Kennedy's intentions.

Attwood had not contacted their intermediary Doctor
Renee Vallejo for many days. Vallejo was often out
of town, visiting patients in remote provinces.
Attwood too, was not always available and the pair
sometimes left messages for one another which went
unanswered for as long as a week.

Fidel very much wanted the accommodation with
Kennedy. Meanwhile, "the thing in Tampa" would
remain in place.

"You're getting too much sun, Lisa. Maybe we should
go back to the Villa." Lisa acquiesced . . . not to
get out of the sun . . . to get into bed with Fidel
and feel his beard tickling her tummy.

**ARLINGTON, TEXAS — A SUBURB OF DALLAS 5:55
P.M.**

On this particular Sunday, Lee Oswald *was not* at
the Paine's visiting Marina and his daughters. He'd
received a call Thursday night from "Maurice
Bishop", asking him to be at the entrance to "Six
Flags Over Texas" amusement park at six p.m.,
Sunday. "Ever been there," Bishop asked. "In
Arlington," Lee replied.

"That's it," Bishop replied, and hung up.

To get to Arlington from Oak Cliff, you had to
drive (40 minutes), or hitch. Buses do not go
there. Oswald didn't own a car and never learned
to drive. To be safe, he started for Arlington at
four. As luck would have it, the first car Lee
"thumbed", picked him up -- an older couple on
their way to "Six Flags", too.

    With over an hour to wait, Lee sat on a bench
near the entrance reading a discarded Dallas
Times Herald.

An article on the front page described JFK'S
upcoming visit to Texas. He would land in San
Antonio at 2 p.m. on the 21st, travel to Houston
that afternoon for a motorcade, attend a dinner
that night honoring retiring Congressman Albert
Thomas. Thence to Fort Worth for an overnight stay
-- a breakfast meeting the following morning with
that city's Chamber of Commerce, followed by a
short hop to Dallas on the 22nd -- a motorcade from
Love Field to downtown Dallas, followed by a
luncheon at the new Trade Mart.

A story about Dallas' Russian Émigré community
caught Lee's eye. Being a recently returned
defector to Russia with a Russian wife made Oswald
and Marina celebrities in this milieu. He devoured
the story hoping to find some mention of his name,
but there was none. Some of the people mentioned
were individuals he was acquainted with.

George de Morhenschildt was identified as a
geologist who taught at a local college. His wife
and the Oswald's had become very friendly, but the
de Morhenschildt's departed for Haiti and hadn't
returned.

Lee smelled cigarette smoke, looked up to find"
Maurice Bishop", staring down at him. "Bishop"
clapped him on the shoulder. "Come on, Lee, we'll
go in. "Bishop" paid for two admissions and Oswald
followed the CIA officer through the turnstiles.
"Have you eaten yet," 'Bishop' asked. "No."

"The hot dogs here are first rate. 'Nathan's' you
know."

This was only the second time Lee had actually
seen "Bishop." Their other meeting was in late

August in the lobby of a large insurance company
at the Southland Shopping Center in Dallas. There,
"Bishop" outlined the assignment he had for Lee to
further undermine the FPCC, this time in Mexico
City where the Communists were quite strong.

He was to get a tourist visa and take a bus to
Mexico City. "They'll never give me a visa" Lee
said. "I was a defector, remember?" "Bishop"
smiled, lit a cigarette before he replied. "I'll
see to it you have one in twenty-four hours. You
can count on it. As soon as you get to Mexico City
go to the Cuban embassy and apply for a visa to
Russia with a stopover in Havana. We'll talk about
the rest later."

In New Orleans, Lee went to the tourist office
and filled out the application. When he returned
the next afternoon, the clerk handed him the
visa. "A miracle," Lee concluded, "a miracle."

Oswald savored the hot dog. "Bishop" hadn't
exaggerated. "How about another one," he
suggested. Lee was soon devouring that one,
too. "Bishop" munched his second and said:

"Let's go see the exhibitions." They began
walking. Lowering his voice "Bishop" told his
young guest: "Done your work extremely well, Lee.
You're a great charade player. If I had three
like you when I started trashing Fidel he'd
already be looking for work."

"I like what I do," Lee replied. Before he
finished the second hot dog, "Bishop" lit another
cigarette. "I've got one more charade for you,
Lee. Your last."

'Last' Lee frowned. "Are you gonna fire me?"

"Hell no, I'm going to make you famous. You're
going to become the man Castro sent to kill
President Kennedy when he got to Dallas."

Lee stopped and stared into the taller man's ice blue eyes. "I wouldn't kill Kennedy for Castro or anyone else."

"Of course not. You'll just fire some shots that miss, leave your rifle behind and vanish. It'll all be traced to you. With your background as a Castro sympathizer 'our friend in Havana' will get the blame."

MONDAY NOVEMBER 11th. 11:45 A.M.

"It being Armistice Day I took John-John with me to Arlington Cemetery for the traditional ceremonies. Being only three it was hard for him to concentrate very long.

After I put the wreath at 'Tomb of The Unknown Soldier', I stepped back and saluted. Listening to taps I thought about Joe and how unfair it all was. We wanted to have him buried in the family plot in Massachusetts but the explosion blew his body into so many bits it was impossible to recover them. Before the bugler finished I noticed John-John pulling on his trousers. 'I want that,' he wailed.

Seeing all the soldiers saluting, he suddenly simulated an attention stance and saluted. That really tickled me."

(Not long afterward John-John's pose would be etched into the consciousness of millions watching his father's funeral on television).

IRVING TEXAS - 12:15 P.M.

Employees of the Texas School Book Depository had the day off, too.

Lee Oswald rode the bus to Irving and spent Monday with Marina and Rachel while Ruth took June and her kids to the movies.

Lee slipped into the living room where Marina was watching a soap opera. Dressed all in black, he had a pistol on his hip, a copy of" The Daily Worker" in one hand, a World War Two, Manlicher Carcano, Italian rifle in the other.

Seeing him, dressed this way, Marina asked if Lee was going hunting.

"No", Lee replied. Get your camera and come into the backyard. I want you to take my picture."

"Why?"

ARLINGTON CEMETERY

When he finished blowing the mournful bugle piece, the bugler herded John-John to the President's side. Kennedy grinned and put his arm around the boy.

Returning in the helicopter to the White House JFK heard a news broadcaster describing the ceremony at Arlington: "The thirty-fifth President, himself a war hero, stood solemnly . . . " the broadcaster's voice was drowned out by the roar of the engine descending to the White House lawn.

"I appreciated not having to hear any more about my heroics in the Solomon Islands. The story was partly an invention of my father's which was very beneficial in my political career. The fact was, that sometime after two a.m. I was at the controls of PT-109 in the Blackett Straight, commanding one of three PT boats watching for Japanese destroyers that we knew were in the area. Two of my crew were sleeping, another two were laying down -- and I was half asleep at the wheel. My radioman was not at his station and missed a warning from one of the other boats.

PT-109 was suddenly rammed and cut in two by the Japanese destroyer, Amagiri which I hadn't seen bearing down on us until it was too late.

Two of the crew were killed. My determination in leading the survivors to safety showed courage I guess, but inattention to duty cost the lives of two men and nearly resulted in my being Court-martialed. General Macarthur said I should have been. Through Dad's friend, Under-Secretary of the Navy James Forestall, I was awarded The Navy and Marine Corps Medal instead.

My brother Joe *was* a real war hero, but newscasters and the print media never mentioned Joe anymore. Like I've always said: 'Life is unfair.' I guess I should add that death is unfair, too."

While John-John ran around the halls of the White House, I worked at my desk for an hour.

Then I went to the pool for a swim sans "Fiddle" and "Faddle" who were off. So I collected John-John and we helicoptered to our home in Virginia.

It was boring being in the country. I rarely rode; I hated that Jackie belonged to a hunt club which chased foxes and killed them. Without any other adults around all I could do was play with the kids while Jackie rode her horse through the Virginia countryside.

I dialed a number in Georgetown. "Hello", a feminine voice came through the line. "Hi Mary,. . Jack. You, going to be around tonight?" "Cord is coming to see the kids." After a pausè, she continued. "I could come to *your place* if that's convenient?"

"Sure" Kennedy replied. "They'll be a pass for you at the gate."

"About nine?"

ISLAMORADA – THE FLORIDA KEYS – 4:30 p.m.

Located on the Ocean side, this CIA sponsored
training site is in the jungle south of
Plantation Key. Here holidays were just like
every other day. Everyone worked. Highly
experienced cadre coached small groups of
paramilitary types slated for assassination
missions in Cuba. With the exception of a few
American soldiers of fortune all the trainees
were Cuban exiles.

This afternoon the cadre was teaching a technique
called "triangulation of fire." The objective
involved pre-positioning three shooters at vantage
points from which they could observe a target, but
the target couldn't see them. The mock target in
the exercise was a dummy dressed in fatigues and a
billed cap. He was seated in the back of a jeep
moving slowly through a clearing in the jungle.

With the use of silencers attached to their
sniper rifles reports of shots could not be
heard. Special gunpowder did not emit smoke
that would give the shooters positions away.
Firing "frangible ammunition" (exploding
bullets) the "dummy's" head suddenly
disintegrated.

Observing the exercise was a civilian in his late
fifties. He had white hair, wore an expensive pair
of dark sunglasses and pressed fatigues. He never
spoke to the trainees, only to the ranking member
of the cadre and that was not often.

Born Fililipo Sacco, the former Capone street
level gangster changed his name to Johnny
Roselli. The cadre knew him only as "Colonel
Roselli," a designation which would have sent
his boss Sam Giancana into hysterics.

At the JM-WAVE station in Miami, very few
officials knew "Colonel Roselli" was a high

ranking member of Giancana's mob. One who did know was "The Wave's" Operations Chief, David Sanchez Morales, aka "The Big Indian." Ostensibly Roselli's role was to coordinate attempt's on the life of Fidel Castro and other Cuban officials. That assignment had recently changed. Now he was working with "The Big Indian" to select a hit team which would rid the world of John F. Kennedy.

PLANTATION KEY: "THE BREAKWATER BAR & GRILL" – 10:11 P.M.

For the trio of Roselli, Morales and Bill Harvey, "The Breakwater" was a favorite watering hole. Harvey could barely squeeze his three hundred pounds between the table and the seat.

They had been drinking since seven-twenty five. "The Big Indian" already consumed most of the fifth of the Black Label he ordered. Infamous for his terrible temper, it got worse when he was drinking. Even close associates like Roselli and Harvey were loath to argue with him.

Speaking in a subdued tone Roselli was going over candidates for their Dallas sniper force. "It's close between Tony Izquierdo and Herminio Diaz. Diaz is probably the best shot."

"Known Herminio since fifty-nine," Morales roared. "Worked together until we shut down the station in Havana." Roselli and Harvey cringed. The Big Indian's voice carried a long way.

"Who else", Harvey asked.

"Tony Cuesta and Eladio del Vallee, Roselli whispered.

"Tony's got a lot of guts, but I'm a much better shot. Put him in the group, anyway", the Big Indian shouted.

Roselli glanced at Harvey. "Maybe we should go into this later," he suggested. "Yeah Dave, it's getting pretty late" Harvey said.

The Indian looked at his watch and responded with a shout: "Late! For Crissake's it's just after ten. What are you – a couple of campfire girls? Gotta be in bed by nine!"

Roselli wisely decided to change the subject. "Tell us about those the little Frauliens you used to boff in Berlin, Dave."

A huge toothy grin spread over the Indian's face. "Hell, Johnny, I'm a family man, I don't do things like that." He paused to look around the room, leaned forward and spoke in a confidential tone: "And I'll never do 'em again." With that, he roared at his own pun.

THE WHITE HOUSE 10:26 P.M.

Lying naked in the President's bed, he and Mary Pinchot were feeling the effects of the LSD pills she brought with her. Locked in each other's arms they kissed and fondled one another. Mary came out of it and sat bolt upright.

"Cord says you shouldn't to go to Texas. He's heard things at Langley that worry, him. Please don't go."

Kennedy's mind was reeling from the effect of the powerful drug. Barely able to respond . . ."*Gotta go,*" and "politics" was all the President could manage. He pulled Mary down, kissed and squeezed her breasts.

In the hallway, Warrant Officer Ira Gearhart (*code name "Shadow"*), sat in a barrel chair, holding a black satchel that those in the know called "the black bag", or "the football." A cousin to "Dr. Strangelove's "Doomsday Machine", the thirty pound *metal suitcase had an intricate combination lock,*

*which only Gearhart and the President knew how
to open.*
Inside were electronic codes designed to trigger a
response to a nuclear counter strike, or to
initiate a preemptive nuclear attack. *The window to
respond to an attack was barely fifteen minutes.*
It wasn't difficult for "Shadow" to figure out what
was happening on the other side of the wall. What he
didn't know was that the President's mind was in
such a state of disorientation, manipulating codes
in "the black bag" would be impossible.

As on other occasions of the kind it was not
John Kennedy at his best.

CHAPTER 8

YBOR CITY - A SUBURB OF TAMPA - 11:05 p.m.

The reflection of a full moon and an array of harbor

lights bounce off the waters of this storied port

for fishing vessels, sailboats and pleasure craft.

Over the wind can be heard the complaining screech

of a seagull, its cacophonous sound an assault on

the ears. When this fades away all that can be heard

are the creaks and groans of the boat hulls nudged

by the tide against their wooden moorings.

Prominent among them are high mast shrimp boats--
their nets gently rustling in the wind. There is no
sign of humanity, commonplace at this hour.

In the distance is YBOR CITY -- its ancient two and
three story hotels and apartment houses framed
against the skyline.

Once a haven for the cigar industry, Ybor City has
fallen on hard times, the victim of an embargo
imposed on trade between the U.S. and Cuba. No more
Cuban tobacco or importing of Cuban cigars. Such
hardships were not envisioned by the President and
policy makers . . . quite often, *not even known.*

Kennedy however, knew about the effect on Ybor
City's cigar industry and would comment on it
during his visit to Tampa. Ironically, the
President smokes mostly Cuban cigars. Where he gets
them is a mystery.

Santos Trafficante walks along the deserted
boardwalk, accompanied by a Cuban in his early

twenties. His name is Miguel Casas Saez. About five-six, Miguel has a stocky build, dark complexion and large brown eyes.
The two converse in Spanish.

"Have you eaten," Santos asks. "No," Miguel replies. I can wait till morning."

"Where are you from in Cuba?"

"Remedios -- a small village in Las Villas - so small the houses don't even have numbers."

"Were you in the military?"

"I trained as a Militiaman while I worked at Department of Construction.

"Any particular specialty?"

"Yes," I trained to be a sniper."

Trafficante was pleased. Raul Castro had sent someone with the right qualifications. The next thing was to put him on ice until the eighteenth. Ybor City was an ideal spot. Santos used his influence with a friend who ran the local "Bolita" (numbers racket) to take Miguel in for a week, or so. At any rate just long enough to do the deed on the eighteenth then hide for a few days before making his way back to Cuba.

Now Santos needed to find a "patsy" -- a fall guy to take the rap.

STONEWALL, TEXAS - 9:20 P.M.

"The hill country" is searing hot and windy in the summer, biting cold in the Winter. In 1960, the population numbered less than one person for every nine square miles.

Had it not been for his father, Sam, a failed
State Legislator, Lyndon Johnson would probably
have chosen an entirely different part of Texas
to put down roots -- Austin, or Dallas perhaps.
Sam Johnson lost the property where "The LBJ
RANCH" is located.

For Lyndon, buying back the property was redemption
for his father's failure and years of disrespect.
He and "Ladybird" spent hundreds of thousands of
dollars to make the LBJ Ranch a showplace.

On this night in mid-November the weather was
clear and warm enough for the Vice President to
sit on his giant patio sipping Jack Daniels before
retiring. His wife, "Ladybird", was forty five
miles away at their home in Austin.

The help had not returned from the Armistice Day
holiday. Except for two Secret Service men, the
fifty-five year old Texan had the ranch to himself.
He heard his private line ringing, and went into
his office to answer it.

"Yeah?" he grunted.

"Lyndon, this is Allen Dulles . . . how are
you?"

"Allen! Haven't talked to ya in a dog's age"

"I heard about some problems you've been having
and decided . . ."

"Hell I got a passel of 'em," Johnson
interrupted. Problems are like assholes,
everyone's got 'em. You in D.C.?"

"As a matter of fact I'm in Austin, promoting a
book I wrote called "The Craft Of Intelligence."

"Why didn't you let me know? I'd of come down and
visited with ya." "I should have dropped you a
note, but . . ."

  "Where ya stayin?", Johnson interrupted a
second time.

"At The Driskill. Just wound up giving a little talk
and signing some books -- and I thought if it wasn't
too late I'd come over and visit for a few minutes?"

"Hell yes! If I'd known I could a sent my plane for
ya. Have ya got transportation or should I come
after ya?"

"I'm driving a rental car. Is Ladybird There?"

"No. Just me and the Secret Service guys."

"Fine. What's the best way to get there?"

LBJ RANCH 11:45 p.m.

Seventy-year old Allen Welsh Dulles and the Vice
President had already been talking for fifteen
minutes. A legend in the OSS during the Second World
War, Dulles was Director Of Central Intelligence
until shortly after the debacle at the Bay Of Pigs
when Kennedy fired him.

His dismissal did not sit well with old-line
members of the Agency. Some took early retirement,
other's resigned. The one's who remained, still
smoldered with resentment. To the old guard,
Dulles was an icon who could not be replaced. To
them, Kennedy was the one who should have
resigned.

In light of the way Bobby Kennedy treated the
Agency, relations had become even more strained,
especially after it came over the transom that his
brother planned to "smash the CIA into a thousand
pieces and scatter them to the wind."

It was not the old spy's first visit to the ranch. He'd been there after the Democratic convention in Los Angeles. An inveterate pipe smoker, Dulles refilled his pipe with a sweet smelling tobacco, fixed Lyndon with a steady gaze and lit up.

"I wanted to give you a heads up, Lyndon. You were always a friend of the Agency, especially when you Chaired the Appropriations Committee. These problems you're having are liable to disappear."

"I don't see how that's possible, Allen. The Rules Committee is fixin' ta hang me and there's nothin' I can do about it."

"Perhaps," Dulles replied. But if I were you, I'd prepare myself to become President . . . very soon."

CIA STATION – MEXICO CITY 8:05 A.M – November 12TH

David Atlee Phillips sat in his office listening to tapes of telephone intercepts retrieved from the Agency's "bug" inside Sylvia Duran's office at the Cuban Consulate. Of course he puffed on a cigarette.

The conversations concerned telephone calls made by a man identifying himself as "Lee Oswald", from Sylvia Duran's desk to someone at the Soviet Embassy.

"Da?" the voice at the Soviet Embassy said.

"This is Lee Oswald O-s-w-a-l-d" the caller announced. "I have to have a visa from you or the Cuban's won't give me a transit visa – and *I must to go to Havana* before proceeding to Moscow."

The caller spoke in a quavering voice. That disturbed Phillips. The real Oswald was confident, often aggressive and never spoke in a timid way.

It was a favorite ploy of Phillips' to identify someone he wanted to compromise by arranging "follow up calls" from the same phone used by the person he was targeting. These "follow up calls" were made by someone *impersonating* Phillips' target.

The purpose behind using a phony Oswald was to demonstrate he had traveled to Cuba thus associating him with Castro and making the charade Phillips arranged with Lee appear more plausible.

The scenario went like this:

A Castro supporter visits Havana, later takes shots at President Kennedy during his motorcade in Dallas and disappears. The trail leads to Lee Oswald who: owns a rifle; works at the Texas School Depository where the rifle is found; signed a phony name (Alek J. Hidel) to order it through the mail; signed that name again as "the Secretary of The New Orleans Chapter of the Fair Play For Cuba Committee" and recently returned to America after defecting to the Soviet Union.

Phillips lit another cigarette, played a different "Oswald" tape.

"Da" said the voice with a thick Russian accent. "This is Lee Oswald", the caller said. "Has Comrade Kostikov received my visa to go to Moscow?"

"Kostikov not here," the Russian replied.

"Kostikov was there when I came, before. I was in his office."

Colonel Valery Kostikov was from the Thirteenth Directorate of the KGB. His mission: Assassinations and sabotage in the Western Hemisphere.

It all fit very nicely except for one gaping
hole in the propaganda specialist's plan.
Knowledgeable people were aware the U.S. kept
all foreign embassies under round the clock
photographic surveillance.

Through some screw-up, the photographer "shooting"
people coming in and out of the Cuban Consulate did
not photograph *the real Oswald.*

There was no picture of him to prove he'd been
there.

On three "subsequent visits" to the Consulate, the
impostor calling himself Lee Oswald *was
photographed.* They had several excellent pictures
of him, but even cursory examination of these shots
would be discredited. It was not the real Oswald.

Phillips ruminated over ways to solve this glaring
discrepancy. The only way out was to say the
camera's weren't operating when the real Oswald
visited the Cuban Consulate. It was weak, but it
was all he had. Phillips reached for another
cigarette using the previous one to light it.

But wait a minute! The counterfeit "Oswald"
brought photographs of himself *for Sylvia Duran to
attach to his visa application.*

Solution: *Replace that photograph* with a
photograph of *the real Oswald and attach it to
the visa application!*

Phillips had plenty of "assets" inside the Embassy
who could see to it they were switched.

CABINET ROOM – THE WHITE HOUSE – 11:30 A.M.

Bobby Kennedy was conducting a meeting of "The President's Special Group."

The group included: Dean Rusk, Robert McNamara, John McCone, Rozwell Gilpatric, Alexis Johnson, Desmond Fitzgerald, Paul Eckel, Richard Helms, Bruce Cheever, Theodore Shackley, Cyrus Vance, General Maxwell Taylor and of course, JFK.

The President's appointment book recorded it as *"OFF THE RECORD MEETING ON CUBA."*

That was a wild understatement. It was, in fact, a top-secret meeting to approve the final date for another invasion of Cuba. Kennedy's pawns, the Cuban exiles, were ostensibly the invaders, but every person in that room knew the world would quickly perceive the United States was the offending party.

It was a reckless gamble by the Kennedy brothers to even up the score for the Bay Of Pigs. The consequence might well result in nuclear war. Many years later Secretary Rusk would say: "They were playing with fire."

ORIENTE PROVINCE – CUBA – 11:13 A.M.

Fidel Castro was furious. He sat at the wheel of his jeep driving slowly through the fields cursing as he surveyed damage to the sugar cane set afire by exile raiders. They were striking from bases in "the Keys", their ninth attack so far this month. In total, the raids accounted for the destruction of over sixty tons of sugar cane in just twelve days. A costly loss.

Sugar cane was Cuba's largest cash crop. Losses like these significantly affected deliveries to the Soviets and others, posing a threat to the Cuban economy.

What Fidel was unable to determine was whether
Kennedy was knowledgeable about these raids and
doing nothing to stop them, or if he instigated the
devastating intrusions.

Cuban Intelligence was doing their best to
determine the answer. Reports were conflicting. One
source claimed Robert Kennedy was behind them; a
second said the brothers Kennedy were shutting down
exile training camps one after the other; a
different source pointed to the escalation of
arrests of exile raiders by the FBI on the orders
of Bobby Kennedy. Could they all be true? Who to
believe?

There had been no further word from Ambassador
Attwood, most likely the result of an extended
absence of his Cuban contact, Dr. Vallejo.

Additional updates from Rolando Cubela ("AMLASH")
were clear enough. U.S. efforts to assassinate
Fidel remained on track.

In light of what was already in motion in Tampa,
the Cuban leader had to weigh his options
carefully.

Of all the possibilities, moving ahead on a
rapprochement with Kennedy was most favored.

NEW ORLEANS 9:45 A.M.

At 544 Camp Street, the office of former FBI Agent
W. Guy Banister, a meeting was in progress.
Banister's secretary, Delphine Roberts, would
later recall one of the participants was the
ubiquitous Johnny Roselli. The other man was in
his early fifties; short, heavyset, wore a hat.

Roberts had never seen him before.

His name was Jack Ruby, age fifty-two. Like
Roselli he was from Chicago. Unlike Roselli Ruby

was just a two-bit wannabe gangster, who commenced his criminal career delivering envelopes filled with cash for Al Capone.

After a hitch in the Air Force, Ruby went back to Chicago. For a time he worked for his brother Earl, who manufactured cheap gaming devices, called "punch boards."

In 1947 he moved to Dallas and became "a nightclub owner." His "nightclubs" were sleazy striptease joints, where he sold liquor after hours, pocketed some of his strippers earnings as prostitutes, operated on the fringes of the Corsican drug cartel and ran guns -- first to Castro, later to those trying to overthrow him.

Ruby had numerous contacts inside the Dallas Police Department.

His "Carousel Club" was just a few blocks from police headquarters.

For "looking the other way", the police had free admission, free booze, free broads . . . anything they wanted.

If what went down in Tampa failed, Ruby's connections inside the Dallas Police Department would be invaluable.

"The biggest thing, Jack," Roselli said, "is keeping an eye on Oswald *and* getting one of your police contacts to knock him off as soon as Kennedy goes down."

"I'll make it happen, Johnnie. You can count on that."

When Ruby left, Roselli and Banister went into other details. One involved coordinating planes to fly the hit teams in and out of Dallas. They would be picked up at remote runways in Miami, New Orleans and Tucson, flown to a Dallas suburb in Garland and another, Red Bird, near Oak Cliff. After "the hit" they would be taken to Red Bird airport where planes would be waiting to fly them home.

Banister reached into the bottom drawer of a filing cabinet, extracted a large roll of papers and gave them to Roselli. "Those are the plans Sergio gave me for the storm drain system in Dallas."

Roselli unrolled the papers and took a quick look. "Great, Guy. I'll have them copied and get them right back to you."

"It's a damned good idea" Banister observed. "How'd you think of it?"

Roselli chuckled.

"I produced a picture called "He Walked By Night" with Dick Basehart. All about a burglar who used the storm drains to escape after he ripped off a place. The cops couldn't figure it out how he disappeared."

Banister was incredulous. "*You* produced a movie?"

"Yeah. They couldn't put my name on the screen because I had a record, but believe me, I produced it."

Banister moved to a different filing cabinet, opened a drawer, withdrew a thick plastic covered folder and handed it to the mafioso.

After leafing through a few pages of the Secret Service handbook on procedures for protecting the President, Roselli whistled softly. "This is gold, Guy."

**U.S. DISTRICT COURT HOUSE —NEW ORLEANS —
10:55 A.M.**

In a Federal courtroom several blocks away, Carlos
Marcello eyed members of the jury. The two who
were "in his pocket" avoided his gaze, in fact
made it a point never to look at him.

Ferrie leaned close to Carlos and reminded him
Roselli and Ruby were meeting at Banister's
office.

Because of his association with Giancana, Carlos had
known Roselli for many years. His acquaintance with
Ruby was fleeting. Something to do with buying up a
stripper's contract from his brother Joe who ran
"The Show Bar" and was out of town when the
transaction took place.

Ruby acted like what he was -- a small time hood,
offering Marcello everything imaginable but nothing
of any interest to "the little man." His
understanding was that Ruby was "babysitting" their
"patsy," Lee Oswald. He learned this from Joe
Civello, the man who looked after Carlos' interests
in Dallas. Civello convinced Marcello that not only
could Ruby keep his mouth shut he had excellent
connections inside the Dallas Police Department. So
Carlos put his stamp of approval on Ruby.

Using Oswald to take the blame for Kennedy's murder
had its genesis when Carlos happened to see him on
TV -- debating an anti-Castro exile about Cuba. A
bookmaker, "Dutz" Murret was in Marcello's office at
the time. "That jackass is my wife's nephew" he
commented.

"Her *nephew is a Communist*", Carlos exclaimed.
"That's a fact" "Dutz" replied. "Kind of a pathetic
little jerk, worked for me running bets until he got
a regular job."

That was the beginning. Using Guy Banister's contacts at the FBI, Marcello learned Oswald's "entire history." He was unaware that "history" was all part of a "legend" Oswald perfected in order to do undercover assignments for various intelligence agencies. He was in fact exactly what David Phillips called him: "a great charade player."

OVAL OFFICE -THE WHITE HOUSE 12:02 P.M.

The 35th President sat in his rocker, listening to The Krupp Works' General Manager, Berthold Beitz, from Essen, Germany.

The State Department's Joseph E. O'Mahoney sat nearby, listening intently to Beitz's pitch in seeking support for the Krupp Works' entrance into American markets.

Their product lines had changed since before World War Two, when they rearmed the Third Reich with weapons of destruction that cost the lives of untold thousands of allied soldiers and innocent civilians in the path of "the Wermacht."

Now, they manufactured coffee makers, blenders and a variety of other kitchen products.

Gustaf Krupp was tried and convicted of war crimes, specifically the brutal treatment of forced labor employed in his infamous armaments factory. The conviction was overturned by John J. McCloy, High Commissioner of the U.S. Zone in Berlin. Krupp went free. (McCloy would soon have a new post -- one of seven members of The Warren Commission).

The meeting lasted barely three minutes before Kennedy signaled O'Mahoney the meeting was over and headed for the swimming pool.

"Fiddle and "Faddle" were already naked,
waiting for the Commander In Chief in the shallow
water.

For him, having the duo close at hand was a
blessing. As he often complained to intimates: "If
I don't have sex for twenty four hours I get a
headache."

CHAPTER 9

TAMPA – WEDNESDAY – NOVEMBER 13TH.

Preparations for Kennedy's visit on the 18th were already in high gear. Floyd Boring, the Secret Service Agent In Charge of the impending trip to Florida, arrived in Miami on the eleventh, went on to Tampa the following afternoon and commenced a "survey". His first stop – the local office of the Secret Service. Here he checked on recent threats against Kennedy and the names individuals which the Agent in Charge in Tampa thought might present a danger when the President arrived. Boring adds these to the list of potential threats given to him by the Protective Research Service (PRC) in D.C. The most recent addition to the list: Gilberto Policarpo Lopez.

Agent Boring's investigation was not the only preparations in anticipation of the President's arrival.

Santos Trafficante was positioning both his sniper (Miguel Saez) and his designated "patsy", twenty-three year Castro sympathizer Gilberto Policarpo Lopez. Policarpo is a highly visible member of the FAIR PLAY FOR CUBA COMMITTEE'S, Tampa branch. Unlike Lee Oswald's phony "New Orleans Chapter", the Tampa operation is real, one which Oswald visited in November. It boasts a membership of 137 and is regularly visited by FPCC national chairman, V.T. Lee, who sends funds to help finance their activities.

During 1963 Policarpo developed a high profile in the city, often getting into fist fights with local anti-Castro exiles -- a parallel to Oswald's staged fist fight in August with Cuban exiles in the streets of New Orleans.

This type of activity generated publicity and Policarpo was frequently in the public's eye. He was known to have a rifle and said to have told associates of his desire "to use it when Kennedy comes to Tampa."

Like Oswald, Policarpo has been trying unsuccessfully to get a visa to go to Cuba. Unlike Oswald his family lives in Cuba. His U.S. passport expired in January and his application for a visa to visit Cuba hasn't gotten a response from Havana.

The motorcade route is the key to everything Trafficante needs to accomplish his mission. Santos has a long standing relationship with a law enforcement official who is directly involved with planning security for the Presidential motorcade. It will travel a circuitous route through the streets of downtown Tampa, often at a pace far less than Secret Service regulations prescribe. When it slows for a hairpin turn beneath a certain multi-storied brick building Miguel Casas Saez will open fire.

Miguel is secreted in the Ybor City apartment of Trafficante's old friend, Guillermo Ruiz, a Cuban gambler who left Havana at the same time Santos did.

Saez brought with him his favorite weapon-- a Czech made model 2-MOA Dragunov 7.62 sniper rifle fitted with a Zeiss telescopic sight. In the hands of even an ordinary marksman, the Dragunov is accurate up to three hundred yards. In the hands of Miguel it is *deadly* accurate, especially since the distance from the window he will fire from will be less than a hundred yards from his target.

The note from Raul Castro only strengthens Trafficante's resolve to kill Kennedy. Alone inside the office located at his modest home in

Tampa, Santos is already envisioning a triumphant
return to Cuba as the kingpin of Havana gambling.
He is keenly aware that plotting his moves must be
accomplished with great care -- which he does.

In the far away Federal Republic of Germany,
U.S. Army code breaker, PFC Eugene B. Dinkin
warned of a plot on the life of President Kennedy.
He was quickly taken into custody by the Secret
Service and hospitalized. Dinkin would stay there
until he changed his story, then was transferred
to the psychiatric ward Walter Reed Army Hospital
where he remained for many years. He is only one
of nine individuals who specifically warned that
Kennedy was going to be assassinated, one of which
came barely thirty-six hours before it occurred.
All nine warnings were covered up when the
President was murdered.

DALLAS - 11:45 A.M..

At the Texas School Book Depository Lee Harvey
Oswald is on a forty-five minute lunch break. He
rides the freight elevator from the sixth to the
second floor where the lunchroom is located.

Lee munches a store bought ham and cheese
sandwich, gets a coke from the coke machine and
sits down at one of several tables.

A heavy rain has been falling for several hours. He
watches little droplets trickle down the second
story windows.

Rain always puts Lee on a downer. When he was
little, his mother couldn't afford to support her
children, so at times she put them in an
orphanage.

Often, while looking out the window waiting for
his mother to come for them on Sundays, it rained.
Lee never forgot his feelings of anxiety and
helplessness, particularly watching the rain
discolor the buildings across the street. Working

as a private nurse, Marguerite Oswald couldn't always get there on time and rarely phoned. Phone calls cost money.

Oblivious to several co-workers sitting close by, the twenty-four year old former "defector" - now a low level intelligence operative, daydreams about his future.

From the time he was fourteen, Lee's favorite TV program was "I LED THREE LIVES". In it actor Richard Carlson portrayed Herbert Philbrick, an advertising executive in Boston who works undercover for the FBI as a counterspy, pretending to be a communist.

The half-hour dramatic series boasted a large audience. Lee watched every one of the hundred and seventeen episodes -- some of them several times. Philbrick's travails totally captured Lee's imagination. To fight communism by pretending to be a communist became his consuming ambition.

In light of coming events, the ex-marine knows one day he will be in a position to tell the world *he's a patriot* and reveal what he's sacrificed for his country. This he expects will motivate a round of interviews on national television, a lecture series and possibly a TV show similar to "I Was A Communist."

All he has to do is keep cool, and wait for November 22nd.

THE WHITE HOUSE - 5:25 P.M.

"I shaded my eyes against the late afternoon sun, listened to the mournful sound of bagpipes and watched a stirring spectacle moving across the White House lawn.

At the moment it served as a parade ground for The Royal Highland Regiment, better known as

"The Black Watch". In their regimental finest,
"the Scots" wore red, white and blue kilts and
tall black fur hats with a red sash at the top.
Their coal black bagpipes wailed ancient Scottish
tunes -- "The Black Bear", The Highland Lassie --
and other *'tunes of glory.'*

"Watching and listening reminded me of the only
other time I'd seen "The Black Watch" perform. My
brother Joe and I saw them in Trafalgar Square a
few days after the survivors returned from the
disaster at Dunkirk. After the pipers passed by
Joe put his arm around me and said:

'What an honor it would be to have the regiment
play at our funeral if one of us got killed. I'm
thinking it would be your funeral Jack since I plan
to live forever.' Then he laughed and pushed me
into the crowd of onlookers. I would love to have
known how to get 'The Black Watch' to play at Joe's
funeral. As it turned out, there wasn't enough left
of him to have a proper funeral."

At the conclusion of the Regiment's presentation
everyone clapped enthusiastically -- none more
loudly than the 35th President who appeared
completely enthralled by their performance. Some of
those standing near him saw tears in his eyes.
Neither he, nor the Scottish soldiers had any way
of knowing that in barely a dozen days the two
hundred year old regiment would return to perform
at his funeral.

" . . . and therefore never send to know for
whom the bell tolls; it tolls for thee."

7:41 P.M. - THE PLANTATION YACHT HARBOR MOTEL

The Big Indian stares into the faces of Roselli
and Harvey with fire in his eye. This time, he is
cold sober.

"If the thing in Tampa don't pan out, I'm gonna
run the operation in Dallas -- right there on the

ground, myself. With me running the show --
there won't be any fuck-ups. With me doing the
shooting they'll ship that sonofabitching double
crossing Kennedy back to the White House in a
goddam box!"

"You'd be taking too big a risk of being seen,"
Bill Harvey observes. "Some of the people in the
crowd will have cameras."

Roselli's only interest is success. If "the Indian"
is willing to risk being recognized in order to get
the job done that was his business. To Johnny,
anything that furthered the prospects for a
successful hit on Kennedy was a plus.

The people occupying an adjacent room were
listening to music. The volume was loud enough to
distinguish Bob Dylan's voice singing the chorus to
his most recent release -- "*Hard* Rain" . . . "and
it's a *hard rai-an-'s* a gonna fall-a-a-ll."

THE WHITE HOUSE - NOVEMBER 14TH

It was going to be a very busy day and evening.

After a breakfast meeting with congressional
leaders, the Chief Executive conferred for two
hours with Presidential aides, Arthur
Schlessinger, Jr., Kenny O'Donnell, Press
Secretary Pierre Salinger and U.N. Ambassador,
Adlai Stevenson. Many subjects were addressed,
including an impending visit from Doctor Martin
Luther King.

King was pressuring Kennedy to take a more forceful
position on Civil Rights, in particular, using
Federal troops in areas of the South where violence
against Negroes was rampant.

Stevenson wanted advice on how to respond to
Krushchev's charge about an impending U.S. invasion
of Cuba. Kennedy assured him their was absolutely

no truth to it whatsoever; blamed the whole thing
on inflammatory rhetoric by Cuban exiles stirring
the pot. None of the other's in the room knew about
"SECOND NAVAL GUERRILLA."

As the meeting broke up, and the advisors departed,
Stevenson lingered. Kennedy looked at his former
Presidential rival with an inquiring smile.

"I want to strongly advise you *against* making
this trip to Texas, Jack," Stevenson confided.

Kennedy replied in a reassuring tone:

"I know you had problems in Dallas recently, but I
have to go. There's all kinds of squabbling between
Lyndon, Yarborough and Connally that's tearing the
Party apart. We have to raise a lot of money in
Texas for the campaign. The coffers are empty."

"It isn't just me they've attacked", Stevenson
replied. Those right wing extremist's are
physically abusive -- they pushed Ladybird and spit
on Lyndon in front of the Adolphus Hotel. I'm an
outsider, but the Johnson's are their own. I think
it's very dangerous in Dallas right now with that
General Walker and the Hunts and Ted Dealey . . .
using his paper to whip up sentiment against you."

"Jerry Bruno and Jack Puterbaugh and the Secret
Service are already in Dallas. Besides, Jackie
decided to come with me. Maybe they'll be a little
nicer with her along."

"I wish you'd reconsider, at least wait until
the campaign begins."

"Thanks for your counsel, Adlai. You know how
much I value your opinion."

Stevenson started to add something, thought better of it, shook the President's hand and left.

As JFK's thoughts lingered on Stevenson's remarks, brother Joe Jr. appeared at his side.

"Listen to him, Jack. Don't go to Texas - and don't go to Florida, either.

"I have promises to keep."

"Promises to whom, Jack?"

"To myself for winning the election."

(Not long afterward Senator J. William Fullbright called Kennedy to add his own caveat:

"Dallas is a dangerous place. *I wouldn't go there.*" Governor Connally echoed those sentiments saying: *"Dallas should be dropped from your itinerary. The people there are too emotional."*)

None of them realized the inherent danger in Dallas made it all the more attractive to a man still competing with his dead brother's heroism.

Doctor King was ushered into the Oval Office. After they shook hands, Kennedy put two fingers to his lips and indicated for the Baptist preacher to follow him through the French doors leading to the outdoor walkway.

King was confused. Seeing this, Kennedy put an arm around the civil right's leader's shoulder, steered him through the doors and along the brick walkway before speaking.

"Hoover has my office bugged -- I'm sure of it."

"He's got taps on all my phones", King replied. "But recording what goes on in your office is beyond outrageous."

"Edgar's going to be seventy the end of next year
and has to accept mandatory retirement. He's
counting on me giving him a waiver, but I'm not
going to. He's out."

Kennedy didn't inform King the taps on his phone
were authorized by brother, Bobby in exchange for
Hoover seeing to it that the Ellen Rometsch story
was killed.

Over the course of the next fifty-five minutes the
two leaders discussed many issues, the most
contentious being timing. King wanted action, now.
Kennedy said additional action would have to wait
until after the election. Moving before then would
further inflame passionate segregationist's in
Southern states whom he couldn't afford to offend.
The South had been a Democratic stronghold since
Reconstruction. He needed those votes.

"Remember, Martin, I can't do anything for
anyone without holding onto the Presidency."

The two parted on cordial terms, but King was not
mollified. By then, Kennedy had no time for
"frolicking" in the pool with "Fiddle and Faddle."
He grabbed a bowl of chowder and a hunk of
sourdough bread, got a shot from "Doctor Feelgood"
and headed for the south lawn of the White House
where a helicopter waited to take him to Elkton,
Maryland for a ribbon cutting ceremony.

DALLAS — 2:15 P.M.

With Presidential visits scheduled for San
Antonio, Houston, Ft. Worth, Dallas and Austin,
manpower at the Secret Service was stretched to
the limit.

Agent Winston Lawson was in the middle of his
maiden voyage as *an Advance Agent* arriving in
Dallas on the ninth to do "the survey" for that
portion of the President's trip.

At times he was joined by various factions with their own agenda's for accomplishing the mission. Jerry Bruno represented the DNC. Jack Puterbaugh's business card read: "Deputy Administrator of State and County Operations of Agricultural Stabilization and Consumer Services", the same division that the murdered Henry Marshall worked for. He also represented the DNC.

Then there was Johnson's man, Cliff Carter, who had been warned by U.S. Attorney Barefoot Sanders that a visit by Kennedy to Dallas was "inadvisable." (Carter later denied this.) There was also Forrest Sorrels, the AIC of the Secret Service's Dallas office, plus Police Chief Jesse Curry and two of his Deputy Chiefs.

Precedence for motorcade routes for similar visits was well established. After getting on Main Street, they continued all the way through the city finally funneling into Dealey Plaza.

Because Governor Connally's backers built the recently completed Dallas Trade Mart, they wanted "The Mart" to be the site for the luncheon. The President would make a speech after the guests had been treated to the typical fare for this type of event: Soggy lettuce and tomato salad, stringy chicken, cold peas, coffee and pudding with a dash of cool whip.

Senator Ralph Yarborough by far the most popular politician in the State, favored the Women's Club at the State Fairgrounds because it could accommodate more guests. Johnson and Connally, bitter foes of Yarborough, insisted on the Trade Mart.

Getting to the Women's Club was simple. The motorcade would continue *straight through Dealey Plaza at the regulation speed of forty-one miles per hour and go underneath "the triple underpass."*

Getting to the Trade Mart could be accomplished using the traditional route . . . except for one detail.

When the motorcade got beneath the triple underpass the cars would have to pass over several planks allowing the vehicles to cross onto *the right hand portion of the underpass* and enter the on-ramp to the Stemmons Freeway. This could be done without violating any Secret Service regulations concerning the minimum allowable speed *--41 miles per hour, when the car was in the open.*

It was decided instead that when the motorcade reached DEALEY PLAZA, the vehicles would *slow to eight mph, turn right on Houston Street, slow even further to accomplish a hairpin left turn onto Elm Street, then proceed down a grade leading to the triple underpass and the on-ramp to the Stemmons Freeway.*

That route, not only violated the speed rules, it took the motorcade underneath twenty eight windows in the Texas School Book Depository and past a "grassy knoll" that rose to a wooded area with bushes and a picket fence. Behind the fence was a parking lot and a rail yard.

Agent Lawson's efforts to follow the rules prescribed in the Secret Service manual crumbled under a morass of conflicting agendas.

A Hollywood production designer couldn't have dreamed up a more likely setting for an ambush.

ELKTON, MARYLAND - 3:45 P.M.

The President cut the ribbon that stretched across the Mason-Dixon line, opening the final link in a turnpike that joined Delaware with Maryland. He was accompanied in this exercise by Governor's Carvel and Tawes. The ceremony having concluded, Kennedy boarded a helicopter at

LaGuardia Airport, where he was met by New York's Deputy Mayor, Edward Cavanah. A motorcade took them to The Carlyle Hotel. The hotel manager escorted the President to his suite, number 34 B.

At seven he and Dave Powers ate dinner. Powers remarked that the President "looked tired." "I am," Kennedy replied. "I'm sending a new bill to Congress -- calling for President's to get paid by the mile. How about diggin up some' *entertainment'* for later tonight?"

HAVANA — 8:09 P.M.

At his office in The Palicio, Fidel Castro said goodbye to Doctor Rene Vallejo and replaced the receiver on the console. The forty three year old physician had finally been in touch with Ambassador Attwood and the news sounded promising. Although not a firm commitment, Attwood reported that Kennedy was disposed to having him fly to a secluded airstrip outside Havana for a meeting with Fidel to discuss an agenda for normalizing relations. The timing for this meeting would be confirmed as soon as the President returned from his impending trip to Texas.

Neither Vallejo or Attwood realized the National Security Agency recorded their conversation. A transcript was immediately relayed to CIA headquarters in Langley, Virginia.

Fidel knew only too well there was little more than seventy-two hours to call off the hit in Tampa. Accomplishing this might prove difficult. Even if Trafficante's telephone number could be found the risk of discussing such information over an insecure phone line was inadvisable. He dialed his brother Raul's private number at the Ministry of Defense. No reply. He called the regular office number and got Senorita Alameda.

"No, Comandante. He left twenty minutes ago." Any idea where he can be reached?" Negative. Fidel instructed her to have Raul call him at the office or the apartment as soon as he checked in.

He dialed Raul's home number. No reply. Must have taken Vilma and kids out for dinner, Fidel concluded. He sent a member of his security detail to Raul's home with instructions for his brother to call him immediately. Two hours passed.

Castro was angry with himself. His acquiescence to Raul's idea about eliminating President Kennedy was foolish. If they couldn't call it off in time the result would surely ruin all hope of normalizing relations with the United States.

NEW YORK CITY — 8:16 P.M.

President Kennedy, Dave Powers and Kenny O'Donnell left the Carlyle via the Madison Street exit and commenced a brisk walk to the President's brother in law Steve Smith's residence on Fifth Avenue. Smith was married to Kennedy's sister, Jean.

They were accompanied by SA's McIntyre, Paolella, Newman and Sherman.

During the brief walk the President wondered if he could get away soon enough for Dave Powers to organize "some entertainment."

FIDEL'S APARTMENT — HAVANA — 12:21 A.M. — NOVEMBER 15th

His phone rang several times, but as yet, no contact with Raul. Fidel's security man called to report all the lights were off at Raul's house. The phone rang again. It was Raul. He and his family had just returned from dinner and seeing a pirated print of Hitchcock's latest movie, "The Birds". The brothers agreed to meet at Jose Marti Park, in twenty minutes.

THE CARLYLE HOTEL — NEW YORK CITY — 12:40 A.M.

Dave Powers came through as usual, landing his boss two hookers from "an escort service," There was of course no time for background checks on these "visitors" so the Secret Service had to settle for frisking them and searching the contents of their purses to make sure they weren't carrying weapons, or cameras. By not following the prescribed procedures such as background checks, etc., the Agents were breaking the law --but their options were severely limited.

They could go along with the program; send the hookers away and incur the President's wrath; wait and report the incident to Chief Rowley who would likely reassign them to S.S. offices in Helena, or Moab -- be forced into early retirement, or just plain fired. (Thirty four years later the agents would relate this type of shoddy incident in the TV program --"Dangerous World: The Kennedy Years.")

Soon, the prostitutes were in the bedroom, giving Kennedy a variety of pleasures he most enjoyed. Kinky sex was definitely his bag. He couldn't get it at home. Aside from Ellen Rometsch,(banished to Germany after pocketing fifty grand of Kennedy's money for dummying up),his 'regulars' wouldn't indulge in this kind of activity. So, he had to wait for trips away from the capitol to satisfy such desires.

Powers had already cautioned the women of the dire consequences they'd face if they dared reveal their 'visit' with the President. He

reminded them he had their names and how to get
to them if they ever 'went public'.

JOSE MARTI PARK — HAVANA — 12:55 A.M.

With their security detail trailing forty yards
behind, the brothers Castro were engaged in grave
conversation.

Raul had already explained that the messenger who
passed his note to Macho Gener *--slipped on a banana
peel*, thereby eliminating any chance for discovering
the source of the communication-- and now,
unfortunately, negating the opportunity for using
him again. Going through Macho Gener a second time
was too risky. Besides the chances of locating him
on such short notice were minimal.

"Then how can we put a stop to this?"

"Probably when the man I sent Santos checks in
with his contact in Miami."

"And when will that be", Fidel asked.

"There's no way to be sure. Chances are he'll be
in touch before "the man" arrives."

"And, if not?"

"Let me think about an alternative and get back to
you."

The clock continued ticking.

CHAPTER 10

MEXICO CITY — 8:15 A.M.

David Atlee Phillips was talking on a secure
telephone line with longtime friend and CIA
associate, David Morales calling from JM WAVE."
The Big Indian" wanted Phillips' media assets to
go into action "as soon as 'the charade' in Dallas
hits the air waves, a week from today. We gotta
make sure the public will blame Fidel for this."

"My people will have the story on the air ten
minutes after the first reports about Oswald
surface."

"And the person who dealt with your 'friend'
when he tried to get the visa, is she still
onboard?"

"Yes. And I took care of that little problem with
the picture on the application form."

"Okay. Has she seen her boyfriend lately?"

"Which one," Phillips laughed. "That little 'puta'
has a new one lined up every night. If he has
blond hair, blue eyes and a dick, she falls over
backward." Phillips laughed again. "Told me she
was with the Ambassador night before last. Still
hasn't gotten that little item installed but she's
going to try again -- maybe tonight. Anything new
on the talks between tweedle dee and tweedle dum?"

"They intercepted another conversation between
Attwood and Castro's doctor, the Indian growled."
Stay close to your radio Monday. Something's
supposed to go down in Tampa."

After they hung up, Phillips pondered how to handle Sylvia Duran's confusion over "the second Oswald" *--and the real Oswald,* whose picture she was unable to identify. This had to be accomplished without her knowing the "blond, green-eyed Oswald" she spoke with was an impostor. That must remain a secret from everyone.

NEW YORK CITY - THE CARLYLE HOTEL - 10:45 A.M.

President Kennedy and Secretary of Labor, Willard Wirtz, left the hotel and started on a round of speaking engagements. At The Americana Hotel they were met by AFL-CIO President George Meany. He introduced the President, who gave speech then departed for The Hilton Hotel.

There, Monsignor's Stevenson and Carroll, of the Catholic Youth Organization (CYO) were on hand to greet Kennedy. After a short speech to the Seventh Biannual Convention of the CYO, the President returned to his suite at the Carlyle and ate lunch.

THE CAROUSEL CLUB - DALLAS - 10:47 P.M.

Jack Ruby sat at a back table across from Lee Oswald. The former Marine was a cheap date -- he only drank coke. To facilitate keeping a close eye on Oswald, Ruby had the former defector working with him on a gun running operation transporting weapons stolen from nearby Fort Hood and delivering them to Cuban exiles who paid cash. The weapons eventually wound up in the hands of Manuel Artime's future invaders, training for "SECOND NAVAL GUERRILLA." The FBI knew all about this operation but were told 'that in the interest of *national security'* they were to look the other way.

"How's the new baby," Ruby asked.

"*Rachel* -- she's fine. I'm glad I only have to listen to her cry on weekends."

The Carousel's headline stripper, "Jada", slipped into a seat next to Ruby. "Who's your friend, Jack?" "Mind your own business" Ruby barked. Jada was mystified. Jack was always congenial around her. She was about to leave when Beverly Oliver, a stripper from the Colony Club next door sat down next to her. "Kind of quiet, tonight, huh Jack" she said. "Yeah", Ruby replied, "those amateur strip joints are really playing hell with our business."

"A lot of them don't even look like they're eighteen," Jada observed. Oswald abruptly got up, said "good night" and left. "Doesn't talk much," Oliver chuckled.

Ruby and the two strippers turned their attention to Wally Weston, the club's stand-up comedian.

"I've learned some important lessons in life," Weston said. "You'll go a lot further with a smile -- and a gun, than just a smile." The audience tittered -- Ruby clapped. Weston was okay.

After Ruby killed Oswald, Wally visited him in the County jail. Weston would later repeat something Ruby muttered during one of their visits.

"Gee, Wally. They're going to find out about New Orleans --they're going to find out about Cuba -- they're going to find out about the guns-- they're going to find out about everything."

Weston disappeared for almost eleven years before Senate Investigators, Gaeton Fonzi and Al Gonzales finally located him. Weston was leery of talking with them but in the end confirmed Ruby's remarks during their visit. Weston disappeared again and never resurfaced.

The President and his party arrived at Idlewild Airport --which soon would be renamed -- "JFK AIRPORT."

United States Air Force #26000 departed for Palm Beach, Florida at 3:04 P.M. -- arrived at West Palm Beach International Airport at 5:15 P.M.

JOSEPH P. KENNEDY'S OCEAN FRONT HOME – PALM BEACH

Agents Norton and Wunderlich who made a preliminary search of the residence two days earlier, did a final sweep of the premises and declared it "sanitized and secured."

Thirty minutes later, Kennedy and his party arrived at his father's mansion. Members of the group included Press Secretary Pierre Salinger, Assistant Press Secretary Malcolm Kilduff, and five additional Secret Service agents.

The President stood on the veranda staring at the tide rolling in. His thoughts turned to one of the family's traditional Christmas vacations in 1930:

Touch football was a tradition with the Kennedy's. A five man game was organized with the Kennedy's and some of the neighbor kids.

Joe (15) captained one team; Jack (13) the other. Jack's team was ahead by one point." The Ambassador" watched from the veranda. As the last play concluded he yelled: "Okay, kids, your mother wants you in the house for dinner." Joe pleaded for one more play and a chance to win the game.

On the ensuing play Joe wafted a perfect pass to a teammate standing at the goal line. Jack crashed into the other boy, illegally preventing him from making the catch. As they moved off the beach

Jack's team was jubilant. Joe ran to his father protesting Jack's interference with the receiver. The Ambassador told him to go inside and wait for another day. As he was about to pass his father, Jack received a big bear hug from him. Reveling in his father's attention, his face lit up. "I know you had to do that to win, Jack", he confided. "Tomorrow it will all be forgotten."

YBOR CITY – NOVEMBER 15TH – 9:50 P.M.

At Guillermo Ruiz's apartment near Tampa Bay, Santos Trafficante and Miguel Saez were going over their plans for Monday.

Twenty minutes before the event, Saez, dressed as an office worker carrying a small suitcase case, would be dropped off in the rear of a large bank building on Grand Central Boulevard.

In a storage loft just below the roof, Miguel would assemble his 7.62 Dragunov rifle, load it with frangible ammunition, attach the Zeiss scope, then stay out of sight and be ready to fire.

On its way from The Armory to The International Inn, the Presidential motorcade had to travel along Grand Central Boulevard at a slow pace until it reached the Howard Frankland Bridge. When it got beneath the bank building, Saez would have ample time to fire. Afterward he would disassemble the weapon and replace it in the suit case. This could be accomplished in 22 seconds.

The difficult part would be returning to the back of the building without arousing suspicion. It involved going down many flights of stairs, through the back of a record's storage building and emerging in the parking lot where the driver who brought Miguel would be waiting to take him to the alley behind Ruiz's apartment.

There he would remain for two days. Then, dressed as a fisherman he would board a boat that would take him to the Gulf of Mexico and put him ashore on a remote stretch of beach near Nuevo Laredo.

Armed with a false passport provided by Cuban Security, Miguel would cross the border and get on a bus to Mexico City. A Cubana Airliner would be waiting at the airport to fly him to Havana.

Santos was well satisfied. The plan had an excellent chance to succeed. The anticipation of returning to Havana as "Cuba's gambling czar" made him light headed.

"The only thing we need now" he told Saez, "is for Kennedy to show up beneath that building. I know you won't miss" "It's an easy shot," Saez observed. "I won't even need the scope for this one."

CAPE CANAVERAL – SATURDAY – 10:32 A.M. – NOVEMBER 16th.

Air Force One landed on "the skid strip" as they called the runway at Cape Canaveral. The President was accompanied by Special Assistant Kenny O'Donnell, six members of the Secret Service, Ira Gearhart (carrying "the football")plus Florida Senator George Smathers.

The Senator and Kennedy were old friends from their days in the House and Senate. The two often "chased skirts" together in the Capitol. During the 1960 presidential primary, Smathers suddenly announced his own candidacy. To protect his State he would run as a "favorite son" against Kennedy and Johnson. This astonished JFK and for a while relations were strained. When Kennedy became President the rift evaporated.

Visiting "The Cape" had special significance to the 35th President. He launched The Space Center on July 1st 1962.

On September 12th, without prior notice or consultation with anyone, Kennedy told the student body at Rice University:

"America is going to land a giant rocket on the moon. And this will be done in the decade of the sixties," he added, closing by asking for "Gods blessing on this most hazardous and dangerous and greatest adventure on which man has ever embarked."

At "The Cape" Kennedy received an orientation on "the Gemini capsule" from astronauts Gordon Cooper and Gus Grissom.

Kennedy asked them if they had any second thoughts going to the moon? "Yes," Cooper replied. "They'll have to drag me inside that death trap." Kennedy's astonished expression produced smiles from the astronauts. "Don't pay any attention to him, Mister President," Grissom advised. "Gordon's our resident joker."

The pair proceeded to brief Kennedy on their present state of readiness. (It took six years, and two more President's, before Neil Armstrong would step foot on the moon.)

Kennedy was taken to "Launch Control Center" by NASA'S Chief Scientist, Doctor Werner Von Braun. The one time darling of Hitler's deadly VI AND VII rocket programs delighted in showing the President the Saturn Missile's Control Center.

An old joke about Von Braun was still circulating:

"He aimed at the moon -- and hit London!"

Von Braun proceeded to brief the President on"
The Saturn Program."
Being on the cutting edge of these programs excited
Kennedy. But he was late for another appointment
and had to bid the astronauts and the scientist
goodbye. (Shortly after his death the facility was
renamed, "Cape Kennedy").

THE PALICIO – HAVANA – 10:56 A.M.

Ninety miles away, Fidel Castro agonized over how
to save President Kennedy from Raul's sniper. The
twenty-three year old Cuban had still not been
heard from. Despite the danger Raul was trying to
locate "his proxy messenger", Macho Gener.

Fidel mulled over alterative scenarios:

Finding *a new* messenger to locate Trafficante in
time to cancel the hit on Kennedy was a daunting
task. Not having access to another source close to
Trafficante made this alternative even more
dangerous. Fidel could instruct Doctor Vallejo to
warn Ambassador Attwood *that Cuban Intelligence had
unearthed a plot by Cuban exiles* to assassinate
Kennedy when he got to Tampa. The Cuban government
was aware that America's National Security Agency
(NSA), monitored all calls to and from Cuba. Since
Cuban Intelligence now knew Tafficante's telephone
number should they run the risk having Raul call
him? That seemed like the most dangerous of all
solutions.

Barely forty-eight hours remained before Kennedy
was scheduled to arrive in Tampa.

What to do? Fidel struggled to reach a
decision.

11:25 A.M. – OBSERVATION ISLAND – (NEAR MERRITT ISLAND) FLORIDA

The President and his party were awe struck when the submerged U.S. submarine, *Andrew Jackson*, launched a Polaris missile.

To see a rocket suddenly emerge from the water and roar into the heavens on its way to the target was akin to something out of Jules Verne. To say Kennedy and the others were impressed would be an understatement. *They were overwhelmed.*

12:52 A.M. – PALM BEACH, FLORIDA

Kennedy and his party arrived back at his father's mansion, relaxed on the beach or beside the pool.

It was time to get busy on the speech he would deliver in Tampa, Monday, or more accurately, three different speeches he would deliver in Tampa -- plus another, in Miami. The Miami speech would contain "the message" that "Comandante Augusto" in Cuba was waiting to hear. Speech writer's, including the masterful Ted Sorenson had already prepared drafts.

Tampa had never been visited by a sitting American President and JFK relished the opportunity of being the first. Castro and Cuba were hot topics all over the state. Anti-Castro exiles were strongest of all in Florida. Strengthening his image as a communist-fighting "cold warrior" was essential for Kennedy.

Crafting the speech for the Inter-American Press Association in Miami was the most important. It had to include "the message" without sounding like what it was. This part was not contained in the text prepared by Sorenson and the others. None of them knew about "SECOND NAVAL GUERRILLA" -- or the President's need to "send a message."

Kennedy worked on "the message", alone. None of those accompanying him knew about "GUERRILLA." When he was finished he used a secure line to call Bobby. "Sounds great," Jack, his brother assured him. "Congratulations. I didn't know you could write anything longer than a postcard."

SUNDAY – NOVEMBER 17TH – FBI'S OFFICE IN NEW ORLEANS – 1:36 A.M.

At this early hour, Sunday morning's were usually slow in FBI field offices.

William S. Walter had little to do today except update the files. Hearing the teletype chatter he moved to the machine and read a message **"From FBI Headquarters,"** warning about an impending attack on the life of President Kennedy by radical organizations when he arrived in Dallas. There is no record of any action being taken on this bulletin by the Dallas office. In fact they claimed they hadn't received it.

A lowly clerk, Walters nonetheless showed keen interest in what the bureau was doing. On a day in August, SA John Quigley went to the New Orleans police station answering a request from a man in their custody, named Lee H. Oswald, who asked for an Agent to come and talk to him. Walters checked the files to see if they contained anything on this individual. He found Oswald's name in the "POTENTIAL CRIMINAL INFORMANT FILE."

In the wake of the assassination, Texas Attorney General Waggoner Carr presented the Warren Commission with what he claimed to be Oswald's FBI informant number and the amount of his compensation . . . two hundred dollars per month. The Commission's way of handling this "dirty little rumor" was to ask Director Hoover to verify whether or not Oswald had ever been a Bureau informant. Guess what his answer was? That was the end of "the dirty little rumor."

WEST PALM BEACH - 10:00 A.M.

The President and Dave Powers attended Mass at
Saint Ann's Church in West Palm Beach. When he
emerged, a crowd of autograph seekers were waiting
for him.

The Secret Service began politely shooing them away.
But Kennedy plunged into their midst, smiling,
shaking hands, signing a few autographs and
conversing with some of the older people.

When, he wondered, would the Agents understand
that the purpose of these trips *was to make
contact with people* in an effort to influence them
to vote for him.

NOVEMBER 18TH - 8:46 A.M.- HAVANA

With slightly less than 3 hours before Kennedy's
arrival in Tampa, Fidel finally made his decision.
Raul would call Trafficante. It was a risky measure
but time had run out. The tactic was to use
metaphors and other language gimmicks to convey
Raul's message: *"The plan must be abandoned."*

Fidel and Raul went over the exact words to use.
Santos was no fool, he would know not to say much.

Since the NSA was not aware of the note Trafficante
received, eavesdroppers would not be able to
decipher what the conversation meant.

Raul initiated the call from a secure number. It
could be recognized as originating from Cuba, but
there was no way to identify the caller --or the
actual number he was calling from. Santos' number
started ringing -- and kept on ringing. Was it

possible, Raul wondered, he left town to avoid suspicion?

"Hello," a voice at the other end said.

"Santos?"

"Yeah?"

"It's your friend from the Hilton Hotel."

"Huh?"

"You remember. The one you came upstairs to thank."

A long silence followed.

"You remember?"

The silence continued.

"Santos? Are you there?"

"O-o-h -- yeah -- sure I remember."

Their conversation continued in Spanish.

"Remember what I said in the note?"

"Yes, everything is on track."

"We don't want it to happen."

Another protracted silence.

"Santos, do you understand -- it must not happen."

The gambler's mind was reeling. How could he call it off? Carlos and the others were counting on him.

"Santos? Did you hear me?"

"I heard. But that's going to be very difficult - maybe impossible."

"Shouldn't be. Tell our friend to call
his contact if he needs confirmation."
Trafficante's head spun as he tried to
figure out how to serve "two masters."

"Make sure he calls his contact. Will you do
that?"

After another protracted silence, the gambler
answered, "I'll tell him."

"Good. It doesn't affect the reward I
mentioned."

"Yes -- I see. Good."

"Adios."

Santos heard the dial tone, put down the receiver
and stared at the wall. Which was more important --
returning to Havana as the czar of gambling -- or
getting rid of John F. Kennedy?

Contacting Saez in time wasn't a problem. Dealing
with the result was another matter. He began
thinking of scenarios he could give Carlos and the
others.

Aside from Raul, no one knew about Saez -- and the
Cuban sniper wasn't about to publicize his role.

Maybe the shooter got cold feet, let Santos down at
the last minute and disappeared? Getting someone
else in time was impossible.

How could anyone prove this was a lie? The last
person they'd think to ask would be Raul Castro.
Contacting him was hardly an option.

Aside from Raul, Fidel was most likely the only person in Cuba who knew. But then, what about Saez's 'contact'? Sounded like he knew.

It was no certainty that Raul's inference about the gambling monopoly would materialize. Was it worth ignoring this possibility to make sure Kennedy died?

It was "a business decision" that had to be weighed very carefully.

MCDILL AIR FORCE BASE — TAMPA — 11:45 A.M.

Air Force one touched down on schedule. Looking tanned and rested, wearing a "midnight blue" suit and striped tie the President disembarked and listened to the local Air Force band play "Hail To The Chief". Color bearers marched forward. An honor guard rendered a brief series of military honors. A half dozen General Officers saluted and shook hands with Kennedy.

He was joined by Senator George Smathers, and Congressmen:

Sam Gibbons, Dante Fascell, and Claude Pepper –– Tampa Chamber of Commerce President James H.Covery, Jr., plus eighteen Secret Service Agents. The President and his entourage motored three quarters of a mile to "Strike Headquarters" where they received a briefing.

MIAMI — "JM WAVE" STATION— 11:57 P.M.

Two-hundred and seventy-nine miles south, in the office of the Chief Of Operations, "The Big Indian", David Morales, already had his radio on anticipating news that his most hated enemy, the President Of The United States, had been gunned down.

Morales already scheduled a celebration with fellow

conspirators, Bill Harvey and Johnny Roselli for early that evening.

NEW ORLEANS - 11:58 A.M.

Six hundred and fifty-seven miles away, Federal Court was in recess until Tuesday.

In his office at The Town and Country Motel, Carlos Marcello played gin rummy with brother, Pete, listened to the radio and watched television, hoping for "good news" from Tampa. In the background Carlos could hear the dulcet tones of Connie Francis singing "Where The Boys Are."

CHAPTER 11

MEXICO CITY - U.S. EMBASSY - 11:58 A.M.

At his office at the CIA Station, the head of Anti-Castro Propaganda and Covert Activities, David Atlee Phillips, was tuned to a radio station that carried international news. Smoke from his fortieth cigarette of the day swirled around his desk.

He had a twelve-thirty "luncheon" appointment at the El Encanto Hotel with Sylvia Duran. Perhaps she had further news about Ambassador Lechuga and had managed installing the bug on his telephone. The nicotine addict couldn't delay his departure much longer. What, he wondered was "The Big Indian" expecting to happen in Florida?

YBOR CITY - 12:02 P.M.

In the end, greed triumphed over murder. Santos decided to follow through on Raul's instructions about calling off "the hit." He entered Guillermo Ruiz's apartment building through a rear door to the alley and knocked on room number sixteen. No response. He knocked again, louder this time. Still, no response. He tried the door. It was open. Santos moved inside and called out: "Guillermo? Miguel?" He searched all three rooms. No sign of either one.

Miguel wasn't due to be picked up for another two hours, but where could he have gone?

There was nothing Santos could do except wait. The gangster sat down on a threadbare couch and rethought his decision. Maybe he should tell Saez to go ahead.

At his office in the Palicio, Fidel and Raul were frantic. Miguel's contact in Miami had not heard from the youthful sniper.

They decided to risk a follow up call to Trafficante. The number rang and rang - no answer.

The brother's Castro were unaware of Kennedy's schedule in Tampa, just that he was supposed to go from there to Miami.

VALDESTA, GEORGIA - 12:10 P.M.

At his home, Joseph Milteer switched from one TV channel to another, trying to get a station covering Kennedy's visit to Tampa. Agitated by not being able to locate a station televising the event he turned on his radio and found a station in Tampa with a live broadcast of the President's visit.

This did not mollify the virulent racist. He wanted to *watch* Kennedy die -- then revel in the aftermath. *Listening* was not a substitute for *seeing.*

The telephone rang. Hoping it was one of his contacts with an update on Kennedy's impending execution he grabbed the phone. "Hello." After a brief silence, the caller hung up. Milteer would never know that the person on the other end was a member of the Dade County Police Intelligence Unit, checking to see if he was home.

THE OFFICER'S CLUB - MCDILL AIR FORCE BASE - 12:15 P.M.

The President lunched with thirty military personnel and thirty civilians. The food was terrible but Kennedy's smile camouflaged his distaste. Sitting on his right, George Smathers grinned. He had eaten

there several times before and knew what they
were in for. It wouldn't be long before the
entourage would depart for Al Lopez Field, where the
President would deliver the first of four speeches
that day.

YBOR CITY — 12:42 P.M.

At Guillermo Ruiz's apartment Santos Trafficante
stared out the window hoping to catch sight of
Miguel. The streets were almost deserted. Many of
the residents in the neighborhood had departed for
the downtown area to watch the Presidential
motorcade.

MCDILL AIR FORCE BASE — 1:16 P.M.

The President's party boarded helicopters which
headed for Al Lopez Baseball field. The trip took
six minutes.

When they arrived, Kennedy mounted steps leading to
bleachers covered with red, white and blue bunting.
After shaking a dozen hands of those invited to
stand next to him, he stepped to the lectern and
spoke to a crowd of several thousand people.

A phalanx of armed Tampa policeman and Secret
Service Agents scanned the crowd looking for several
individuals who had made threats on the President's
life. These included Gilberto Policarpo Lopez, the
Cuban involved with the local chapter of The Fair
Play for Cuba Committee. Although they possessed
only a superficial description of another Cuban,
Miguel Casas Saez, the lawmen were watching for him,
too.

Following perfunctory opening remarks, Kennedy
launched into a blistering attack on the Castro
regime. Later, he paid tribute to some three
thousand Tampa cigar makers, put out of work by the
continuing embargo against Cuban tobacco.
Virtually all of them worked in Ybor City. While
his address was in progress the Special Agent In

Charge (SAIC) Emory Roberts, went over assignments with five other Agents. Will Greer would be at the wheel of the President's limousine. He had chauffeured Kennedy on every trip since he became President.

SA McHugh and SA Boring would ride in the front seat with Greer. Roberts would control things from the follow-up vehicle accompanied by Agents Blaine, Yeager and Rybka, who would alternate between standing on foot holds in the back of the President's limo, or riding on the running boards of the follow-up car. Salinger and Kilduff would also ride with Roberts.

Security all over the city was maximum. Overpasses were manned by police and military units toting rifles and shotguns. Tampa Sheriff's personnel secured the roofs of major buildings in the downtown area, *including the bank building from which Saez planned to shoot the President.* All tolled, six hundred personnel were involved.

OAK PARK - ILLINOIS - TAM O'SHANTER GOLF COURSE - 12:53 P.M.

Even with all the rounds of golf Sam Giancana was logging his game was getting worse. Previously an *eleven* handicap, he was now a *sixteen*. This aggravated the mob boss. Driving alone in his golf cart, his tiny transistor radio was tuned to the local CBS affiliate. In five minutes they would switch to network news coverage. "Moony" had high hopes for Trafficante's operation in Tampa. If it succeeded they would be rid of the double crosser occupying the White House. Giancana noticed his nemesis --the FBI'S Bill Roemer, making his approach shot in the twelfth fairway. Like Inspector Jobert, in "Les Miserables", Roemer was relentless in the pursuit of his quarry.

With Kennedy out of the picture, Bobby Kennedy would be a eunuch and Roemer would be finished. The

golf cart passed over a depression in the cart
path, jolting the cart so violently it nearly
dislodged Chicago's mob boss. Out of the corner of
his eye he saw Roemer grinning at him.

AL LOPEZ FIELD - TAMPA - 1:56 P.M.

The Presidential motorcade left the ballpark and
commenced a seven and a half mile, forty-five
minute trip through Tampa heading for Fort Homer
Hesterly Armory.

Crowds lined the streets. Even though Tampa was a
bastion of conservatives that voted for Nixon in
1960, some waved banners proclaiming: "JFK IN 64."
Kennedy smiled and waved. They waved back.
Suddenly, he stood erect, making himself an easy
target for an assassin. Agent's Blaine, Yeager and
Rybka vaulted out of the follow up car and rushed
to take up positions on the back of Kennedy's
limousine.

THE PALICIO - HAVANA - 2:01 P.M.

Saez had not checked in and Raul still wasn't able
to contact Trafficante. Secreted in Fidel's office
the brothers Castro were resigned to hearing news
that Kennedy had been assassinated. Prospects for a
rapprochement would be over.

"It will be a winter of hard cheese," Fidel
prophesied.

YBOR CITY - GUILLERMO RUIZ'S APARTMENT

Miguel Saez opened the door and found Santos
Trafficante sitting on the couch staring at him.
"Where were you," Santos asked. "In Church, asking
Mother Mary for her blessing" Saez replied. The
irony associated with this request was lost on the
gangster.

"It's almost time for me to be picked up -- is

something wrong?" "Yes," Trafficante replied.
Raul telephoned me several hours ago and called it
off." Saez was puzzled. "Why?", "Didn't tell me",
Santos replied. "Said you could call 'your contact
in Miami' if you wanted confirmation."

THE MOTORCADE

Despite repeated protests from the Agents on the
back of the limousine, Kennedy remained erect,
posturing defiance in the face of assassination.

In the follow-up car SAIC Emory Roberts scowled. He
didn't like Kennedy. A Southerner, Roberts resented
the President's civil rights policies, thought him
a reckless womanizer who used drugs and constantly
compromised the Service's ability to protect him.

Worst of all, was his habit of isolating himself
from Warrant Officer Gearhart -- and "the
football." During these times the President would
not have been able to discharge his duties. If
Kennedy was assassinated, Agent Roberts would not
mourn.

The balance of the Tampa visit passed without
incident. The President's remarks at the Armory,
and later to six hundred members of The
Steelworker's Union assembled at the International
Inn were well received.

The motorcade proceeded to McDill Air Force base.
Air Force one, bearing the President and his
entourage, departed for Miami at 4:20 P.M.
At his home in Miami, William Somersett's phone
rang. The caller was Joseph Milteer.

"Kennedy should have been killed in Tampa, but
someone called the FBI and gave the thing away and
of course he was well guarded and everything went
'pfluey'."

There was "no joy in Valdesta, Miami, New

Orleans, Chicago, or Mexico City --- the
assassins had "struck out."

THE PALICIO - 4:55 P.M.

Something *akin to joy* was going on in Fidel
Castro's office.

He and Raul, were able to breathe again.
Intelligence agents in Miami had monitored a
broadcast from Tampa confirming that the
President's visit to that city had not produced
any untoward incidents.

Now all they had to do was wait for Doctor
Vallejo to hear again from Ambassador Attwood.

MIAMI INTERNATIONAL AIRPORT - 5:00 P.M.

The danger in Tampa had been dealt with. JFK'S
visit there had been a great success. He and
Senator Smathers discussed this during the flight
to Miami and hatched plans for a winning campaign
in Florida the following year.

To JFK the best news of all was a whisper from
Smathers that he had "a really hot number" waiting
in the wings to meet the President. An hour's lag
time between their arrival at the Americana Hotel
and the President's attendance at a cocktail party
would allow for "an introduction."

"Of course", Smathers said, "if you're tired and
would rather take a rest, I can arranges omething
with her the next time you visit Miami."

"Tired! I'm not tired!! Let's meet her as soon as
we get to the hotel."

Air Force One landed on the main concourse where a
noisy rally greeted the 35th President. The event
was of course staged by Miami's Democratic
Headquarters. Even though he was aware the event
was "scripted", JFK basked in his reception. A

small band of Cuban-exile protesters were
swallowed up by the huge crowd. Their presence went
virtually unnoticed.

The Presidential party arrived at the Americana at
5:50 P.M. The hotel manager escorted Kennedy to
the Presidential suite. Complaining that he *needed
"a rest,"* Kennedy shooed the Secret Service and
Pierre Salinger out of his room.

Fifteen minutes later, Smathers arrived with "the
hot number" on his arm and promptly excused
himself.

"What do you do", Kennedy inquired. *"You"*, she
grinned.

MIAMI — 7:08 P.M.

At *"The Breakers"*, the celebration Morales planned
turned into a wake. Johnny Roselli and Bill Harvey
listened as "The Big Indian" outlined plans for
"the operation in Dallas" on Friday.

Two hit teams, composed of three shooters each,
were being flown in from Miami, New Orleans and
Tucson. Guy Banister and David Ferrie made all of
the arrangements to get them to Garland, a suburb
of Dallas. They would arrive two hours before
Kennedy's speech at the Trade Mart. Team one, would
take up positions in Dealey Plaza; team two would
cover the Trade Mart in case something queered the
first team's ambush in the Plaza.

Their "patsy" was being run by David Phillips who
thought the plan in Dealey Plaza was part of an
elaborate *charade* designed to make the world believe
a Castro inspired assassination failed. The "patsy's
background" -- and the discovery of his rifle would
quickly lead to "exposing" Fidel Castro as the
mastermind behind "the attempt on Kennedy's life."
*Neither Phillips nor the "patsy" knew Kennedy would
actually be killed.*

A Dallas police officer was being recruited to shoot the patsy "while attempting to avoid arrest."

A last minute component involved an assist from two Secret Service Agents on the Dallas portion of the trip. Their knowledge of Morales' operation was limited to what was planned to occur in Dealey Plaza. They had no information about the genesis of the plot or names of the individuals involved in the ambush.

THE AMERICANA HOTEL - MIAMI - 8:10 P.M.

Eleven miles from "The Breakers", President Kennedy reached the crucial point in his speech to The Inter-American Press Association containing his message to the "Guerrilla" leader in Cuba.

"The genuine Cuban revolution, because it was against the tyranny and corruption of the past, had the support of many whose aims and concepts were democratic."

"The goals proclaimed in the Sierra Maestra were betrayed in Havana. A small band of conspirators has stripped the Cuban people of their freedom and handed over the independence and the sovereignty of the Cuban nation to forces beyond the hemisphere. "This and this alone, divides us."

"As long as this is true, nothing is possible. Without it, everything is possible. Once the barrier is removed, we will be ready and anxious to work with the Cuban people."

"Once Cuban sovereignty has been restored, we will extend the hand of friendship and assistance to a Cuba whose political and economic institutions have been shaped by the will of the people."

The speech was received politely but without the enthusiasm Kennedy and his speech writers hoped for.

If Cuban exiles had been in the audience they would have cheered.

In a safe house not far from Havana, Comandante "Augusto", Guerrilla's leader and his comrades rejoiced. Kennedy had make good on his promise of support -- and done so in unmistakable language. "Muerto a Fidel" they shouted. (Death to Fidel).

A PAY PHONE IN TAMPA – 8:15 P.M.

Santos Trafficante was talking to Carlos Marcello at his office in The Town & Country Motel. "The Little Man" was not happy. "Should'a had a back-up!" he growled. "I did", Santos lied. "He chickened out, too. So many people guarding him must'a spooked 'em. So I got a hole in my pocket and the sob is still walking around." He carefully avoided any mention of Miguel Saez, which would surely provoke inquiries from the street-wise Marcello.

"Friday's our last chance," Carlos croaked and hung up. It had been an awkward conversation. Santos was not sure Carlos bought it. He salved his guilty conscience by speculating that Raul Castro would come through for him.

Carlos still pondered what Santos related. Something was wrong. He glanced at a sign over his office door, which read: "THREE CAN KEEP A SECRET IF TWO OF THEM ARE DEAD."

MIAMI

At 9:20 P.M. Air Force One took-off for a two hour flight to Washington. The President slept most of the way. The plane touched down at Andrews Air Force Base at 11:15 P.M.

Fifteen minutes later, Kennedy arrived at the White House via helicopter. He went upstairs and fell into bed.

Before falling asleep he remembered an incident

that happened while he and Joe played in high school championship baseball game. Joe pitched so hard his catcher went to their manager and said his catching hand hurt so bad he couldn't continue. Jack volunteered to replace him. Joe burned them in with such ferocity Jack's left hand swelled up and turned purple. They won the game and on the way to the locker room the Ambassador put his arm around Joe, praising him for pitching a two-hit shutout. Jack tagged along expecting some recognition for his part in the victory. It didn't come. That his hand was a bloody pulp didn't bother him. Seeing Joe get all Dad's attention was unbearable.

TUESDAY — NOVEMBER 19TH

Reaction to Kennedy's speech with its thinly veiled threat against the Castro regime was swift and pointed.

United Press International observed:

"President Kennedy all but invited the Cuban people to overthrow Fidel Castro's Communist regime and promised prompt U.S. aid if they do. The President added: "It would be a happy day if the Castro government is ousted."

The New York Times was a little more subdued:

"Kennedy says the U.S. will aid Cuba once Cuban sovereignty is restored under a non-Communist government."

In Havana, the government controlled newspaper, "GRAMMA", excoriated Kennedy for his speech, branding him an agent of imperialism bent on destroying a peace loving nation -- adding: *"the threat of another invasion of Cuba is eminent."*

The Soviet Union's PRAVDA echoed these sentiments and reminded Washington of Khruschev's recent edict:

"A U.S. invasion of Cuba would mean war."

RENEE VALLEJO'S APARTMENT —HAVANA — 6:50 A.M.

Fidel's doctor and trusted confidante put the phone down ending a three and a half hour conversation with Ambassador Attwood.

Castro sat next to him the whole time, listening and occasionally whispering suggestions. Infuriated by Kennedy's bellicose remarks in Tampa and Miami, Fidel insisted Attwood extract assurances from Kennedy that this was merely political rhetoric -- not a turnaround in efforts to reach a rapprochement between their two countries. The speech had taken Attwood by complete surprise and now he worked at damage control. The Ambassador had not spoken with the President since their meeting in New York, but was scheduled to see him at the White House later that day.

John Kennedy awoke well rested and ready for a series of appointments plus wrestling with mounds of paperwork accumulated during his absence.

He was happy to have his valet George Thomas help him into his clothes, even happier when "Doctor Feelgood" showed up with his shots of cortisone, procaine and amphetamines which he'd gone without for five days.

He looked forward to "time in the pool" with "Fiddle and Faddle" whose "company" he sorely missed. If it wasn't for his "surprise visitor" at The Americana, the President would probably have a severe headache, perhaps a migraine.

The switchboard put a call through from Jackie.

"Hi, stranger -- how did it go?"

"Fine, honey, how are my kids?"

"I thought they were "ours", Jackie chided."

Here, Caroline wants to talk with you."

"Daddy! Did you bring me something?"

"I might have something -- that is if you haven't been eating candy while I was gone." After a suspicious silence, Kennedy continued his interrogation. "Well, "yes" -- "no", or "maybe?"

"Here," she said, "talk to mommy, again."

That really tickled Kennedy.

"Jack?"

"Uh-huh. That girl has the makings of a great politician."

"Oh, swell! Here's John-John." Jack heard his son giggling in the background.

"Hello? John-John? -- How are you?"

The giggling continued, followed by a shout.

"I want pancakes, mommy!"

"Jack . . . I'd better get busy before he starts screaming. Talk with you later, honey." Then she hung up.

The President had forgotten to check with Jackie about her wardrobe for the trip to Texas. He wanted her to bring the pink outfit with the pillbox hat.

THE OVAL OFFICE

By 9:25 the President was at his desk scanning a half dozen newspaper while Evelyn Lincoln shuffled through the paperwork she felt her boss should see first. Out of the corner of his eye he spied a message from Bill Attwood, requesting a meeting as early as possible. Kennedy correctly surmised that his speech in Miami provoked a reaction from Castro.

"The Attorney General wanted to know if you had time for lunch, today."

"Tell him okay for lunch --*here* --one-thirty. Have Ambassador Attwood meet me in the Rose Garden at three-thirty. "Yes, Mister President," Lincoln responded. She put the data she wanted him to read in front of him and returned to her office.

CHAPTER 12
MARKET HALL - DALLAS - 9:40 A.M.

Lyndon Johnson hadn't appeared in the nation's capitol for a month. He preferred to remain holed up at his ranch with his ear to the ground-- assessing prospects for staying *on the ticket* and *out of jail*. Rumors that he would soon become President continued coming in over the transom. He had a sudden rash of visits from "big oil", -- in many cases, men he hadn't seen in a long time.

At the moment the Vice President was mingling with various politicos on hand for the Pepsi Cola Bottler's convention, a body he was scheduled to address in forty minutes.

"Working the room," was a Johnson specialty. These conclaves presented targets of opportunity for hearing and dispensing salacious gossip and significant intelligence about state and local politics.

Explaining the First World War is much easier than explaining the intricacies of Texas politics in 1963.

Since Reconstruction (1869) the Democratic Party was effectively *the only party* in the State. The candidate who won the Democratic primary automatically *won* the general election.

(Finally, in May 1961, Republican John Tower became

the first Republican Senator from Texas, elected
to fill the seat vacated when Johnson became Vice
President.)

The "Junior Senator" was currently a non-entity, but
his election was a harbinger of a monumental
turnaround in the political landscape of "The Lone
Star" State.

In November 1963, *Democrat* John Connally was
Governor, *Democrat* Ralph Yarborough was the Senior
Senator, and *Democrat* Lyndon Johnson was Vice
President. The bad news was Johnson and Yarborough
hated one another. Connally distanced himself from
old friend and patron Johnson and did everything he
could to undermine and embarrass Yarborough. He was
known as "the little people's Senator" and was
easily the most popular of the three.

Big oil and big business abhorred his ultra
liberal beliefs.

Headquartered in Dallas, that clique supported
Connally and mistrusted Johnson because of his
alliance with an Administration that was pushing
Civil Rights. They despised the "Yankee President"
for being "soft on communism" and a threat to the
oil depletion allowance. He was in the words of one
of them:

"A liability to the free world."

Dallas was known as the "Right Wing Capitol of
America" for a good reason: It was. Organization's
like The John Birch Society, The Minutemen and The
Klu Klux Klan thrived in "Big D".

It was contributions from these groups and
private parties which paid for billboards all
over the state that read:

"IMPEACH EARL WARREN"

The "Warren Court" was responsible for a 9-0

decision upholding Brown v.s. The Board of Education thereby eliminating segregation in tax-supported institutions.

John Kennedy was poised to travel to Texas and immerse himself in this morass of virulent hatred and political infighting.

While Johnson was addressing the bottlers, an edition of The Dallas Times Herald hit the streets featuring the President's motorcade route on the front page. Two citizens who bought copies were Lee Oswald and Jack Ruby.

Johnson insisted the President and his wife spend the night at the LBJ Ranch after the festivities in Austin were over.

Jackie Kennedy had never been to Texas . . . and she would never return.

THE WHITE HOUSE - 11:15 A.M.

JFK was still reading the newspapers when Mrs. Lincoln informed him that National Board for The Poultry and Egg Association were waiting for him in the garden outside his office.

There he was presented with a live thirty-five pound turkey for Thanksgiving. Holding the bird was awkward. He got feathers on his suit but continued smiling. Ordinarily he would have passed this ceremonial chore on to a Presidential assistant, but since the powerful Senate Minority Leader, Everett Dirksen, *from Illinois* promoted this meeting it was smart politics to do it himself.

At 12:55 Kennedy hurried to the pool. He was overjoyed to see "Fiddle and Faddle" frolicking naked in the shallow end while Dave Powers kept watch. As usual, the Secret Service was not invited.

"Having" the young secretaries again elevated

Kennedy's consciousness.

THE PRESIDENT'S PRIVATE DINING ROOM — 1:45 P.M.

Jack and Bobby dined alone. It was a safe place for their meeting since the President was positive the Oval Office was bugged.

Harry Williams had received confirmation that "Guerrilla's" leader in Cuba, heard and heartily approved the assurances Kennedy delivered in his speech the previous night. From their perspective, "all systems were go."

The *bad news*: The speech went so far it fueled speculation that an invasion of Cuba was eminent.

More *good news*: A CIA Officer (Nestor Sanchez) was scheduled to meet "AMLASH" (Rolando Cubela) in Paris on Friday to finalize plans for "an inside job" to murder Fidel. The assassin would be supplied materials that included a ballpoint pen containing deadly shellfish toxin.

"We're playing with fire, Bobby."

"The opportunity to get rid of Castro is worth it, Jack."

"Yes —— as long as it works." While the President gobbled down the remainder of his crab salad he thought of a different subject.

"What's going on with that fellow in New Orleans?"

"It's going to the jury the end of this week. My people there say he's a cinch to be convicted. And speaking of convictions, Senator Williams over at The Rules Committee thinks Lyndon will be referred for prosecution on at least eleven counts of accepting bribes."

The President groaned. This was the worst news of all. The younger Kennedy was overjoyed. He thoroughly despised Lyndon Johnson.

THE ROSE GARDEN — 3:33 P.M.

"I know what I said in the speech sounded inflammatory Bill, but Fidel must understand with an election year around the corner, I have to posit a strong anti-Communist stand, especially on Cuba."

Attwood continued pushing for the Cuban initiative:

"To keep this alive I need to give him something concrete --like authorization from you to proceed with talks outlining an agenda for reaching agreement.

Kennedy's attention was diverted by three placard-carrying civil rights advocates picketing on the sidewalk just beyond the wrought iron fence.

"Action now!" they chanted *--over and over again.*

Returning his attention to Attwood, Kennedy said:

"Tell Doctor Vallejo I'm leaving for Texas for a couple of days on Thursday. When I come back, I'll talk with Dean Rusk and put together an agenda we think appropriate for your discussions."

He didn't bother to inform Attwood that a meeting with his Secretary of State was scheduled to take place in a few minutes. If the "Comandante Augusto" -- or AMLASH, succeeded in offing Fidel, negotiations for a rapprochement would no longer be a problem. From a political standpoint, Castro's demise was by far the most desirable.

When Attwood departed, the President instructed

Mrs. Lincoln to have the Secret Service invite the civil rights protesters to come to the Rose Garden right away.

MEXICO CITY - 2:55 P.M.

David Phillips was burning. He'd just put down the phone after talking with The Big Indian and lit another cigarette. Oswald, he learned was involved with Ruby transporting stolen guns from Fort Hood to Cuban exiles that shipped them to the insurgents training in Nicaragua.

This had to be stopped, pronto. Phillips couldn't have his "patsy" sitting in a jail cell when the President's motorcade rolled past the Schoolbook Depository. Had Oswald taken leave of his senses? Did he have any in the first place?

THE ROSE GARDEN - 4:05 P.M.

Smiling and all charm, the President shook hands with the three stunned civil rights protesters. He asked each one their names and where they were from.

"Look," he said, "it takes a lot of courage to come up here and protest and I admire that. The Attorney General has Federal Marshall's working around the clock in hot spots all over the South. We're making progress. I hope you realize this administration is sincere about addressing your concerns."

Kennedy's words and the eye contact he established with each of them carried the day. They departed convinced he meant business and anxious to tell their comrades about "their dialog with the President."

THE WHITE HOUSE PRESSROOM - 4:29 P.M.

Pierre Salinger briefed reporters on the trip to Texas. The press plane would depart from

Andrews Air Force Base Thursday at ten a.m. and arrive in San Antonio at 11 A.M, CST.

Assistant Press Secretary Malcolm Kilduff would stand in for Salinger who was accompanying Cabinet members on a flight to Honolulu.

THE OVAL OFFICE – 4:34 P.M.

Kennedy sat in his rocker, listening solemnly to Dean Rusk point out that the President's challenging remarks the night before were not playing well in many parts of the world. Soviet Ambassador Dobrynin in was on the phone with him for forty-five minutes, warning that Khruschev meant what he said regarding "war" over an invasion of Cuba.

When Rusk finished, Kennedy soft pedaled the whole thing as "election year politics" which everyone should be able to decipher. During the balance of their thirty minute meeting Kennedy failed to bring up the short fuse on his Cuban invasion plan or the "rapprochement" issue with Fidel Castro.

1027 N. BECKLEY STREET – OAK CLIFF, TEXAS – 5:45 P.M.

The pay phone in the hall outside "O. H. Lee's" room rang several times before Earlene Roberts got there to answer it.

Oswald was shaving when he heard her knock.

"It's for you, Mister Lee," she said.

"Okay," Oswald muttered, scraped the shaving cream off his face and went to the phone.

"Yeah?"

"It's Jack. Can you come to my apartment, tonight?

Kennedy was on the phone with DNC Chairman John
Bailey. The Chairman had developed a list of
potential replacements for Lyndon Johnson. As
the President listened to Bailey rattle off a
roster of candidates he scrawled one name on
a scratch pad: **Terry Sanford**. Sanford, the
same age as Kennedy, was a highly decorated
paratrooper during the war and a very popular
Governor of North Carolina.

"Okay, John," the President said. "Let's go with
Sanford. But keep that to yourself. I'm going to
Texas this week and I don't want Lyndon hearing
about this."

Ten minutes later, the President listened to a
report from CIA Deputy Director Of Plans, Richard
Helms and Herschel Peak, the CIA'S man in Venezuela.
Peak told Kennedy of a coup in the works to
overthrow Venezuelan President Romulo Betancourt.
The putsch was being planned by a terrorist group
calling themselves "ARMED FORCES FOR NATIONAL
LIBERATION (FLN) which had been receiving arms from
Castro.

After hearing them out Kennedy told Helms: "I think
we should stay out of it. This seems like it ought
to be referred to The Organization of American
States."

Then he went to the pool for the second time
that day.

DALLAS - 8:01 P.M.

At Jack Ruby's apartment, located just over a mile
from Oswald's rooming house, he and Lee were
involved in a discussion with a third man, Dallas
Patrolman Jefferson Davis Tippit, whom everyone
called "J.D."

He was one of Ruby's closest contacts inside the DPD. When he worked nights, J.D. stopped in at The Carousel Club quite often.

Tippit was addicted to Ruby's generosity. He got free drinks, free food, free broads and cash for persuading fellow officers to drop charges against Jack's girls for prostitution, lewd conduct, minor drug violations even an occasional speeding ticket.

Tippit's knowledge of the plans for November 22nd was limited. After Oswald fired at the President, J.D. would pick him up in back of the Depository. The officer would have a policeman's uniform in his car, which Oswald would don on their way to Red Bird Airport. There, Oswald believed a plane would be waiting to fly him to Mexico.

Ruby told the former Marine it was too risky for him to continue working on the gun running operation out of Fort Hood. With the President due to arrive in Dallas in three days, staying out of harms way was essential. "Okay", Oswald shrugged and left.

"The little prick is going to shoot Kennedy on Friday," Ruby said. The news startled J.D. Surely Jack was kidding.

Ruby took five one hundred dollar bills from his pocket, offered them to Tippit, and confided:

"When your patrol car gets to Houston Street tell Lee to get out -- then shoot him." Tippit was taken aback. He didn't realize this was the type of thing Ruby would be involved in.

"How am I gonna explain that," he asked.

"Oswald was resisting arrest. You're gonna be the cop who bagged the President's assassin! You'll be famous . . . and a cinch for a promotion."

J.D. stared at Ruby as he thought his proposition over. Finally, he took the currency and stuffed it in his pocket.

"There's something else I want you to do," Ruby continued. "Bring me a medium sized police uniform with a badge and gun. A man wearing that uniform will be waiting for you in the parking lot behind my club *at exactly noon, Friday*. Drive him to the Depository and let him out in the parking lot. That's all you gotta do for this cee-note."

On a Policeman's pay, and working two other jobs, a man supporting a wife and three children was always up against it. J.D. took the hundred and put it in his pocket.

At one-fifteen in the morning, Ruby's telephone rang. Donnell Whitter, his auto mechanic and occasional gun running cohort was calling from jail. He and another man had been arrested by FBI and the Dallas Police for stealing guns from THE TEXAS NATIONAL GUARD ARMORY. "Don't talk to anyone," Ruby told him. I'll have a bondsman there in half an hour."

During a preliminary hearing in Federal Court, defendants Lawrence E. Miller and Donnell D. Whitter, apprehended following a ninety mile an hour chase were represented by hastily recruited counsel. In the trunk of their Thunderbird car, police discovered a cache of military type weapons. Now they faced the judge who asked them for their plea. Before their lawyer could respond, the prosecutor said: "One moment your Honor, if you please." He and defense counsel approached the bench. The prosecutor whispered to the Judge that he had been instructed by the Department Of Justice to ask that all charges against the defendants be dropped. It was, they said, "a matter of National Security."

Whitter and Lawrence walked. The prosecutor, the Judge --and the public never knew the stolen guns were destined for Manuel Artime's invasion force in Nicaragua.

Bobby Kennedy's operation "SECOND NAVAL GUERRILLA" dodged the bullet again.

However, the sands of time flowing through the hour glass of his brother's life were rapidly disappearing.

THE WHITE HOUSE –11:25 P.M.

When the President retired, he found a stranger in his bed -- Jackie. She and her husband slept together for the first time in many weeks. Their lovemaking didn't last very long -- not long enough for Jackie, anyway. After having his way with her Jack rolled over and was asleep in less than a minute.

What else was new, Jackie mused. If she and Angie Dickinson ever compared notes it's a good bet Jackie would concur with Angie's comment about her husband:

"The best twenty seconds of my life."

It was the final sexual contact between the President and The First Lady.

Jackie's thoughts turned to her wardrobe for the trip.

Earlier that day she'd asked Texas Senator Ralph Yarborough's wife what the weather would be like. "Well," Mrs. Yarborough replied, "that depends on which twenty minutes of the day you have in mind."

THE WHITE HOUSE – WEDNESDAY – NOVEMBER 20TH – 8:45 A.M.

John Kennedy's last full day in The White House began with a "Legislative Leaders Breakfast." The group consisted of five Congressmen and Senators, including future Warren Commission Member, Hale Boggs, of Louisiana.

The half hour breakfast was consumed over wrangling about which bill should be receiving the most attention and what could be done to speed up progress in various committees.

The President's focus was on his trip to Texas. He was having second thoughts and ran through a list possible excuses for canceling.

SECRET SERVICE H.Q. – THE TREASURY DEPARTMENT – 9:17 A.M.

Key members of The White House Detail (WHD) who weren't already in Texas, listened to Chief James Rowley's final briefing before departing with the President the following day.

Rowley emphasized that extremists might seize this opportunity to harass Kennedy. Feelings of hatred in Texas against his administration were especially vociferous in Dallas.

Ambassador Stevenson was assaulted there in late October, Vice President Johnson and "Ladybird" were shoved and heckled in front of the Adlophus Hotel earlier in the year.

He told the Agents that their office in Dallas had received *no reports* of threats against the President. (There had been many, *but none had been passed on to the Dallas office.*) They were confident there would be no trouble.

Special Agent Floyd Boring, ordinarily in charge of this type of travel wouldn't be making the trip. Neither would the Agent In Charge Of The White House Detail, Jerry Behn.

SA Roy Kellerman would take Boring's place. The absence of Behn and Boring exacerbated an already serious lack of experienced personnel. With Kennedy visiting five cities in two days the Service was seriously undermanned.

When the meeting broke up, ASAIC Emory Roberts, told Agent's John Ready and Clint Hill:

"The President has to have an unrestricted view of the crowd during the motorcade. He doesn't want agents riding on the back of the limousine."

Clint Hill thought this especially strange. He had been with the Kennedy's since the beginning and didn't recall the President ever complaining about having Agents on the back of the limousine or running alongside.

In fact Kennedy was always very cooperative and never second guessed directions from The White House Detail.

Hill was looking forward to the Texas trip. Jackie had not accompanied her husband on a domestic political junket since the primaries during the 1960 campaign. He was confident her charm and beauty would enhance the whole experience.

ASAIC Roberts made a mental note to tell limousine driver Will Greer to watch him for a signal in case of trouble -- which he knew was coming.

THE OVAL OFFICE - 9:38 A.M.

When the President arrived in his office he found three students from The Federal Republic of Germany's *BERLIN HIGH SCHOOL* waiting to meet him.

Two of them, Heidi Marie Mueller, and Johann Hessing, enthusiastically informed Kennedy they were at "the wall" in June when he addressed a million of their countrymen.

"It was the most exciting moment of my life," Mueller gushed. Then she handed Kennedy a photograph of himself and asked him to autograph it. The President obliged, adding his famous comment on that day in June, "Ich bin einBerliner." The other two lamented the fact that they had no pictures for him to sign.

"That's alright. Give your names and addresses to Mrs. Lincoln and she'll see to it you get them."

"With the quotation?", Hessing asked.

"Of course," Kennedy smiled.

They were in for a bitter disappointment. Mrs. Lincoln was too busy to attend to their request before she and her boss left for Texas.

11:30

The President met for ten minutes with DNC Chairman John Bailey, who brought with him singer Lena Horne and actress Carol Lawrence the star of Broadway's WEST SIDE STORY. Both were Kennedy supporters who'd volunteered to make appearances for the President during the campaign. That earned them ten minutes with JFK.

11:40 A.M.

After a fifteen minute meeting with THE INTER-AMERICAN COMMITTEE, Kennedy hurried to the pool. Jackie was in Glenora, packing and not due at the White House until 1:15. So the President had precious little time for what would be his final "frolic" with "FIDDLE" and "FADDLE".

At the Federal Courthouse, Carlos Marcello paid
no attention to the lead prosecutor's summation to
the Jury. Marcello's thoughts were on the
conversation he had with Santos night before last.

In his mind he replayed what the Tampa mob boss said
to him. The thing that stuck out was Santos making
no reference to doing something about the hit men
who ran out on him --*with his money.* This was not
like Santos. Restitution and retribution was
mandatory. Maybe Santos didn't want to discuss this
on the telephone.

Carlos would bring it up when they saw one
another.

His focus turned to preparations for Friday and
hopes there would not be a repeat of what happened
in Chicago and Tampa.

He already spent over five-hundred thousand of his
own cash on planning, equipment, transportation
and payments to personnel involved with "the hit"
in Dallas.

Guy Banister received the cash and "laundered" it
through a dummy corporation in the Bahamas. A
courier brought the "sanitized cash" back to the
States where Banister saw to its "distribution."
Marcello was a business man. He expected results
for the money he laid out.

Marcello leaned over to whisper in David Ferrie's
ear. "How long you gonna be gone on Friday?"

"Two, maybe three hours -- unless we run into bad
weather. I just deliver 'the painters', turn
around and fly home." ('Painters' is mob-speak
for *people who kill people.)*

CHAPTER 13

VERADERO VILLA - HAVANA - 12:56 P.M.

Fidel Castro puffed on the remains of a Monte Cristo cigar and tried to unravel a puzzling situation.

Sitting opposite him in the living room, French journalist, Jean Daniel was recounting his meeting with Kennedy in the President's office at the White House in late October.

Kennedy, Daniel said, was disheartened by the history of American involvement with Cuban dictator Flugencio Batista. He sympathized with the Cuban people's suffering under the former despot and hoped that the Cuban revolution would eliminate enemies of the people.

The humiliation and exploitation of oppressed people in the world was in no place worse than in Cuba.

"I am still in agreement with the first Cuban revolutionaries regarding the sins of the United States for supporting this scourge of humanity, "Daniel said the President told him.

Castro insisted Daniel repeat Kennedy's denunciation of Batista three times.

While he was doing so, Fidel was having difficulty separating fact from fiction. In his breast pocket was a decoded message from double agent, Rolando Cubela informing Castro he would meet his CIA case officer again in Paris on Friday. The Agent had promised Cubela assassination tools for eliminating the Cuban Premier.

Earlier that day, Doctor Renee Vallejo had a telephone call from Ambassador Attwood informing him that Kennedy was set to approve the diplomat's travel to Cuba for discussions that would produce an agenda for the full fledged negotiations outlining a rapprochement between Cuba and the U.S. The President would see to this as soon as he returned from a short visit to Texas.

Was all this part of some bizarre misunderstanding? Or was the President trying to deceive Fidel, all the while advancing plans to murder him? If the latter was true, the Cuban leader would have to reassess his decision to recall Miguel. There was still time to send him to Texas.

THE WHITE HOUSE - 1:20 P.M.

Returning from Glenora, Jackie Kennedy breezed into her bedroom consulting her notes for the items of wardrobe which she was taking to Texas. Jack had been very explicit about the importance attached to what she would wear. A different outfit was selected for each part of the trip. She had to hurry to be in time for her appointment at the beauty parlor in Georgetown.

BOBBY KENNEDY'S "HICKORY HILL" HOME IN VIRGINIA - 8:31 P.M.

A band of family and friends gathered to celebrate Bobby's thirty-eighth birthday. This included all his children, Jackie and her kids, plus an assortment of other nieces and nephews.

Ethel Kennedy arranged for an elaborate spread to be brought in from Bobby's favorite restaurant in Georgetown. The President was there for a half an hour then begged off to return to the White House and complete last minute preparations for the trip to Texas.

Harry Williams and a handful of other Cuban exiles were also on hand. The exile contingent had become permanent fixtures at the Attorney General's residence.

PRESIDENTIAL PRIVATE DINING ROOM – THE WHITE HOUSE 9:15 P.M.

One of the "last minutes details" on the President's agenda was entertaining Mary Pinchot with a late supper which included twenty four-year old French champagne.

When he greeted her, Mary said she had a present for him. Kennedy assumed it was LSD, perhaps another hallucinogenic drug, or possibly some esoteric sexual technique.

In his bedroom Mary withdrew a package from her purse and handed it to him.

Inside he discovered a toy monkey with a pair of brass symbols. When he wound it up, the monkey slammed the symbols together and hopped around.

"Give it to John-John," she said. "I haven't seen him for so long. I thought if you didn't have something to give him tomorrow he could play with it while you're away."

"This is just the type of thing he'll be crazy about. That's really thoughtful of you, Mary. Thanks."

Mary withdrew a second package and gave it to him.

Inside he found a tiny black patent leather purse.

"I know Caroline has the shoes that go with this. She's so dainty and feminine I thought she might like it."

Kennedy was visibly moved by Mary's gesture. He hadn't remembered to buy anything for his kids.

"Have you considered what Cord said about Dallas?" she asked.

"I haven't forgotten. I'd like to get out of it-- but I have to go.

"Have to --*or want to?*"

"*Have to*", he replied.

"You know something, Jack? I think you'd rather die than lose the election."

EUNICE, LOUISIANA. - 11:50 P.M.

State Police Lieutenant Francis Frugue was enroute from Eunice to the State Hospital in Jackson. Seated next him, wearing a straightjacket was ROSE CHERAMIE, a woman in her late thirties. Earlier that evening, Cheramie had been found bruised, disoriented and wandering on highway 190 a few miles outside the small town of Eunice where Lt. Fruge was stationed.

At a private hospital she was treated for abrasions and diagnosed: "Controlled Substance Addiction." As a person "of no means", Cheramie was summarily discharged and turned over to Lt. Fruge who "worked narcotics."

He put her in a jail cell and left. Several hours later he was told to return. Cheramie had been "climbing the walls", obviously suffering severe symptoms of withdrawal. A doctor gave her a sedative. He suggested the woman be committed to the State Hospital in Jackson, where she could receive proper treatment.

During the almost three hour drive to Jackson, Cheramie was quite lucid. Fruge asked her how she got the abrasions.

She had she said been traveling from Miami to Dallas with two "Italian looking men, who might have been Cubans."

Along the way she heard them talking about the fact that Kennedy would be killed when he got to Dallas."

Not being persuaded by this part of her story Fruge dismissed it.

At the hospital he turned her over to doctors in the psychiatric ward and left. She repeated her warning to several doctors: "Kennedy is going to be killed when he gets to Dallas." With nearly two thousand mentally disturbed patients in their midst this type of pronouncement didn't provoke any curiosity.

On Monday, following the assassination, Frugue took Cheramie back into custody and questioned her regarding the statements by her companions as to what was going to happen to the President. To this she added having worked for Jack Ruby and having seen him in the company of Lee Oswald.

Fruge called the Dallas Police and told the story to Captain Fritz, the detective in charge of the investigation. Fritz told Frugue they were "no longer interested." The case had been turned over to the FBI. The Bureau noted her story. No mention of this account was included in their report to the Warren Commission.

(Nineteen months later, Cheramie was found around two in the morning lying on a deserted highway near Big Sandy, Texas, apparently the victim of a "hit and run motorist." Shortly thereafter she died at the Gladewater hospital.)

The President and Mrs. Lincoln were packing his briefcase for the trip to Texas.

"Will Mister Johnson be joining you in San Antonio," she inquired.

"Yes, but Lyndon won't be on the ticket next year. Governor Terry Sanford is my choice for Vice President."

DALLAS — 9:00 A.M.

Five Thousand hand bills were being distributed in the streets of "Big D."

Similar to "WANTED" posters, they had a profile and front view of the President. The text began:

"WANTED FOR TREASON"

"This man is wanted for treasonous activities against the United States."

It went on with a list of particulars that included:

"Betraying the Constitution." "Turning the sovereignty of the U.S. over to the communist controlled United Nations." Betraying such friends as Cuba, "being wrong on innumerable issues", including Cuba and the Test Ban Treaty, encouraging race riots, "invading a sovereign State with Federal troops," upholding The Supreme Court "in its anti-Christian rulings" and appointing "anti-Christians to Federal offices."

Finally, it charged: "He has been caught in fantastic lies to the American people, including personal ones like his previous marriage and divorce."

(This last referred Jack's marriage to a Palm
Beach socialite named Durei Malcolm which spanned
several days before the Ambassador found out. He
paid someone to remove the documents from the cities.
files and destroy them. Rumors about this continued
to circulate after his marriage to Jackie.)

ANDREWS AIR FORCE BASE − 12:30 P.M. Nov. 21st.

The President and his party took off for San
Antonio, a journey of just over two hours.

Preparations for visiting five cities in three
days, plus a sleep over at the LBJ Ranch, was like
a mini version of "Operation Overlord."

It involved:

Air Force One, (AKA "Angel One"), transporting the
President and Mrs. Kennedy, a battalion of
Presidential Assistants including Dave Powers, Kenny
O'Donnell, Assistant Press Secretary Malcolm
Kilduff, five Democratic Congressmen who would
accompany the President during official functions
and motorcades, Senator Ralph Yarborough, Warrant
Officer Ira Gearhart (toting "the football"), valet
George Thomas, White House staffers, the airplane's
Commander, Colonel James Swindal, General Godfrey
McHugh, Air Force aide to the President, an
assortment of additional military personnel, Evelyn
Lincoln and six other White House secretaries, plus
Pamela Turnure, Press Secretary to Mrs. Kennedy.
"Fiddle & Faddle" stayed home to rest, pretty up and
be ready for duty when the President returned.

Tail number 86970, or "Angel Two" as it was
referred to in code carried the press corps,
Signal Corps personnel, plus half a plane load of
communications gear and baggage for all the people
on "Angel One" and "Angel Two".

"Angel Two" would arrive in San Antonio an hour before "Angel One' and revert to the Vice President's use while the President was in Texas.

TEXAS SCHOOL BOOK DEPOSITORY 11:01 A.M.

Lee Harvey Oswald got into the freight elevator with a push cart full of book orders and rode it down to the second floor. He got a coke out of the machine and went back to the elevator. On his way, he encountered Ruth Paine's neighbor Wesley Buell Frazier. "Okay if I ride home with you, Wes?"

"Today is Thursday, Lee."

"I know," Oswald replied. "I'll see you in the parking lot after work." Lee climbed aboard the elevator which lurched toward the first floor.

Frazier wondered why Oswald was coming to Irving *today*. He always rode home with him on *Friday's*. Glancing outside he saw a constant drizzle continue to fall. It would be slow driving home tonight.

DALLAS - 11:15 A.M.

At the entrance to a one story office building less than a mile away, two Latino's dressed in dark suits, wearing ties and sunglasses, stood at the front door to one of the offices. Each carried a satchel similar to what athletes bring to practice.

The shorter one, Tony Cuesta, took a key from his pocket, opened the door and went inside. The other Latino, Felipe Vidal, followed.

The office had a desk two chairs, a divan, an old TV (with "rabbit ears"), a telephone and a lot of dust on the floors and windows.

Cuesta disconnected the phone, took *another* out
of his satchel and plugged it in. His phone was
equipped with "a scrambler", i.e. a device used to
transform what the caller was saying into
"gobbledie goop." It also blunted the telephone
company's ability to determine where the call
originated. The recipient of the call employed "a
de-scrambler", to hear what the caller was saying.

"Check the closet in the other room and make sure
the rifles with silencers and the police uniform
are there. "Felipe went into the inner office.
Several moments elapsed before he appeared in the
doorway with a grin on his face. "They're here," he
said. "And the ammo too."

"Good," Cuesta grunted. Now black out the
windows."

Vidal took a can of dark shoe polish from his
satchel and began rubbing it on the windows. Cuesta
dialed a number. After a moment he said: "Hello --
we're at home base." Then he hung up.

MIAMI - 12:16 P.M.

Fourteen hundred and thirty miles away, "The Big
Indian" put the receiver down with a satisfied
grunt. The safe house in Dallas was now manned by
team leaders in charge of the shooters. They were
experienced in "liquid affairs" and had worked with
him before. Morales would be joining them early the
next morning to manage the operation to off the
President - an assignment he eagerly looked forward
to. Most of the Brigade members who died on the
beach were people Morales had trained. Tomorrow
would be pay-back time for the double-crosser who
canceled air support for his men.

With the teams he and Roselli had assembled,
plus the type of weapons and ammunition the
shooters would employ, there wouldn't be any
screw-ups this time. As insurance Morales

himself would be one of the shooters. He dialed a number in New Orleans.

At 544 Camp Street, Guy Banister's secretary put Morales' call through to her boss.

"Guy," 'the Indian' said. Any word from Ferrie?"

"They're still in court," Banister replied." Usually calls me during the lunch break." Then, glancing at his watch he added: "That should be any minute now."

"When he calls ask him to check the plane to make sure it's gassed up and ready to scoot tomorrow."

"He'd do that anyway, but I'll remind him.

"And this bird with the Dallas cop?"

"Jack Ruby?"

Yeah. I'm worried 'cause I never met him."

"Ruby's solid, Dave. We'll hope for good luck tomorrow."

"When things are done right," 'the Indian' growled, you don't need to rely on luck."

MEXICO CITY — 12:10 P.M.

In the lobby of the El Encanto Hotel, David Atlee Phillips loitered near a pay telephone. He was expecting a call from Lee Oswald. The call would be made from a pay phone on the first floor of the Book Depository. There was always a possibility someone else was using it. He didn't want to talk on a non-secure telephone, but for conversations with Oswald he had no choice.

While he waited, he lit his thirty-ninth
cigarette of the day and inhaled, deeply.

SAN ANTONIO INTERNATIONAL AIRPORT - 12:22 P.M.

Lyndon and "Ladybird" Johnson arrived in their
Beechcraft Twin Engine Bonanza an hour and a half
before Air Force One was scheduled to land.

"I'm gettin' a haircut, 'Bird'. You wait for
John and Nellie's plane to get in."

"Bird" smiled and went inside the departure lounge.
It wasn't a problem. In those days there were no
security checks. Passengers and bystanders could go
anyplace they pleased without a boarding pass or
any other good reason to be in the terminal.

Sitting in the barber chair, Johnson ruminated
about his future. He wasn't worried about becoming
President, just the effect of referral by the
Rules Committee to the Justice Department.
Insurance broker, Don Reynolds was testifying in
front of the Rules Committee tomorrow. Reynolds
had given kickbacks to Johnson on policies sold to
people the Vice-President recommended, bought air
time he couldn't use on radio stations Johnson
owned; given him a TV and a high-fi set. That was
something to worry about. Johnson didn't want to
become the first President who went from the White
House to "The Big House."

MEXICO CITY - 12:25 P.M.

David Phillips heard the telephone ring and
hurried to answer it.

"Bishop, here," he said.

"Sorry, Mister Bishop. Some stupid girl was on the
phone to her boyfriend."

"Okay. I just wanted to go over plans for tomorrow one more time."

"Sure."

"We don't want anybody getting hurt, remember."

"Uh-huh."

"Wait till the car reaches the Stemmons Freeway sign, then fire two shots. Then fire another right away and that's it. Hide the rifle and meet your contact."

OAK PARK, ILLINOIS - 12:41 P.M.

On his way home from TAM O'SHANTER, Sam Giancana pulled into a gas station and told the attendant-- "fill her up." Out of the corner of his eye, he spotted Agent Bill Roemer and another Agent cruise to a stop at the curb. The mobster stepped inside a pay booth attached to the station's office, put in a dime and dialed. "Please deposit ninety cents for three minutes," an operator said. After doing so, the number he dialed in Tucson began ringing. Johnny Roselli's baritone voice boomed a "hello" into the receiver. The men never used names - they didn't need to.

"Yeah," Giancana intoned. "Are the pieces in place down there?" "Sure, relax," Roselli replied. "All we gotta due is wait for tomorrow." "Okay," Giancana said and hung up.

LAREDO, TEXAS - 12:43 P.M.

In a motel room on the outskirts of the city, Miguel Casas Saez heard the telephone ringing on a pay phone attached to the wall outside. He bounded off the toilet seat, hurried to the phone and grabbed the receiver. "Bueno?," he said. "Bueno, Miguel?" the caller replied. They continued conversing in Spanish.

"Take the bus to Dallas. Find a motel room near
The Trade Mart -- 2100 Stemmons Freeway. When you
get in call this number: five-two eight-zero-seven-
one- zero . . . and ask for *'Manny'.*

"Okay," Miguel said. The caller hung up. Miguel
ran back inside his room and wrote down the
information.

Six minutes later, he paid his bill and asked
the manager to call a taxi. When it arrived he
told the driver to take him to the Greyhound
bus station. There he learned the next bus for
Dallas would depart at 1:15. It would arrive at
eight that evening.

CHAPTER 14
SAN ANTONIO INTERNATIONAL AIRPORT- 1:32 P.M.

Hot air greeted the visitors when the aft door to
Air Force One swung open and a ramp was rolled
into place.

The First Lady emerged at the top of the stairs. She
wore a white dress with a black belt and a barrette
in her beautifully coiffed auburn hair. The crowd at
the airport broke into a frenzy screaming: "Jackie!
- Jackieee!" A familiar figure appeared behind her
smiling and waving at the crowd assembled to greet
him. Below them a political welcoming committee
advanced to the bottom of the metal stairs. The
group included:

Governor Connally and his wife, Nellie, the
Johnson's, the Mayor of San Antonio and a group of
twenty other local dignitaries staring up at the
Kennedy's.

Unaccountably, the President began to giggle.
Looking down at Lyndon's large, oafish face he
remembered Lincoln's remark when the press accused
him of being "two faced." "If I were 'two faced',
Lincoln said, "do you think I'd wear this one?"

With Congressman Henry Gonzales, Senator Ralph
Yarborough and a host of others behind them,
Jackie and her husband descended the steps and
began shaking hands.

After dispensing with the Connally's, the
Johnson's and the Mayor, the President greeted
every dignitary by their first name, a feat which
always amazed Jackie. How did he remember?

While the motorcade was being formed, Senator
Yarborough spurned riding with the Johnson's,
preferring instead to join Representative
Albert Thomas in the car behind them.
Reporters had a roster of who was supposed to
ride with whom. They noted Yarborough's
'change of address.'
With over three thousand cheering them on, the
precession began the trip to San Antonio's brand
new *Aerospace Medical Health Center* which the
President was going to dedicate.

In the 1960 election, the city and surrounding
areas was Kennedy country, votes sorely needed to
offset a sixty thousand Republican majority in
Dallas. Polls showed if Goldwater became the
candidate, Kennedy would have an uphill battle to
win Texas.

TAMPA — 3:02 P.M.

Santos Trafficante and his attorney, Frank Ragano
had lunch in Ybor City and were on their way back
to the International Inn where Ragano's girlfriend
was visiting him.

"I read that Kennedy went to Texas, today,"
Ragano said, fishing for a response. Trafficante
did not acknowledge the statement. After a few
minutes, Ragano continued:

"They say he's visiting five cities in three
days."

Again, Trafficante failed to respond.

Ragano remembered the chilly reception he got from Marcello and Trafficante in New Orleans and dropped the subject.

As Trafficante was letting Ragano off, he asked: "Any plans for tomorrow night, Frank?" "Nothing special," Ragano replied.

"Let's have dinner here, huh?" "Sure," Ragano replied. "Can I bring my girlfriend?"

Trafficante hesitated before replying. "Yeah. "See you in the restaurant at eight."

As he drove away, Trafficante hoped dinner on Friday would be cause for celebrating the end of John F. Kennedy.

AEROSPACE MEDICAL HEALTH CENTER – SAN ANTONIO – 2:55 P.M.

The President was addressing a crowd numbering over nine-thousand people.

". . . we stand on the edge of a great new era, filled with both crisis and opportunity, an era to be characterized by achievement and by challenge. It is an era which calls for action and for the best efforts of all those who would test the unknown and the uncertain in every phase of human endeavor. It is a time for pathfinders and pioneers."

When he concluded his remarks, the crowd jumped to their feet roaring their approval. Nearly five minutes of thunderous applause followed, accompanied by shouts of *"JFK in sixty-four!"*

For a trip which engendered so much foreboding it was an auspicious beginning. The bad news:

The Washingtonian's were suffering from heat

exhaustion.

Sitting next to her husband on the way back to the airport, Jackie squeezed his hand and whispered: "You were great, Jack." Kennedy smiled and whispered back: "That's nothing compared to what I'm going to be in bed, tonight." "Big talk, little do," Jackie whispered back. They both giggled. Seated in front of them, John and Nellie Connally wondered what they were laughing about.

DALLAS

Rain no longer fell as Lee Oswald rode toward - Irving in Wes Frazier's battered car. The streets were still wet. Vehicles skidded on the slick oily asphalt like "bumper cars" at the pike. Buildings with wet plaster lined the freeway reminding Lee of the houses across the street from the orphanage when he was little. He would sit at the window steeped in depression hoping his mother would come for him. Even now Lee got those same feelings when it rained.

He liked Wes because small talk didn't interest him. Not a word was spoken during the twenty-eight minute journey to Irving.

In the driveway of Wes' sister's house, Lee got out holding two neatly folded sections of brown wrapping paper. "See you in the morning," Lee said, and walked half a block to Ruth Paine's house.

He found Marina bathing one-month old, Rachel.

"You don't call," she frowned. "Wanted to come today, Lee said. "You shouldn't do that. Ruth may not have enough."

Marina's pale blue eyes still fascinated Oswald.

"Where's June," he asked.

"Garage, I think," Marina replied. That worked out well. Lee ducked into the garage and put the wrapping paper over his Marine blanket roll. Tucked inside it was his Manlicher Carcano rifle.

"Whatcha gonna do with the paper, poppa", June asked.

"Nothing," he smiled, "let's go outside and play catch."

PALICIO

Fidel and Raul Castro drank coffee and contemplated events about to unfold in Dallas. Miguel Casas Saez would arrive there about eight, Central Standard Time. He would contact Manuel Orcarberro Rodriguez. "Manny" is a prime mover in the ultra violent *anti-Castro 'DRE'*. In reality, he's a double agent, working for Raul. It had been the latter's brainstorm to hook Saez up with Oscarberro and revive the plan to "hit" Kennedy, this time, in Dallas.

For Fidel the idea of assassination was repugnant. In this case however it was motivated by self preservation. Seven attempts on his life and another being solicited in Paris was ample evidence of how dangerous Kennedy was. Not being able to trust him to pursue the projected talks about rapprochement was a bitter disappointment. So Fidel resigned himself to continuing his relationship with the Russians.

HOUSTON INTERNATIONAL AIRPORT − 5:37 P.M.

Air Force One pulled to a stop and waited for the ground crew to roll the metal stairs into place. The President was almost an hour behind schedule.

What followed was a repeat of San Antonio, except this time the crowd was much more raucous. A girl about eight was nearly trampled when she tried to get close enough to shake hands with the President. The "big people" shoved her aside trying to accomplish the same purpose. The girl started sobbing. She and her mother had come a long way and she didn't get to touch the President.

Agent Clint Hill was flanking Jackie who juggled a large bouquet of yellow roses and shook people's hands at the same time. Seeing the little girl's plight Hill mentioned it to Jackie. She shouldered her way to her husband and informed him. He moved against the crush, spotted the little girl crying and plunged into the crowd, trying to reach her. Reacting with alarm, Agents Ready and Roberts went in after him. They were quickly swallowed up by a swarm of humanity surrounding the President. Bending over caused him considerable pain but Kennedy hoisted the girl with the tear streaked face in his arms and began talking to her. "What's your name," he smiled.

"M-m-ol-ly," she blubbered. "I didn't get to shake your hand. I put my hand out, but everyone had bigger arms than me so they got to shake your hand," she said and sobbed again. The President took a handkerchief from his breast pocket and blotted Molly's tears. "Where's your mother, Molly?"

The crowd was so humongous no one saw the mother trying to push her way through. "Come on, Molly," Kennedy said, "we'll go to my car together."

The President wasn't a baby kisser. But he was a soft touch for a female in distress -- even those who weren't. As they neared Kennedy's limo Molly's mother emerged from the crowd and gratefully took Molly from Kennedy's arms. "Thank you for bringing your beautiful daughter today," Kennedy grinned.

Molly's mother was so overcome she was couldn't speak.

The President was distracted and failed to notice several negative signs in the crowd:

'COEXISTENCE IS SURRENDER' -- 'WATCH KENNEDY STAMP OUT YOUR BUSINESS' -- 'KENNEDY KHRUSCHEV AND KING'

As the entourage climbed into their cars, Agent Rufus Youngblood took Senator Yarborough by the shoulder and dragged him toward Johnson's car. The Senator wrested free and hopped into Congressman Thomas' car.

PRESIDENTIAL SUITE – THE RICE HOTEL – HOUSTON – 6:55 P.M.

Jackie fell on top of the bed, grateful for the rush of cold air from the air conditioner.

She could hear her husband and Johnson having a set-to in the hallway. It was mostly about problems between Lyndon and Yarborough.

Johnson glowered at him. "The Dallas Morning News is running a story tomorrow, quoting Dick Nixon sayin' I won't be on the ticket next year."

"I don't know where Nixon gets his information but you're getting it *from me*: *You will be on the ticket next year.*"

They were due at the Houston Coliseum at nine for a dinner honoring retiring Congressman Thomas. Jackie knew she should take a bath and get ready but the thought of expending that much energy was too much. She heard her husband come into the room. Without moving she said: "What's with Lyndon?"

"Oh, he knows he's in trouble," Kennedy chuckled, "so I had to humor him." "Is he going to be on the ticket, Jack?" "No," he replied. "What are you going to wear tonight?"

NEW ORLEANS — 8:35 P.M.

At the Town & Country Motel, Carlos Marcello was
slumped in one of the office chairs. It was a long
day in Court. The trial had been going since
November first, but the case still hadn't gone to
the jury. That irked the fifty-three year old
mobster. It was a simple case which shouldn't have
taken that long. Tomorrow promised to be a big day
in Dallas and he wanted to be by a radio and a
telephone to keep abreast of things. Of course,
being in the courtroom gave him a perfect alibi.
They couldn't pin Kennedy's murder on him.

HOUSTON — 7:45 P.M.

At the Houston Coliseum over two hundred well
wisher's paid five dollars each to dine on" Chicken
Virginia", (a breast of chicken broiled on a slice
of ham), rolls, green beans and pumpkin pie.
Hundreds of others with five dollars in their hand
were turned away because there wasn't enough food.

In the Grand Ballroom at the Rice Hotel, the
Kennedy's and the Johnson's were being serenaded by
a mariachi band from "The League of Latin American
Citizens," (LULACS).

Following perfunctory remarks by the President he
nodded at Jackie who was wearing a beautiful long
black dress and a diamond necklace. In flawless
Spanish she addressed the audience of three-
hundred and fifty eager listeners:

"I'm very happy to be in the great state of Texas
and I'm especially pleased to be with you, who are
part of the great Spanish tradition which has
contributed so much to Texas.

This tradition began a hundred years before my
husband's State, Massachusetts was settled but it

is a tradition that is today alive and vigorous.
You are working for Texas and the United States.
Thank you and Viva Las LULACS."

The LULACS went crazy. Kennedy was tickled.
Jackie was the best vote getter of them all.

DALLAS

Miguel Casas Saez sat in the back of a taxicab,
looking at the tall buildings. He had only seen
Chicago during the day. A big city in America with
lights on tall buildings was a new experience for
someone from a tiny Cuban village.

"Do you know any motels near The Trade Mart," he
inquired. "Sure," the cabbie replied. "Are you
lookin' to get laid?"

Miguel did not understand. "What do you mean," he
asked. "If you don't know, I guess you're not," the
cabbie sighed.

HOUSTON COLISEUM — 9:10 P.M.

While The Waltrip High School Band played 'Hail To
The Chief', the President and his party walked into
the testimonial dinner.

Kennedy sat down next to Congressman Thomas, who
introduced Johnson. After very brief remarks
saluting Thomas, Johnson sat down.

Thomas introduced the President, saying:

"He is a great, great, friend of Texas, and I mean
in more ways than one. We took him to our hearts
three years ago and Texas will take him to its
heart come next November. For our President will go
down in history as one of the greatest men this
nation has ever produced."

That received a standing ovation.

Kennedy went to the lectern and smiled at the guests seated below him. After acknowledging half the people in the room, he began his speech:

"When I went to Washington in nineteen forty seven as a freshman congressman from Boston, I spent the first six months wondering how I got there -- and the next six months wondering how the others got there. But that did not include Congressman Thomas. It has always been clear tome why he is in Congress.

Next month, when the U.S. fires the world's biggest booster, lifting the heaviest payroll into . . . uh, that is *the heaviest payload* into space . . ." Kennedy couldn't stifle a giggle adding: "It will be *the heaviest payroll*, too."

The crowd laughed.

After extolling Thomas' virtues and accomplishments the President concluded his address with a quote from the scriptures:

"Your old men shall dream, dreams, your young men will see visions. Where there is no vision, the people will perish."

"Thank you very much."

With that the Presidential party left the Coliseum and headed for their next stop - Fort Worth.

DALLAS –SPUR MOTEL – 2000 BLOCK STEMMONS FREEWAY 10:10 P.M.

Miguel Casas Saez listened to the phone ringing for the number he was given for "Manny." He was about to hang up when a husky male voice said: "Bueno."

"Manny" esta?, Miguel asked. "Si -- es Manny."

Their conversation continued in Spanish. "Who's this?" "Miguel. A friend in Miami told me to call."

"Yes. Where are you?" "The Spur Motel, "I'll be there in fifteen minutes."

IRVING TEXAS — RUTH PAINE'S HOUSE — 10:22 P.M.

Oswald lay in bed. Marina had been watching
television, hoping her husband would be asleep
when she retired. She was shivering when she
slipped between the covers. Lee put his leg over
hers. "No", she said, and pulled her leg away. It
had become a familiar pattern of rejection which
Oswald was barely able to tolerate. He was unable
to tell Marina this might be the last night they
would ever spend together. Lee turned over and
tried to sleep. Tomorrow would be his opportunity
to become famous.

One day soon the world would finally learn who and
what he really was --a *patriot*.

THE SPUR MOTEL — 10:41 P.M.

"Manny" Oscarberro straddled a chair and stared
into the youthful face of Miguel Casas Saez.

"This won't be easy, but it can be done," Manny
said. "The best place to get him is in the parking
lot. You don't have to have any I.D. to get in
there. He isn't due until twelve-thirty, so we'll
have plenty of time to go over this again. There's a
guard tower where a security guy watches what people
are doing. I'll take him out and give you his
uniform. No one will pay any attention until after
you shoot the bastard."

"How will I get away," Miguel smiled.

"A friend at my apartment house has a horse
trailer. I'm going to park it across the highway
from the parking lot. You'll have to climb the
fence and get inside the trailer, before *they get
you.*"

THE CABANA MOTEL - DOWNTOWN DALLAS - 11:27 P.M.

Jack Ruby had a busy evening and his work wasn't finished yet. Inside room 235A he shook hands with fifty year old "Jim Braden", a career criminal who had been in and out of prison since he was nineteen. He specialized in fraud, larceny -- and early on in his career, counterfeiting gasoline ration stamps.

Ruby eyed him suspiciously. "Lenny told me your name was Gene." "It is, 'Jim' replied. "I changed it a couple of months ago to *'Jim Braden'*, because I . . . I was *'in school'* for a while, so it's easier using my new name."

"Uh-huh," Ruby nodded. "How long you known Lenny?" "Since I was a kid, living in Chicago." "What part?" "Cicero." Ruby was satisfied that this was the person Lenny Patrick sent to meet him.

"You got something for me," Ruby asked."

Braden nodded, went to his suitcase, produced a large manila envelope stuffed with cash and gave it to Ruby. The nightclub owner counted the contents --forty-five thousand dollars -- and nodded. "Okay," Ruby said. He handed 'Jim' a Carousel Club business card. "Come in anytime. The drinks are on me."

THE TEXAS HOTEL - FT. WORTH - NOVEMBER 22ND - 12:50 A.M.

By the time her husband climbed into his bed Jackie was already asleep in the other room. Neither of them realized this would be their last chance to sleep together.

In "The Will Rogers Suite", five floors above them, Lyndon and Ladybird Johnson were entertaining friends. Their suite was much nicer than Kennedy's, but the Secret Service deemed it unsafe for the President.

After receiving a telephone call the Vice President promptly excused himself left the hotel and drove to oilman Clint Murchison's house in Dallas where a party was in progress.

He went into a room and huddled with a battery of powerful Dallas oilmen for twenty minutes.

On his way out, he ran into Madeliene Brown, a girlfriend of many years with whom he had sired an illegitimate son. The attractive brunette was surprised to see him. She would later relate an ominous remark Lyndon whispered to her:

"After tomorrow, those godammed Kennedy's will never embarrass me again. That's no threat -- that's a promise"

HOTEL TEXAS - ROOM 850 - 1:16 A.M.

Before sleep overcame him the President's thoughts turned to warning's he'd received about visiting Dallas.

CIA Officer Cord Meyer's caveat funneled through his ex-wife, Mary -- 'Tell Jack not to go.'

Adlai Stevenson's recounting his own ugly experience with citizens in Dallas and pointing out what happened to Lyndon and Ladybird.

Senator Fulbright's admonition: "Dallas is a dangerous place. I wouldn't go there."

John Connally's pointed remark: "Reconsider the stop in Dallas. People there are too emotional."

"Well, the fat was in the fire. If Joe could volunteer to fly ten tons of dynamite to a target in France knowing the Luftwaffe would be gunning for him, I could certainly risk going to 'Big D' guarded by eighteen Secret Service Agents and the entire Dallas Police force."

He noticed Joe, Jr. standing at the foot of the bed.

"*Wrong!* What I did came out of insecurity -- not a desire to die for my country. I felt your becoming a war hero diminished me. I was wrong. Hubris and competitiveness cost me my life, Jack. That didn't help our family - it didn't help you -- and it sure as hell didn't help me."

"I have to show those who hate me can't intimidate the President," Jack replied.

"You're still trying to prove yourself to the Ambassador, Jack. You don't have to prove anything to him, yourself or me or anyone else. Don't go to Dallas. You'll be riding into an ambush."

OFFICE BUILDING NEAR DEALEY PLAZA −1:15 A.M.

Tony Cuesta and Felipe Vidal poured over a sheaf of plans of the Dallas City sewer system. Cuesta marked a place with his forefinger located at the Northwest end of a stockade fence, a few feet from where it joined the North end of the triple underpass.

"This is the closest entrance to the sewer at that end of the parking lot," Cuesta declared.

"The only way we can be sure it's still there is to drive over there and look," Vidal replied. There won't be anyone around to see us at this time of night. Besides, it's really dark out."

The Secret Service's midnight to eight shift,
prowled around The Hotel Texas checking exits and
entrances.

SAIC Roy Kellerman made a final inspection of the
garage where Kennedy's blue limousine arrived before
his party got in. Satisfied that all was in order,
he went to bed.

Nine other agents on the White House detail were in
a celebratory mood. They gathered at "THE CELLAR",
an after hours saloon where booze and topless
dancers were plentiful.

Three other Agents from the midnight to eight shift
left their posts in front of Suite 850, went to
"The Cellar" and hoisted a few with the others.
Four of these Agents would ride behind the
President's limousine including ASAIC Emory
Roberts, a man who detested John Kennedy. He dwelt
on *his own* agenda for the motorcade.

RAILROAD YARD – BEHIND THE TSBD – 1:29 A.M.

The yard and the parking lot in back of the grassy
knoll were so dark it took Cuesta and Vidal a few
minutes to orient themselves. Where the stockade
fence joined the North end of the triple underpass
they verified the existence of an entrance to the
storm drain. Looking at Elm Street they were
surprised to see how close it was to where they were
standing. The pair walked East where the branches of
a tree hung over the stockade fence. It was less
than fifty yards from the place where Kennedy's
limousine would pass. Cuesta slapped Vidal on the
back.

"I could throw a rock and hit him from here," he
grinned.

CHAPTER 15

"THE GRACE RANCH" - TUCSON, ARIZONA - 5:15 A.M.

When mobsters with interests in Las Vegas needed a secure meeting place, they came to "The Grace Ranch". It was owned by mobster Pete Licavoli, one of five ruling "Dons of Detroit" and a murderer thought to have been one of the gun men in the "St. Valentine's Day Massacre." The ranch's half dozen rooms were located close to a small landing strip used almost exclusively for CIA "special operations."

Johnny Roselli lay in one of the rooms. The other members of the team lay in their's. Roselli had been staring at the clock for nearly an hour.

Finally he roused himself, showered and dressed.

The Big Indian" arranged to use the Agency's airstrip for the team's operation.

"Team B" was composed of: Tony Izquierdo, Arthur Espaillat and Rafael Villaverde. Cuban exiles all, they trained together in the Florida Keys and were superb marksmen. Their assignment for today -- The Trade Mart, a back up location in case Team-A's effort in Dealey Plaza didn't succeed.

The trio were shivering and sipping coffee outside their rooms when Roselli appeared. They piled into a station wagon which Johnny drove to a twin engine Cessna. The pilot already had the craft ready to go. Three minutes later "Team B" was airborne on its way to Dallas. Filing a flight plan with Air Traffic Control wasn't a problem -- the strip didn't have one.

A PLAIN WOOD FRAME HOUSE IN OAK CLIFF, TEXAS —6:15 A.M.

Marie Tippit had her husband's breakfast on the table.

"Come on, J.D. -- it's getting cold." The thirty eight year old Dallas patrolman was already in uniform. He sat down, sipped his coffee and toyed with his breakfast. For a man with a voracious appetite this was highly unusual. Receiving a very low score on a crucial test for advancement, J.D.'s chances for moving up the ladder were poor.

Marie noticed a look of intense preoccupation on his face. "What's the matter?" she asked. J.D. remained silent. He took his coffee cup and went into the kid's room. They were still asleep. Tippit stared at the serene look on their faces. The youngest boy was sucking his thumb. J.D. gently removed the thumb from his son's mouth and wondered if this would be the last time he would see the boy. Working two other jobs, security guard at Austin's Barbecue and Stevens Park Theater he barely saw his kids except on Sundays.

As he was leaving, J.D. gave his wife a hug. "No matter what happens today, I love you and I love the kids."

After he left, Marie thought about his comment. The remark wasn't like him. He was an undemonstrative person.

7:18 A.M. – PRIVATE AIRSTRIP IN NEW ORLEANS

"Team A", consisting of: Herminio Diaz Garcia and Eladio del Valle was already onboard another twin engine Beechcraft, this one with David Ferrie at the controls. Flight plans were required here but Ferrie didn't file one. A twenty dollar bill in the controller's pocket facilitated this.

Ferrie was awaiting the arrival of the third
member of "Team A" and the operation's overall
leader, David Morales. Unbeknownst to them,
Morales had been delayed at JM WAVE awaiting up to
the minute information from his Secret Service
contact about the motorcade. He was also expecting
a telephone call from CIA Agent Nestor Sanchez who
needed instructions for his meeting with "AM/LASH"
in Paris at noon that day.

Now, finally, Morales' plane touched down.

During the flight to New Orleans, "the Big Indian"
mulled over his attack plan for teams "A" and "B".
A half hour before the motorcade arrived in Dealey
Plaza, "Team "A" would take up positions in the
Dal-Tex building and the entrance to the storm
drain. Eladio del Vallee, a light skinned Cuban who
spoke English without an accent would be at the
stockade fence dressed in the uniform of a Dallas
Policeman. If "Team A" was stymied by a last minute
change in the motorcade route or some other
deviation, "Team B" would be in positions at The
Trade Mart to accomplish the hit.

Irving, TEXAS – RUTH PAINE'S HOUSE – 7:03 A.M.

Lee Oswald, who from that day forward be known as
LEE *HARVEY* OSWALD zipped up his jacket, took off
his wedding ring and placed it in a small China
cup on the bureau in Marina's room. To this he
added $185.00 in cash keeping just $13.56 for
himself.

For security reasons leaving Marina a note was out
of the question. He would like to have seen her
pale blue eyes one more time. But it wasn't to be.

Lee went into the garage, turned on the light,
withdrew his Manlicher Carcano from the blanket
roll, disassembled the weapon and slipped it

into the pre-folded pieces of brown wrapping paper.

Nagging doubts about Ruby's plan to have J. D. Tippit waiting behind the depository to pick him up continued to plague Lee. The presence of a police car would surely focus attention on them.

Outside Oswald was greeted by a light rain falling on him as he made his way toward Wes Frazier's Chevy. Wes was already behind the wheel. Eyeing the bundle in Lee's hands he asked: "What's that?" "Curtain rods," Lee replied, "for my room."

SUITE 850 - THE TEXAS HOTEL - 7:08 A.M.

"There was a lot of noise in the hallways most of the night. When finally I fell asleep, I dreamed my brother Joe and I were on the porch at Hyannis, talking to the Ambassador. He told us how much he loved us and our brother's and sisters. 'Having you kids has been the best part of my life.'

Then I heard George Thomas' gentle knock at my door. I roused myself enough to mutter 'Okay. 'As the door opened and George padded into the room the effects of my dream lingered.

Eyebrows were raised when George came through the lobby with me last night. The management must have instituted a temporary moratorium on their "White's Only" policy which I knew would be reinstated when I left. Well, one day . . . maybe, one day.

I liked George. He had plenty of dignity, conducted himself more like a co-worker than a servant. George deposited a stack of newspapers at the foot of my bed, laid out my clothes and disappeared into the bathroom. Soon I heard water running in the bathtub.

Glancing through **The Dallas Morning News** I was confronted by an advertisement featuring a **"WANTED"** poster, with a front and profile view of myself. The caption underneath it read:

"WANTED FOR TREASON"

John F. Kennedy.

Ted Dealey, the paper's editor, was a right-wing nut who hated me and Bobby. At a meeting of sixty newspaper editors in the White House earlier in the year he insulted me with stinging sarcasm I'll never forget. After reading a couple of paragraphs describing my 'crimes against America,' it made me more determined than ever to campaign in Dallas. I tossed the 'Morning News' on the floor. Not a way to begin the day.

Results in **The Houston Chronicle**, were better.

It quoted Congressman Al Thomas introducing me:

'Our President will go down in history as one of the greatest men this nation has ever produced.' I was relieved that Jefferson, Lincoln, and the Roosevelt's weren't around to read that! At the same time it made me heartsick that Joe didn't live to be President. *He* might well have been 'one of the greatest men' Congressman Thomas spoke about -- more likely than I.

Another article caught my eye:

CHRONICLE POLL SEES GOLDWATER OVER KENNEDY

'Senator Barry Goldwater's conservatism would carry him to victory over President Kennedy if the presidential election were held today in Texas.'

Well, we'd see about that. If Barry is the candidate he won't win ten states. With first time Negro voters and all the money we've spent in Houston and Ft. Worth -- Texas won't be in his column. Of course there was the 'minus Lyndon factor.'

(*Johnson became the candidate in sixty-four.* *Goldwater* *won just six states and received less than 37% of the vote in Texas.*)

"The other national newspapers fixated on "the rift" between Yarborough and Johnson. This was exactly what I'd hoped to avoid. The press was making it even harder for me to create harmony here. Yarborough would ride with Johnson today or I'd break his goddam neck!"

Returning to the Dallas Morning News I found the article Lyndon feared: **"NIXON PREDICTS JFK MAY DROP JOHNSON"**.

That *sonofabitch* Ted Dealey was using everything he could to throw gasoline on the fire.

"Your bath's ready when you are, Mister President."

As I got up, the telephone rang. Kenny O'Donnell was on the line. He reminded me that Union workers and their wives were in the parking lot getting rained on while they waited for me. Kenny and Bobby were at Harvard together where he'd been a great Rugby player and the team's captain. Now he was my Appointment's Secretary. Aside from my family, if you wanted to see me you had to talk with Kenny first.

"Meet you in the parking lot in twenty minutes, "I said, "And tell Yarborough if he doesn't ride with Lyndon today he's going to walk!" "Okay", Kenny replied. I put the phone down. The shouts from the parking lot were growing louder. **'Jackeee!'** **'Jackeee!'** I lowered myself into the water and began musing about turning the rest of the trip over to her.

WASHINGTON D.C. 8:15 A.M.

Robert Francis Kennedy was speeding, again. This time he was going to be late for a meeting with his "Task Force On Organized Crime."

The trial in New Orleans had dragged on far longer than his people predicted. Well, getting Marcello convicted was worth the wait.

Jack hadn't called since he left for Texas. Probably, had his hands full Bobby surmised. Dallas would be the least hospitable stop on his itinerary. It was known as 'the hate capitol of America' for good reasons -- it was.

There were other considerations on the Attorney General's mind. The CIA'S Nestor Sanchez would be meeting with Rolando Cubela ("AM-LASH") today in Paris, to give him a ball point pen designed to prick the thumb when the top was depressed and inject poison into the flesh of an unsuspecting user. It could also fire a bullet. Harry Williams would be reporting on the Brigade's state of readiness in Nicaragua. With a positive report the invasion of Cuba could proceed in a couple of weeks.

It promised to be a busy day he mused. Bobby had no conception of how prophetic this prediction would be.

CASTRO'S APARTMENT OVERLOOKING VERADERO BEACH – 8:31 A.M.

The Jefe Maximo had been prowling around his beachfront home and staring at the blue Caribbean waters for three hours. He had an appointment at the Palicio with French Journalist Jean Daniel at one o'clock.

Considering today's plan in Dallas, the interview with the Frenchman was a minor matter.

If Miguel Casas Saez was successful Fidel would have to decide about the country's state of military preparedness. This was a real conundrum. Ordering a **"Maximum Alert"** *prior* to startling news from Texas would inevitably be interpreted as foreknowledge of an attack on Kennedy. If he waited too long, the U.S. might mount a strike against Cuba that would bring planes and missiles over the island within ten or fifteen minutes of receiving the order.

Fidel had a hole card the American's were unaware of. Cuba possessed *tactical nuclear weapons* which could be launched in less time.

Why was Kennedy taking such a precipitous path? He was a man of considerable education, political experience, intelligence and humanity. Certainly he could perceive the consequences of his reckless actions. Was he actually responsible? Or were the CIA and the military acting without his knowledge?

THE HOTEL TEXAS – 8:08 A.M.

"Scanning the daily National Intelligence Estimate I concluded the country might be safe for another day.

Outside, shouts from the parking were now *even louder.* Dave Powers is right. Jackie was enough to win Texas in spite of me!

Hurrying into Jackie's room I found her still in bed, staring at the ceiling, eyes brimming with tears.

"What's the matter?" "I miss the kids," she whispered. I kissed her on the forehead. She managed a smile. "You have to get up. If you're late for the breakfast it's liable to start a riot. And be sure and wear the pink suit with the hat!"

Jackie grinned, threw the covers back, marched into the bathroom and ran water in the bathtub. "See you downstairs," she shouted.

"When I opened the door I saw Warrant Officer Ira Gearhart standing in the hallway holding' the football'. Poor guy had nothing to look forward to except nuclear war. "Ira," I said with a straight face -- "stay close. If the Dallas Morning News prints another ugly story about me we're going to nuke their offices." Gearhart managed a weak grin. I chuckled and gave him a mock punch on the arm.

TSBD - 8:10 A.M.

By the time Wes Frazier's Chevy arrived at the Depository the rain had ceased. Before he turned the engine off Oswald hopped out of the car and made for the rear entrance toting his package "of curtain rods".

Anxious to avoid meeting fellow employees, or worse, Manager Roy Truly, the soon to be accused assassin of the President hurried to the freight elevator and rode it to the sixth floor.

A considerable portion of that floor was under repair but for some reason the work had been suspended. Except for order clerks like Oswald there was no reason for anyone to be there.

Lee slipped the package containing the rifle in a corner behind a large box of equipment for repairing the floor, then rode the elevator to the second floor.

GARLAND AIRPORT - (NORTHEAST DALLAS)

With the difference in time, David Ferrie's Beechcraft made it to Garland airport at eight fifteen. A 1959 Oldsmobile Station Wagon with Oklahoma plates and a "GOLDWATER FOR PRESIDENT" sticker cruised up to the plane and stopped. Felipe Vidal was at wheel.

With the exception of Ferrie the other occupants of the plane disembarked. At Morales' direction they climbed into the Olds station wagon. The rest got into a green and white Nash Rambler station wagon driven by Tony Cuesta. By that time, Ferrie's Beechcraft was already taxing down the runway.

The Olds wagon cruised off the tarmac and headed for the exit with the Rambler trailing.

Morales looked at his watch. The twenty minutes he lost in Miami left less time for orientation and preparation. But he didn't tell Vidal to hurry up. The last thing they needed was a cop to stop them for speeding.

MEXICO CITY - 8:57 A.M.

David Atlee Phillips took a carton of Camel's from the front seat of his car locked the door and walked into the lobby of the American Embassy. Inside his office he used a secure telephone to call Oswald. Dialing specially coded numbers he rang the rooming house.

Mrs. Earlene Roberts answered.

"Mister Lee, please," Phillips said. "I'm sorry," she responded, "I haven't seen Mister Lee, this morning. He wasn't here last night, either."

"Oh, thanks" Phillips said, hung up and lit his ninth cigarette for the day. Where the hell could he be? Lost his nerve maybe and left town?

Irritated, Phillips sucked in two long drags and
searched for the number of the pay station on the
first floor of the Depository.

"Hello!" a gruff voice barked. "Is Lee Oswald
working, today," Phillips asked. "Dunno. Who wants
him?" "Uh, it's not that important." "Gruff voice"
hung up before Phillips could. The nervous CIA
Officer took two more deep drags. He shuddered to
think what "the Big Indian" might do if Oswald
didn't show.

DALLAS

By the time the Rambler station wagon reached the
small office complex, Roselli and his team, were
already inside. They had arrived in an old black
Ford.

The atmosphere was very businesslike -- no time for
niceties.

Morales opened his briefcase, withdrew maps and
drawings. They were too large to fit on a desktop so
he spread them out on the floor. A knock at the door
distracted him.

Tony Cuesta opened it a crack. "Yeah?" he
growled.

"Good morning," a voice on the other side of the
door said. "I'm the mail carrier on this route.

Is Mister Jacob M. Kaufman still at this address?
"No," Cuesta replied. "He moved out." "Any
forwarding address for him?" "No." "Okay, thanks."

Cuesta closed the door.

It was getting late. Morales gave team members
pocket sized Motorola sub-miniaturized low
frequency transceivers, confined to 100 Kilohertz
range, which the assassins could use to communicate
without being detected by standard radio receivers.

Each of them was already armed with a 6.5
Manlicher Carcano rifle fitted with silencers and
telescopic sights plus ammunition that came from
the same store where Oswald purchased his ammo.

"The Big Indian" commenced the orientation,
explaining who would be where, what they would do
and when they would do it.

OUTSIDE THE TEXAS HOTEL - FT. WORTH - 8:48 A.M.

"Johnson, Connally, Yarborough, Congressmen Henry
Gonzales, Jim Wright and a half dozen Secret
Service Agents followed me through a light drizzle
across Eighth Street where the large group of Union
workers still waited. I waded into the crowd
smiling and shaking hands: "Thank you for coming
out in the rain."

To their shouts, demanding "Jackie! Jackie!!
Jackeee!!! I said: "She's still organizing herself.
It takes her a little longer than us but she looks
better than we do when she finishes." The crowd
reacted to this with laughter and applause. I
mounted the back of a truck and was handed a
microphone. "I'm happy to see there are no faint
hearts in Fort Worth!" The crowd roared their
approval.

Inside the suite, Jackie heard her husband
speaking. She hoped the rain would continue so "the
bubble top" would be mounted on the limousine and
prevent her hairdo from wilting.

NEW ORLEANS FEDERAL DISTRICT COURT - 9:49 A.M.

Carlos Marcello felt a combination of relief and
excitement when he saw David Ferrie coming to take
the seat next to him.

"Everything okay," Carlos asked. "Right where it
ought to be," the bizarre looking Ferrie replied.

Carlos lowered his voice and bent closer: "Whose picking them up?"

"I don't know. Morales took care of that."

Carlos settled back and tried to concentrate on the lead prosecutor's rebuttal to his attorney Jack Wasserman's closing argument. But he was unable to do so. His thoughts focused on revenge for what the Kennedy's did to him. Two and a half years was a long time to wait. Killing Kennedy would be worth it.

PARKING LOT – THE HOTEL TEXAS – 8:47 A.M.

"The Texas trip was turning out better than I expected. The rain had turned to a fine mist and the Union Worker's enthusiasm continued mounting.

The TFX fighter isn't being made in Washington, by lobbyists, Cabinet Members, or myself -- they're being made in Fort Worth by people like you," I shouted. This really hit the mark. The applause was loud and lasted so long all I could do was keep on smiling as I waited to continue.

I wished Jackie had met me down here. That would really have put the finishing flourish on my appearance.

Instead, I shouted: "We are moving forward! With support from organizations like yours and others, America will continue to show the communists and other enslaved people in the world the fruits of freedom. Thank you!"

THE CAROUSEL CLUB – 8:56 A.M.

Jack Ruby concentrated on preparing the weekend ad-copy which had to be in to The Dallas Morning News before noon. People in Chicago and New Orleans were depending on him. The money

Braden delivered wasn't from Lenny Patrick.
He was just an errand boy for Sam Giancana. If
anything went wrong, Sam would . . . well, Ruby
couldn't even think about that. Would J.D. do
what he'd been paid to do? Or would he renege
and leave Ruby holding the bag?
The night club owner got plenty of money from Guy
Banister, too. If New Orleans didn't get the
results they expected . . . well, he didn't want to
think about that, either.

After turning in the copy, Ruby thought about
hanging around to watch 'the fireworks' through
the windows of the ad department. But first he
needed to deposit some money in his bank account.

CASTRO'S OFFICE IN THE PALICIO - 10:58 A.M.

Fidel and brother, Raul were debating whether or
not to institute a **"MAXIMUM ALERT"**.

"If we don't do it we're putting the lives of
eight million people at risk. We have to do it,"
Raul insisted.

Fidel spent the morning puzzling over the problem.
Raul had a good argument but if the attempt on
Kennedy's life didn't materialize how could he
explain a "MAXIMUM ALERT" to the people? And if
Casas Saez succeeded wouldn't a preemptive alert
point the finger at him as being the party
responsible for murdering the American President?

THE SPUR MOTEL - 9:01 A.M.

In room number five, Miguel Casas Saez looked at
himself in the mirror. Outfitted as a Security
Guard, he felt confident he could pass inspection.
One detail still worried him. Texan's were racists.
Would The Trade Mart hire Latinos for such jobs? He
should have asked "Manny" about this.

"I stood in the kitchen pantry waiting to walk into the Chamber of Commerce breakfast, steaming after an encounter I had with Ralph Yarborough."

"You're raining on my parade, Ralph. "The newspapers are full of it and you're goddamned well going to cut this out! You either ride with Johnson today or you no longer have a friend in the Oval Office."

I spotted Clint Hill out of the corner of my eye and motioned him over. "Go tell Missus Kennedy she's late and I need her --now! "Yes, Mister President," Hill answered and quickly shouldered his way toward the elevator.

"Okay, let's go," I said and went through the swinging doors into the Grand Ballroom. The Johnson's, Connally's, Yarborough, Ft. Worth Congressman Jim Wright, and the rest of my entourage trailed after me as I made my way to the dais. A band struck up "Hail to The Chief" which Jackie delighted in telling everyone was my favorite song. The applause was spontaneous. I nodded and waived.

While Chamber of Commerce President Raymond Buck introduced everyone I looked toward the door hoping Jackie would appear. When Buck finished, the band played "The Eyes of Texas Are Upon You". As if on cue, Jackie walked in.

Most of the two thousand guests stood on their chairs, clapped and roared their approval.

Wearing her pink suit with the pillbox hat and white gloves, she accepted a huge bouquet of *red roses* on her way to the dais. (They were supposed to be yellow, but all of them had been sold.)

Jackie was radiant, smiling, and oozing class as she went to her seat. I smiled at her from the lectern then looked at the crowd and tried to speak but they wouldn't have it. It must have been three minutes before I was able to say:

"Two years ago I introduced myself in Paris by saying that I was the man who had accompanied Missus Kennedy to France. I'm getting somewhat that same sensation as I travel around Texas."

The crowd laughed, clapped, and stomped their feet.

When the noise subsided I launched into my speech, extolling the virtues of Ft. Worth and its citizens."

SECOND FLOOR LUNCHROOM – BOOK DEPOSITORY – 10:13 A.M.

Just before the break the rain let up again. Moments later the sun pushed most of the clouds aside sending spears of light bouncing off shallow puddles in Dealey Plaza.

Lee Oswald spied a copy of THE DALLAS TIMES HERALD lying on top of one of the lunch counters and began reading it.

The front page carried a detailed diagram and timetable of the President's motorcade route. His limousine should reach Elm Street at 12:15.

Lee's mouth was suddenly dry. Numbing fear consumed him. In two hours, he would pull the trigger that would send tremors into the lives of millions around the world. He put the paper down and rode the elevator to the sixth floor.

CIA STATION – MEXICO CITY – 10:45 A.M.

In David Atlee Phillips' smoke filled office he went over a list of media contacts who would receive compromising information about "the former defector to Russia, Lee Harvey Oswald."

A secure telephone in his bottom drawer rang.
Phillips answered. He was not surprised when he
heard Dave Morales' voice on the line. "Everything
set with your friend 'in the school' he said. "I
wasn't able to reach him at his home or at 'the
school' this morning. His landlady told me he
didn't come home last night."

A long pause ensued before Morales' barely
controlled rage filtered through the telephone
line. "Where the hell is he?"

"I don't know Dave, but he's not the type . . .

"Call him again," Dave snapped and hung up.

Phillips withdrew the last cigarette from his
first pack, lit it with his old cigarette, took
three deep drags then dialed the number for the
phone booth on the first floor of the Book
Depository.

A feminine voice came on the line with a
pleasant "Hello?"

"Yes, good morning," Phillips said. Is Lee
Oswald working today?"

"I saw him in the lunch room a few minutes ago. Do
you want me to see if he's still there?"

"No, uh . . . no. Thanks anyway." Elated,
Phillips depressed the button and initiated
another call.

CHAPTER 16

AIR FORCE ONE – ON FINAL APPROACH TO LOVE FIELD

"Jackie sat next to me during the thirteen minute flight to Dallas. I bombarded her with kudos for her performance in Fort Worth."

"I hope we can have the bubble top this time," she said.

"The weather is great," I replied. "People don't want to feel shut off from us."

Jackie glanced out the window. "The weather changes here every fifteen minutes. If you really want me look nice why not put the top on? You said yourself, 'Dallas is nut country.' The bubble top will shield us in case somebody throws something at you."

"That's the real reason I brought you. They won't throw anything as long as you're sitting next to me!"

"Oh, great," Jackie groaned then turned to look out the window again.

OFFICE COMPLEX NEAR DEALEY PLAZA – 11:25 P.M.

"The Big Indian" was ready to accompany his troops into the field. While the shooter's tested their radio's and made a final check of their weapons, Morales reiterated to start firing as soon as they heard "the decoy's first shot." After five seconds elapsed, all shooting had to cease. That would make the idea of *a single assassin plausible.* The shooters would get just one shot each. "Make 'em count," The Indian growled.

The small television set was broadcasting Air
Force One's arrival at Love Field. The door opened.
Jackie began descending the steps with the
President right behind her. He was smiling and
waving at the enthusiastic crowd jammed against a
fence hoping to shake hands with "the Kinnedee's."

Morales looked at the set and yelled:

"Smile, asshole," "We'll wipe that off your face
pretty quick."

LOVE FIELD

Bright sun replaced the rain and the temperature was
rapidly rising.

"I saw Secret Service Agents Roy Kellerman and Emory
Roberts organizing the motorcade, checking the
manifest showing who would ride with whom.

Kenny and Dave were putting the heat on Yarborough.
Ralph looked like he was weakening.

Jackie and I moved along the fence, 'pressing the
flesh' and exchanging "hellos" with supporters. A
few of them said:

'We come all the way from Amarilla ta see ya.' "That
was hundreds of miles from Dallas so I pumped their
hands and thanked them profusely. One of them asked
if I had 'an extra PT-109 tie clip'. I took mine off
and gave it to him. The guy looked like he'd just
been given the keys to Fort Knox.

Six other Secret Service Agents, including Clint
Hill, Jack Ready, Rufus Youngblood and Henry Rybka,
were at our side, watching for trouble. Except from
a few dissident's carrying **"YANKEE GO HOME"**
placards, everything was going well. If this was
'the hate capitol of America' I wanted to come
back."

TEXAS SCHOOL BOOK DEPOSITORY (TSBD)

Workers were knocking off for their forty-five minute lunch break.

On the sixth floor, Lee Oswald lifted the gate of the freight elevator, stepped inside with a cart full of books and pushed the button for the first floor. It was hot and he was nauseated. All Lee wanted for lunch was a coke. After unloading the books, he took the stairs to the second floor lunchroom, bought a coke and glanced at the clock.

OAK CLIFF - 11:51 P.M.

Driving Dallas Patrol Car #10, Officer J. D. Tippit, was on his way to meet a man who would be waiting in the parking lot of the Carousel Club wearing the DPD uniform J.D. had given Jack Ruby.

Tippit "signed out" for lunch at 11:29. His standard routine was to eat what Marie fixed for him and get back "on the air" by 12:15. Today he had to be faster. J.D. wolfed down his lunch then bolted for the door telling his wife it was important to remain alert for possible problems associated with the President's visit.

If traffic didn't delay him he'd meet his "contact" at the appointed hour . . . noon.

BOBBY KENNEDY'S HOME - HICKORY HILL

The Attorney General had just arrived after a three hour meeting of the ORGANIZED CRIME TASK FORCE. He was scheduled to return to the Justice Department for an afternoon session. After a quick dip he sat down at a picnic bench where Ethel had clam chowder, sandwiches and potato salad ready for him and his two guests, Manhattan D.A. Robert Morgenthau and J.D. assistant, Silvio Mollo.

Jack still hadn't called. He'd probably phone tonight. Bobby wanted to relay Harry Williams' update on the Brigade's state of readiness and confirm a final date for the invasion.

REAR OF THE CAROUSEL CLUB - 12:05 P.M.

Eladio del Valle stood a few feet from the back entrance to the club waiting for the cop who would drive him to the parking lot behind the Book Depository. Time was critical. He had only ten minutes to get into position behind the stockade fence. In his holster he carried a **.357 Magnum** equipped with a silencer. Using his miniature transistor radio he informed "base" he was waiting for his "contact."

FEDERAL COURTHOUSE - NEW ORLEANS - 1:10 P.M.

Following a few minutes absence, David Ferrie returned to his seat next to Carlos Marcello, leaned close and whispered: "Guy's watching it on television. They're at Love Field."

Marcello remained impassive staring at the jury as they listened to final instructions from the Judge. Jurors number six and eleven steadfastly refused to look at "the little man."

FIDEL CASTRO'S OFFICE - THE PALICIO - HAVANA

The Cuban leader tried to concentrate on French newsman Jean Daniel's opinion about Kennedy's intentions toward Cuba.

The clock on Fidel's desk revealed the time was 1:08. In that era, simultaneous satellite transmission had not yet come into being. So the Jefe Maximo could only speculate on what was transpiring fifteen hundred and twenty-five miles from Havana. In the end Fidel had overruled Raul's insistence about initiating a "MAXIMUM ALERT."

Instinct told him to wait for news from Texas.

THE MOTORCADE

"With everyone aboard, the procession of vehicles moved forward heading toward downtown Dallas, thence to The Trade Mart.

Agent Greer was driving. Agent Kellerman sat next to him. John and Nellie rode in the 'jump seats' behind them. Jackie and I sat in back. Nellie was a chatterbox. Except when he was giving a speech or collaborating with me on political plans, getting a word out of John was as rare as finding trout in your bathtub.

Mayor Earle Cabell and Dallas Police Chief Jesse Curry rode in the lead car. Agent Emory Roberts and five other agents, including Clint Hill were behind us in the follow-up car. Ralph Yarborough pouted as he sat next to Lyndon and Ladybird in the car behind them.

Yarborough's acquiescence was a relief. Out of the corner of my eye I saw Agent Henry Rybka trotting behind our limousine.

Agent Roberts shouted: *'Come back! Henry! Come back!'* That struck me as strange. The Agents usually alternated between standing on the rear steps of the limousine, running behind it, or riding on the running board of the backup car. Looking over my shoulder I saw Rybka wearing a puzzled expression. Roberts yelled at him again to 'come back.' Rybka threw up his hands in frustration and started back."

THE PARKING LOT AND RAILROAD YARD BEHIND THE STOCKADE FENCE

Railroad employee Lee Bowers stood behind the glass in his fourteen foot tower overlooking

the area. As the 'tower man' he coordinated
the flow of rail cars moving in and out of the
yard. Below him a police car stopped momentarily.
An officer got out and began walking slowly down the
fence line peering into parked cars as he went. The
patrol car turned around and drove away. The cops,
Bowers concluded, would earn their money today. He
suspected the motorcade would be along any moment.
Glancing at his watch, Bowers saw it was eleven
minutes past twelve.

Eladio

The former Brigade member knew the man in the tower
might be watching. With this in mind he didn't dare
use the transistor to report that he was in
position. A hundred and fifty feet further West,
Eladio saw movement near the corner of the triple
underpass. He recognized Herminio's head just
barely protruding from the storm drain.

MOTORCADE

"I was distracted by a beautiful brunette holding a
child high in her arms so he could see me. She was
tall, wore a purple sweater and a black scarf on
her head. I waved at her.

'Beautiful, isn't she, Jack', Jackie said.
"Who," I replied, feigning confusion. Jackie let
it drop and waved to some enthusiastic
supporters on her side of the limo.

She had her sunglasses on again. "Honey, take
them off, please. People want to see your eyes."

THE TRADE MART

"Team B" was dressed in business suits, armed
with proper identification -- and weapons
hidden beneath their raincoats. They filtered
into a huge dining room where most of the 2500

guests who'd coughed up a hundred dollars each to have lunch with the President, were already seated.
There were no metal detectors or body searches. Anyone with a ticket and an I.D. was admitted.

Posing as Secret Service Agents, "Team B" acted out their parts, scanning the rafters, checking entrances and emergency exits, occasionally asking a guest for identification.

The legitimate Agents assumed these men were plain clothes Dallas detectives. If the real Agents checked them Morales' men could produce credentials that would pass muster.

Kennedy would be an easy target sitting near the lectern while he waited to be introduced. All they had to do now was wonder if he would show up.

KENNEDY

"In the windows of the buildings along the route, I looked up and saw people throwing confetti down on us. We passed hundreds of open windows. Normally all windows had to be closed during a Presidential motorcade but in this case the rule was either forgotten, ignored, or more likely impossible to enforce.

The closer we got to the center of downtown Dallas, the larger the crowds became. They were ten deep by now and getting bigger every block. Over the roar of the crowd I shouted at Jackie: "I hope they're all registered voters!" She responded with a giggle and said: 'I wonder who'll they'll vote *for!'*

"I laughed and continued waving.

They waved back and screamed, mostly focusing on Jackie who was fast becoming Dallas' most most popular visitor. She was totally absorbed in communicating with them. It was like finding

friends for an instant, then, finding new one's
the next, creating a moment of intimacy which some
would never forget."

TSBD

In the Southeast corner of the sixth floor, Lee
Oswald had arranged cartons of books in the window
which would give him a place to crouch low enough
to fire from a kneeling position.

A radio announcer's voice describing what was
happening in the motorcade drifted up from the
fifth floor:

"The President's out of the car now, shaking hands
with people crowded against the ropes. People on the
other side of the car are surging against the ropes,
waving and shouting at Missus Kennedy."

Lee brought his rifle to the window, aimed it down
Elm Street where he planned to fire several shots
when the President's limousine reached the Stemmons
Freeway sign. With the triple underpass just beyond
it, the sidewalk would be deserted making it easy
not to hit anyone.

THE DAL-TEX BUILDING

On Houston Street, across from the TSBD, David
Morales crouched in a maintenance closet on the
fourth floor. It had a window that looked directly
down Elm Street toward the triple underpass. His
Manlicher Carcano rifle leaned against the sill
while Morales looked up Houston Street. He was
getting anxious. According to the schedule the
motorcade should have already arrived.

Morales had trained many of those who died on
the beaches at the Bay Of Pigs and many more who
languished in a Cuban prison for nineteen months
after seeing dozens of friends die on the beach,
victimized, Morales felt, by Kennedy's cancellation
of the air support the Brigade had been promised.

Pay back time for his treachery was close at
hand.

HOUSTON STREET

Officer J.D. Tippit sat in his patrol car parked a
hundred feet from the rear entrance to the
Depository.

He hadn't called in since checking out for
lunch. J.D. reached for his microphone and
called the Dispatcher.

"Unit 78."

"78," the Dispatcher replied.

"Back in the car . . . central Oak Cliff."

"Roger 78. Remain at large."

"78 out."

**WHERE THE STOCKADE FENCE JOINS THE TRIPLE
UNDERPASS.**

Herminio Diaz Garcia had a something for the
President. The Cuban exile wanted to make sure he
was in position to deliver it. He sighted his
rifle through an opening in the fence which
afforded an unobstructed view of Elm Street. Aside
from Morales, Diaz was the only professional
assassin in the group.

He had murdered many people, some for Dominican
Dictator Raphael Trujillo, others for former Cuban
President, Flugencio Batista.

Johnnie Roselli, Tony Cuesta and Felipe Vidal
watched the small television set where the local
station continued providing coverage of the
President's motorcade. They heard the transistor
radio hiss.

"A-three to base. In position . . . Out."

All three cheered. Ruby's man had come through
after all.

Roselli looked at his watch. "They're late,
dammit!

DALLAS MORNING NEWS ADVERTISING OFFICES

Jack Ruby had been at the ad department almost
forty minutes. His business with them was
completed, yet he lingered. From this vantage
point he'd have a perfect view of "the fireworks."

Ruby was thinking ahead. With funds he received from
"The Outfit", he could pay back taxes to the I.R.S.
and have enough left over to move his Carousel Club
to a better location.

THE CROWD ALONG HOUSTON STREET

Scrunched in the midst of a battery of Kennedy
supporters was a person of the opposite persuasion -
- *Joseph Milteer*. Anxious to be on hand for the
President's "execution," he'd driven all the way
from Georgia and spent a restless night in a motel
waiting for "the finale." Pulse racing, wiping
perspiration from his face, he hoped the current
occupant of the White House would not escape this
time.

KENNEDY

"I saw a group of five or six nuns in their
traditional habit trying to get my attention. I
leaned forward and shouted at Agent Greer to stop.
Jackie smiled as onlookers armed with cameras

screamed: 'Look *this way,* Jackie!'

"The limousine stopped. I made my way through the crowd to where the Nuns were jabbering excitedly."

In the follow up car, AAIC Emory Roberts ordered three Agents to go into the crowd and bring Kennedy back. This was not the action he'd been anticipating. It should happen soon.

"The Nuns were a delight, praising me for my visit and reaching out to touch me."

"We want to take your picture," one of them smiled.

"I stepped back and the other's crowded around me. The shutter clicked twice.

"If you mail them to Missus Evelyn Lincoln at the White House, I'll sign them and she'll send them back."

By that time, Agent Ready was at my shoulder. 'We're really late, Mister President,' he advised.

ELADIO

"Waiting was making me loco. I was worried a real cop might show up and ask questions I wouldn't know how to answer.

In the distance I saw the cop in the Patrol Car I came in parked on the street. What was he waiting for? After I took my shot I would race into the storm drain behind Herminio. I stole a look at the man in the tower. He was concentrating on railroad cars and manipulating his controls. In the distance I heard shouts coming from Main and Houston streets. "They're coming!" "Here they come!" "They're coming!"

Reacting to the chorus of shouts Herminio Diaz

raised himself a little further out of the storm
drain and aimed his rifle up Elm Street.

6TH FLOOR - DEPOSITORY

Lee Oswald was battling a case of nerves. He heard
the same shouts, checked to make sure there was a
round in the chamber of his rifle then peered toward
the intersection of Main and Houston. The lead car,
carrying Chief Curry and Mayor Cabell moved into
view and made a hard right turn onto to Houston
Street.

MOTORCADE

Agent Clint Hill was standing on the back of the
President's limousine directly behind Jackie. Seeing
the sharp right looming up he dropped off the back
and rejoined his fellow agents in the follow-up car.

Agent Emory Roberts knew whatever was supposed to
happen would occur very soon. From his vantage point
he could make out the triple underpass in the
distance. He was acutely aware that slowing the
motorcade to make the right on Houston followed by a
left on Elm Street was a glaring deviation from
prescribed rules: '41 mph when traveling in an open
area.'

KENNEDY

"I noticed one of the flags attached to the left
wheel guard missing. Probably the victim of a
souvenir hunter I concluded. Dealey Plaza was on
Jackie's left. Named for the founder of the Dallas
Morning News, I thought about the ugly ad in their
morning edition. It was a paid advertisement. The
paper didn't have to accept it, they elected to.
Ironically, Dealey Plaza was full of cheering
people. I hoped Ted Dealey was watching.
As we turned onto Elm Street, the crowd noise
was still ear splitting. A smiling Nellie
Connally turned to me and shouted:

"You can't say Dallas doesn't love you today, Mister President."

TSBD

Through his telescopic sight, Lee Oswald had been tracking the Presidential limousine since it turned onto Houston Street.

As it turned left onto Elm Street, the figure of the President filled his telescopic sight. If he'd wanted to kill Kennedy, this would have been the moment. But Oswald had no intention of killing him, just creating *the impression* that a supporter of Fidel Castro had attempted to. While waiting for JFK'S limo to reach the Stemmons Freeway sign two large trees obscured Lee's vision of "the target".

KENNEDY

"The motorcade was beginning its descent down a grade leading to the triple underpass. From barely moving, we were slowly gaining speed. A sign looming up on my right read: *STEMMONS FREEWAY*."

STOCKADE FENCE – BEHIND THE GRASSY KNOLL

Eladio del Vallee leaned against a tree trunk to steady his aim, the 357 Magnum clutched in both hands. Thick bunches of bushes hid most of his image from scattered onlookers on the opposite side of Elm Street. Among them he noticed a woman with a bandanna and a light colored overcoat, holding a small motion picture camera. Eladio tightened his grip on the 357 Magnum and moved closer to the tree's branches to help shield him from view.

STORM DRAIN

Herminio Diaz's finger was on the trigger. Kennedy's head and shoulders filled the glass in the telescopic sight and was growing larger.

TSBD

Lee Oswald continued tracking the limousine which by now had almost reached the Stemmons Freeway sign. Kennedy was barely seventy five yards away. Lee aimed at the pavement near the entrance to the triple underpass.

STORM DRAIN

Diaz squeezed the trigger a split second sooner than he should have. The shot went through the windshield and hit Kennedy in his Adam's apple.

KENNEDY

"I'd just finished waving to a little boy on a patch of grass to my right when I felt a sharp burning sensation in my throat. Instinctively, I covered it with both hands. At the same time, I noticed a hole in the windshield."

TSBD

Oswald fired simultaneously with Diaz's shot, creating a report that directed attention to the Book Depository. He activated the bolt and fired a second immediately. At the triple underpass, tiny bits of concrete flew up and hit bystander James T. Tague in the cheek. Scores of pigeons nesting underneath the eaves of the Book Depository took flight.

Oswald fired one more shot. This one buried itself in the grass embankment. Only then did Lee notice the President clutching his throat.

DAL—TEX BUILDING

Morales fired a shot that hit Connally. He cursed.

KENNEDY

"I heard another shot and Connally lurched forward. 'They're going to kill us all', he said.

DAL-TEX BUILDING

Morales fired again.

KENNEDY

"A shot struck me in the back, hurling me forward. I wanted to get down on the floorboard, but my back brace kept me from bending over. I slumped to my left and leaned on Jackie who was still trying to grasp what was wrong.

MOTORCADE

In the follow up car, Agents Ready and Hill started to leave the vehicle.
"HOLD!" Agent Emory Roberts roared. Hearing this command, Agent Greer took his foot off the gas pedal, turned and looked over his shoulder at Roberts, allowing the limousine to glide almost to a stop. Agent Ready obeyed Roberts. Agent Hill ignored him, sprang from the car and rushed toward the back of the President's limousine.

LIMOUSINE

As Agent Greer looked at Roberts again, Eladio fired his 357 Magnum. The round exploded Kennedy's head momentarily creating a red halo around it. Fragments of bone, brain tissue, blood and bits of reddish brown hair flew through the air. The shot left a puff of smoke underneath the tree. The impact knocked Kennedy into Jackie's lap.

Simultaneously, bystander Mary Moorman depressed the shutter of her Polaroid camera, focused on the limousine. (The print would become perhaps the most famous image of the assassination).

Standing near Moorman aiming in the same direction, stripper Beverly Oliver was filming with her 8mm camera. Directly across from her, dressmaker Abraham Zapruder continued filming what would become the most famous *twenty second movie in history.*

KENNEDY

"My head felt like it collided with a wrecking ball. That was the last thing I felt.

I didn't hear Jackie cry out:

'They've killed my husband! I'm holding his brains in my hand.'

Agent Hill scrambled onto the trunk of the limousine. Seeing the President's head devastated him. He began pounding his fist against the trunk. Hill knew Kennedy was dead.

The limousine was barely moving.

"Come on, Bill," AIC Kellerman bellowed at Greer. "Let's get to Parkland Hospital!"

The limousine lurched forward, swerved out of line and sped underneath the triple underpass.

"I was aware of my spirit leaving my body. I saw Jackie holding what was left of my head in her arms. I will never be with her or my kids again . . . so many things left undone.

Will God forgive my sins and take me into his house -- or send my soul to eternal hell?

Hail Mary, full of grace . . ."

Joe Jr. was hovering just above his brother and

Jackie.

"Come on Jack" he said, I'll show you around. Jack's
spirit wasn't there. Joe began searching for him.
"Jack . . . Jack . . . where are you?"

CHAPTER 17

TSBD - OSWALD

"My mind was spinning out of control. Bishop lied! It wasn't a charade -- it was the real thing. *I saw Kennedy's head explode.* Ruby and Tippit snookered me. The President is *dead* -- and now I'm it! If I kept my appointment with J.D. he'd kill me and the frame would be complete. Marina and my kids would forever think I was a murderer.
Aside from my rifle which I wasn't about to carry out of the Depository I had no way to defend myself. If I went to Red Bird Airport I'd get a one way ticket to where Kennedy went.

I needed to make it to my rooming house, get my pistol, find Ruby and kill the bastard.

The police would be inside the building soon. I buried the rifle at the bottom of stacks of book cartons, rushed to the stairwell and raced down the stairs. On the way, I heard footsteps coming up. I got off at the second floor, bought a coke from the machine, took a sip and tried to appear relaxed.

Manager Roy Truly barged into the lunchroom with a cop who had his gun drawn and leveled it at me."

"Who's this?" Officer Marion Baker demanded.
"He's okay, he works here" Truly replied.

Satisfied, Baker and Truly continued upstairs.

HOUSTON STREET - IN FRONT OF THE DAL-TEX BUILDING

With his partially disassembled rifle stowed beneath his raincoat David Morales pushed

Through the crowd of shocked onlookers and headed for Commerce Street where Tony Questa would pick him up. The two spent cartridges from the rounds he fired were safely in Dave's coat pocket.

TSBD

Lee Oswald was on his way out the front door of the depository when a tall blond man confronted him. "Can you tell me where I can find a telephone" "At the end of the hallway," Oswald replied, and hurried outdoors. (Much later, the man he encountered was identified: NBC newsman, Robert McNeil).

THE PARKING LOT

J.D. Tippit stood behind the back entrance to the depository trying to make it appear he was there to seal it off. Fellow officers Mabra and Orville rushed up behind him. "Ya see anything, J.D." Mabra asked. "Nope, just a couple of tramps running toward those freight cars."

Mabra and Orville sprinted toward the tracks where freight cars were parked.

Many people raced up the grassy knoll and converged in the area behind the stockade fence. Walking toward his patrol car J.D. picked up the pace. He could wait no longer. The Dispatcher had probably already called him. The cop was now confident Oswald would be a no show.

THE STORM DRAIN

Herminio Diaz Garcia and Eladio del Vallee were in full flight, splashing through knee high filthy water on their way to where Industrial Street met the Commerce Street Viaduct. Herminio had disassembled his rifle and put it underneath his raincoat. Eladio ditched the police shirt, cap and badge. Finally, they crawled out the Commerce Street viaduct where Felipe Vidal had the car waiting for them. They piled into the back seat and tried to catch their breath. Felipe headed for THE TRADE MART, then on to Red Bird airport.

PARIS

A meeting between Rolando Cubela ("AM-LASH") and the CIA'S Nestor Sanchez was interrupted when Sanchez was called to the telephone. He returned ashen faced and confided that President Kennedy had just been assassinated in Dallas. The plan for Cubela to kill Castro had been placed on hold.

OFFICE BUILDING

As they moved around the office, wiping off finger prints and packing their gear, Roselli, Tony Cuesta and Morales were exuberant. Vidal was already out picking up members of Team A and B.

Roselli and "The Indian" would drive the remaining car to Red Bird.

"Johnnie!" Morales shouted, "We finally evened up the score with that motherfucker Kennedy!"

EMERGENCY ENTRANCE - PARKLAND HOSPITAL

AAIC Emory Roberts came to the side of the car, lifted the President's arm and realized his condition was hopeless.

"I'm going to Johnson" he told Kellerman. "You stay with them." *This was strange. Kellerman was the Agent in Charge, but Roberts issued the orders.*

NEW ORLEANS FEDERAL COURTHOUSE

The Judge was almost finished reading instructions to the Jury when a bailiff handed him a slip of paper. He looked annoyed, then shaken.

"Ladies and gentlemen President Kennedy was assassinated in Dallas a few minutes ago."

A devastating look from Marcello inhibited any reaction from David Ferrie who was getting ready to clap.

The Judge completed reading instructions to the jury and ordered them to begin deliberating. Then he rapped his gavel on his ornate desktop and declared Court would be in recess till two that afternoon.

HOUSTON STREET

Lee caught a bus that would take him to Oak Cliff. He was low on funds and would need more money to get to Mexico City. With his new "high profile" he had to find a way to contact Castro for an invite to Havana. If he got there he'd use the first opportunity to kill the commie rat.

MEXICO CITY - CIA STATION

The news from Dallas sent David Atlee Phillips' into shock. Normally unflappable, Phillips was trembling. "The Big Indian lied! *The assassination was for real.*

He forced himself to focus on lighting his forty-fourth cigarette for the day.

Kennedy's murder presented a golden opportunity. The original plan was to portray Castro as having motivated Oswald's *attempt* on President Kennedy's life -- which failed. Now Fidel could be posited as the "mastermind" behind Kennedy's *murder*.

Phillips dialed the private number of a friend --
Miami based Pulitzer Prize winning reporter, Hal
Hendricks and asked him to stand by for damning
evidence against Kennedy's assassin. After the news
broke Phillips would alert other contacts like John
Martino and Carlos Bringuer to call local news
media and relate Oswald's "communist activities" in
New Orleans.

THE PALICIO - HAVANA

Celia Sanchez, Fidel's longtime lover, secretary
and confidante from the earliest days in the Sierra
Maestra, interrupted the discussion between Castro
and French newsman, Jean Daniel. "Comandante," she
said, "President Kennedy has been shot in a place
called Dealey Plaza, Texas."

Daniel was visibly shaken. Fidel was confused. He
had no idea where "Dealey Plaza, Texas" was.
Speaking rapidly he addressed Celia in Spanish.

"Do they know who did it," he asked.

"No Celia replied, Kennedy's been taken to a
hospital."

"Bring a radio in here, please" he said "I want to
follow what's transpiring." (Contemporaneous live
satellite broadcasting didn't commence until April
1965).

Turning to Daniel he spoke English again: "This is
very bad news. Watch how fast the CIA tries to blame
us." His private telephone rang. When he answered,
Raul said simply: "It wasn't us," and hung up.

HICKORY HILL

Kenny O'Donnell called Robert Kennedy from Parkland
Hospital and informed him several shots had been
shot fired at his brother. "One hit him

in the back, at least one more hit him in the
throat, another hit him in the head." "Is he still
conscious," Bobby asked. "No." "Have someone call a
Priest." "I did that already. I'll call you back."
Two minutes later, his nemesis, J. Edgar Hoover
called. "The President has been shot." "Yes, Edgar,
I know" Bobby said and hung up. He was fighting to
control his emotions. Clear thinking was mandatory.
Bobby answered another call, this one from White
House aide, Tazwell Shepherd. "Bob, the President
is dead. I'm awfully sorry." "Thanks, Taz -- keep
me informed," Bobby replied. Is Clint Hill
available?" "Yes." Hill came on the line. Before he
could unburden himself about losing the President,
Bobby cut him off. "Clint - get the President's
body onto Air Force One, immediately." He hung up
to answer another phone. It was Lyndon Johnson
wanting to know the exact language for officially
swearing him in as President. "You became President
the moment my brother died" Bobby said dryly. "I
know, but I think it's very important for the
public's perception of continuity to be
photographed being sworn in." Bobby paused while it
sunk in. "I'll have one of my people transmit the
language to you." Johnson tried to add something
but got the dial tone before he could speak.

Now Bobby was organizing his thoughts for what must
be done. Kenny said several shots had been fired,
from the front and the rear. A conspiracy was
obviously in play. Constraints had to be put in
place to keep any hint of Cuban involvement from
surfacing. If "Second Naval Guerilla" was revealed
it could mean nuclear war.

Johnson knew nothing of the impending invasion. He
would have to be briefed about the need to limit
any investigation which might reveal this *secret
of all secrets.*

The cover up was about to begin -- with the highest ranking law enforcement official in the country orchestrating it.

TRADE MART

Miguel Casas Saez never made it to the parking lot. Police had it cordoned off. When he heard them talking about the President being shot he made a call from a pay phone at The Spur Motel and received instructions to get to Laredo, cross the border and make his way to Mexico City. There, comrades would arrange for his return to Cuba. Miguel paid his bill and took a taxi to the bus station.

DALLAS – A BUS MIRED IN TRAFFIC

Lee Oswald was panicked. Police cars swarmed all over Dealey Plaza bringing traffic to a standstill. He went to the driver, asked for a transfer to another bus and got off.

Lee walked hurriedly through the crowds of stunned people and made his way to the Greyhound Bus Station where a taxi stand was located. He piled into a cab. An old woman entered from the other side. Oswald got out, telling her he'd take another cab. She thanked him.

Fifteen seconds later a new arrival pulled in and picked up Oswald. He told the driver to take him to North Beckley Street in Oak Cliff.

Concurrently, Miguel's taxi deposited him at the station. He went inside, bought a ticket for Laredo, and sat down to wait an hour for it to depart.

TIPPIT

J.D. knew Oswald lived in Oak Cliff. He was crossing the Houston St. Viaduct on his way there when his radio crackled.

"ATTENTION ALL SQUADS. THE SUSPECT IN THE SHOOTING AT ELM STREET IS REPORTED TO BE AN UNKNOWN WHITE MALE, APPROXIMATELY THIRTY;SLENDER BUILD; HEIGHT SIX FEET; WEIGHT 165 POUNDS -- ARMED WITH A THIRTY-THIRTY RIFLE. OUT"

J.D. wondered who in the hell that might be? It certainly didn't fit the description of Lee Oswald. He picked up the mike.

"78".

"What is your location, 78?"

"Central Oak Cliff."

"Roger. Remain at large, 78. Out.

The Gloco Gas Station loomed up on Tippit's right. Oswald, J.D. reasoned, had to be on foot or in a taxi. The quickest way to get to Beckley Street was by crossing the Houston viaduct --three miles from the book depository. It was 12:45. Exactly fifteen minutes had elapsed since Eladio's shot blew off the side of Kennedy's head.

Tippit cruised into a Gloco's parking lot where a pay phone was located. He put in a dime and dialed the number for The Carousel Club.

Ruby answered.

J.D. yelled into the receiver: "Jack! He never came out!"

"What!" Ruby shouted.

"Give me his address!"

Half a block from his rooming house, Oswald told
the driver to stop, paid him, then walked north to
1027.

12:59 P.M.

Mrs. Earlene Roberts was watching television in the
living room. The front door burst open and slammed
shut. "O.H. Lee" rushed to his room and closed the
door. Mrs. Roberts wondered why he was in such a
hurry.

Lee stripped off his shirt, put a fresh brown one
over his white t-shirt, donned a pair of dark
trousers, stuffed a .38 Smith and Wesson into his
waistband and searched for a jacket.

While that was transpiring, Mrs. Roberts heard two
short beeps from a car horn. Through the window she
saw a Dallas Police Patrol car with an officer
behind the wheel. A policeman's blouse could be seen
through the back window, hanging on a coat hanger.
Presently the patrol car inched into the
intersection, lingered a few seconds then drove
away.

Moments later, "O. H. Lee" emerged wearing a white
nylon jacket which he zipped up on his way out the
front door.

Curious about his behavior, Missus Roberts looked
through the window again. She saw "O.H. Lee"
standing beneath a bus sign. Roberts shrugged and
returned her attention to the disjointed coverage
on TV. It was a few minutes past one p.m.

TIPPIT

J.D. was frantic. Oswald didn't respond to the horn
and was obviously "off the reservation. The Police
radio crackled again.

J.D. ignored the dispatcher and gunned the patrol car in a southerly direction. He pulled to a stop in front of "TOP TEN RECORD" store and raced inside. Brushing people aside he hurried to the pay phone and called The Carousel Club, again.

No answer. J.D. slammed down the receiver and hustled back to his patrol car.

(Customers at "Top Ten" would remember the cop's abrupt actions and relate them to investigators).

PARKLAND MEMORIAL HOSPITAL – TRAUMA ROOM ONE

President Kennedy's nude body lay on the examination table.

He was being treated by Dallas' finest doctors: Clark, Perry, Carrico, Peters and McClelland.

An incision had been made to widen his throat wound and facilitate the insertion of a tube that would enable him to breathe. (Autopsy doctors later mistook this for *an exit wound.)*

The doomed President had a three inch hole in the back of his head, a wound of entry in the upper right portion of his back and the wound in his Adams's apple. When he was first brought in, the needle on the blood pressure dial barely moved.

Moments later, all vital signs confirmed what every one of the doctor's knew when they first looked at the patient. He was dead.

For the living, November had thirty days.

For John F. Kennedy it had only twenty-two.

HALLWAY — OUTSIDE TRAUMA ROOM ONE

Jackie Kennedy sat in a chair staring into space.
Her eyes reflected shock and grief associated with
the brutal events she had experienced. Her pink
suit and her hands were covered with blood.
Ladybird Johnson moved close and murmured: "Would
you like me to send for a change of clothes?" "No,"
Jackie replied. "I want them to see what they did
to my husband."

TRAUMA ROOM TWO

Doctors attending Governor Connally were confident
he would live. Presently they moved their patient
to the fifth floor for emergency surgery on his
back and chest. Nellie Connally prayed.

NEW ORLEANS FEDERAL COURTHOUSE

Twelve Jurors filed into the jury box and sat
down. Marcello and Ferrie searched the twelve
faces looking for some reaction that might reveal
"the little man's" fate.

"Mister Foreman, has the Jury reached a
verdict?" the Judge asked.

"Yes, your Honor, we have," the Foreman replied.

"How do you find, the defendant . . . guilty or
not guilty?"

Marcello and Ferrie each took a deep breath.

"Not guilty, your Honor."

Attorney Jack Wasserman descended on his client
and pumped his hand. Mindful that all eyes were
focused on him, Carlos whispered, "Thanks, Jack."

Going down the courthouse steps, "the little man" was besieged by a crowd of reporters shouting questions, including: "What comment do you have about the President being assassinated?" "*No* comment," Carlos replied and stepped into a waiting car.

HICKORY HILL

Bobby and Ethel rushed around the house answering four different telehones. One of the calls was from Silvio Mollo, who along with Morganthau had returned to the Justice Department. He advised Kennedy that Carlos Marcello had been acquitted. As devastating as this was it was low on the scale of devastations. Fielding a call from younger brother Teddy, Bobby asked him to fly to Hyannis and inform their parents about Jack's death. To a second call from Hoover informing him his brother was dead, Bobby replied that he had already known this for half an hour and hung up.

TENTH STREET — OAK CLIFF

Lee Oswald walked South in this mostly residential area of the city. He was perspiring, his heart was racing, adrenaline raced through his body.

He could hear radio's blaring reports about *"the shooting on Elm Street."*

But Oswald's thoughts were focused on what would be lost if he didn't reach Cuba and accomplish his mission: to kill Fidel Castro. Only then could the former Marine, former "defector", former "Secretary of THE FAIR PLAY FOR CUBA COMMITTEE" reveal his true identity -- *American patriot*.

Like the character in "I Led Three Lives", he had sacrificed everything for his country.

Out of the corner of his eye he saw a black and white patrol car loom up alongside him.

"Hey!" he heard a voice yell from the car.

Oswald, stopped. Tippit's patrol car stopped. The two eyed each other for several moments before Tippit motioned Lee closer.

"What the hell happened to you!" Tippit bellowed.

Lee leaned on the open lip of the window and shrieked: "I'm wise to you and that bastard, Ruby!"

"Get in the car," Tippit ordered.

"Fuck you," Oswald yelled.

Tippit opened the car door, drew his gun and started around the hood.

Oswald snatched the pistol out of his waistband and shot the officer four times. Tippit hit the ground . . . and lay there, dying.

His assailant trotted away, emptying spent cartridges on the lawn in front of a mortuary as he hurried from the scene. At Ballews Texaco on East Jefferson Boulevard, he stripped off his jacket and threw it underneath a car. While still in flight "the patsy" began reloading his pistol. Presently, he reached the main shopping area in Oak Cliff.

TIPPIT

Domingo Benevides witnessed the shooting from the opposite side of Tenth street. He and several others approached the policeman lying in a pool of blood near the front wheel of his patrol car. His cap lay nearby. He wouldn't need it anymore.

On Channel One, *Police Dispatcher Hulse* heard the voice of Domingo Benevides say:

"Hello, Police operator . . .?"

"Go ahead -- go ahead, citizen on the police radio," Hulse responded.

"We've had a shooting out here," Benevides continued.

"Where?" Hulse asked.

"Tenth Street -- 404 Tenth Street. It's a policeman. Someone shot him."

MIAMI

Like most people in America, police informant William Sommerset was watching TV.

His phone rang. Sommerset was annoyed. He didn't want to miss anything.

"Bill", said the voice on the other end of the line, *"Joe Milteer.* Were you watching?"

Sommerset stretched as far as he could to pull a recording device from a table onto the couch. "Yeah, Joe . . . I saw it.'

"Happened just like I told you, didn't it?"

"Uh-huh, Joe, you were right on." Sommerset punched a button on his recorder.

Milteer continued crowing: "They'll pick up someone in a few hours just to make it look good. Doesn't matter, he won't know anything. The Patriots outsmarted the communist's this time!"

CONFERENCE ROOM — PARKLAND HOSPITAL

Assistant Press Secretary Malcolm Kilduff faced a
battery of noisy reporters. Camera's were trained
on Salinger's stand-in; still photographers were
snapping pictures.

"President John F. Kennedy," Kilduff intoned,"
died today at one p.m." A barrage of questions
burst from the mouths of scores of reporters. Out
of this mish-mosh, Kilduff zeroed in on one of
them: *"How was he shot?"*

*Placing his right index finger at his right
temple, Kilduff replied:* **"It was a simple
thing. A shot right through the head."**

HICKORY HILL

Director John McCone, a close friend of the
Kennedy's, drove the short distance from CIA
headquarters to the Attorney General's house. On
the spacious lawn sloping down to the road in front
of "Hickory Hill", McCone and Bobby engaged in
quiet conversation. Bobby put forth a dread
suspicion: "On your honor as a Catholic and on the
lives of your children can you swear to me that
Agency people were not involved in murdering my
brother?"

Looking directly into his friend's searching ice
blue eyes the older man replied: "They didn't do
it, Bobby -- I'm sure of that. I feel confident it
was Castro."

This was not welcome news to the thirty-eight year
old Attorney General. A thorough investigation of
the Cuban leader's complicity in the death of the
President would ineluctably expose secrets which
had to remain secret. Revealing the Kennedy
brother's sponsorship of attempts on Castro's life,
plus the existence of Operation Second Naval
Guerrilla would be catastrophic for the image of
the Kennedy's and the country. Americans were not

ready to learn about such horrors and the younger Kennedy was determined to make sure they never did. Incredibly, McCone had not been briefed about "Guerrilla." The country's top spy was totally in the dark -- and Bobby intended to keep it that way.

DEALEY PLAZA

With many eyewitnesses claiming that shots had been fired from the TSBD, police quickly sealed the building. Other reports claimed shots had been fired from "the grassy knoll". A search of the area yielded nothing except three tramps, hiding in nearby freight cars. They were marched to the Sheriff's office and soon thereafter released . . . without documenting who they were.

FBI agents took Mary Moorman's Polaroid picture from her and impounded Beverly Oliver's eight millimeter camera assuring her it would be returned. (It wasn't). Moorman's Polaroid *was* returned and soon became one of the most familiar images of that fateful day.

FBI Agents accompanied Abraham Zapruder to the local Eastman Kodak processing lab, turned in what he shot and waited for technicians to develop *the original and three prints. Time-Life purchased the original from Zapruder for a reported $150,000.*

TSBD

Chief of **HOMICIDE & ROBBERY,** Captain Will Fritz arrived to take charge of searching the building. He thought the assassin(s) might still be there -- or may have left evidence behind. Fritz and other officers started on the first floor and worked their way up. Another group of officers started on the seventh floor and worked their way down.

CHAPTER 18

JOSE MARTI PARK - HAVANA

Fidel and Raul Castro were having a discussion at their favorite outdoor meeting place.

Things were critical and might get worse. The airwaves already bristled with suggestions that Cuba was behind the President's murder. Nonetheless, Fidel decided against a **"MAXIMUM ALERT"**. Miguel Casas Saez, whom they learned took no part in what happened in Dealey Plaza was already on his way to Laredo. Evidence of his presence in Dallas would be catastrophic. Additionally, Manuel Oscaberro's cover had to be preserved. His importance as a double agent reporting on anti-Castro activities provided vital intelligence which could not be compromised.

HICKORY HILL

Mindful of O'Donnell's report that shots had come from the front and the back, Bobby Kennedy called the hospital and instructed him to: "Get my brother's body back here as quickly as possible." The embattled Presidential assistant mentioned problems with Texas officials who wanted an autopsy performed prior to releasing the President's remains. "Tell Clint Hill I said to get the body on the airplane and to hell with the Texans."

RED BIRD AIRPORT

Planes carrying both assassination teams had just departed for Tucson, New Orleans, and Miami. The only problem "Team A" faced was powerful turbulence over Texas and Louisiana. Their Beechcraft was rocking and rolling. This did not deter the conspirators from passing a quart of Black Label around. Soon, "The Big Indian" was feeling no pain. The mission had been executed with the highest degree of professionalism. Now he would focus on his second most hated enemy . . . Fidel - Castro.

OAK CLIFF

While sirens blazed all around him, "the patsy" lingered near the entrance to a shoe store until the police cars passed. He needed time. The Texas movie theater was just a few doors away. Trying to act casual he sauntered past the remaining shops. The cashier was busy counting the receipts so he moved inside the theater unseen . . . or so he thought.

Shoe store manager Johnny Brewer noticed Oswald loitering in front of his display windows until the police passed. Brewer went onto the sidewalk in time to observe "the loiterer" disappear inside the Texas Theater . . . without purchasing a ticket.

He told cashier Julia Postal a suspicious looking individual went inside the theater sans ticket. She called the police.

LOBBY OF PARKLAND HOSPITAL

Dallas Times Herald reporter, Seth Kantor, was reviewing notes of the afternoon's events. The President was dead and Governor Connally was in surgery where doctors were confident he would recover. Kantor, thirty seven, was ready to write his story, call the copy desk and dictate what would be published under his byline. A tug on his sleeve distracted him.

"Hi Seth. Isn't it terrible? Kantor recognized Jack Ruby, a man he had known for many years. "Yeah. A real black eye for Dallas, huh?

"Terrible, just terrible. I can barely keep from crying. I'm considering closing my club for the weekend, Seth. Whatta ya think?"

"That would be a very nice gesture, Jack. I gotta find a telephone and call in my story. See ya, huh?"
Ruby lingered a few moments, eyeing people moving back and forth. He sauntered over to a pair of elevators where two gurneys stood, *unattended*. The man who would soon be known as "the patriotic nightclub owner," surreptitiously deposited a spent 6.5 millimeter bullet on the gurney nearest the elevator then walked out of the hospital. (An orderly named Darrell Johnson would one day reveal neither gurney was used to transport Kennedy or Connally.)

(Kantor and Ruby both testified to the Warren Commission. Kantor told about their meeting in the hospital. Ruby claimed he didn't go there. The Commission elected to believe "the patriotic nightclub owner" and said so in their Report).

THE TEXAS THEATER

Lee Oswald sat in the darkened theater, panting and near exhaustion. On the screen Audie Murphy's heroic exploits during the Second World War were being recreated in a movie entitled, "WAR IS HELL" -- starring, Audie Murphy.

There were only fourteen patrons in the house.

The theater was a good temporary hiding place. Lee decided to wait there until dark. By then police activity in Oak Cliff would have subsided. Meanwhile, he could refine plans to reach Mexico City, thence to Havana.

The sound track slowly drowned out. Sunlight poured into the theater from both back exits illuminating the interior. Policemen began moving up the aisles. Officer Nick McDonald focused on a young man sitting in the third

row. McDonald continued checking a few other
patrons but kept an eye on the third row. Shoe
store manager Johnny Brewer stood in front of the
darkened screen talking with two policemen
surveying the patrons. Oswald saw Brewer point to
him.
By then, McDonald was walking in the row in front
of Lee. The quarry knew the cops could shoot him
and claim he was resisting arrest. Since he was a
cop killer little attention would be given to
investigating what actually happened. Oswald
reached into his waistband and took out his pistol.
Anticipating Oswald's move, McDonald leapt over the
seats at the suspect, and tried to wrest the pistol
away. McDonald unleashed a stream of invectives as
the struggle continued.

Officers Walker, Bentley and Hawkins waded in to
help McDonald. Even with their numerical advantage
a prolonged battle was required to subdue "the
suspect".

Sergeant Gerald Hill rushed downstairs from the
balcony to lend a hand. McDonald finally wrenched
the Smith & Wesson out of Oswald's hand. Oswald
punched him. McDonald laid "a lick" on Lee's
forehead.

This created a swelling and a bruise over his left
eyebrow. The other officers slammed Lee face down
on the concrete. Sgt. Hill and Officer Hawkins
eventually managed to snap handcuffs on the ex-
Marine. As they led him out of the theater Oswald
shrieked: "I am not resisting arrest! I am not
resisting arrest!"

A crowd of nearly two hundred onlookers had
gathered in front of the theater.

"Let us have him!" one of them yelled. "Hang him!",
another screamed. "String him up", a woman
demanded. Sgt. Gerald Hill hustled Oswald into the
back seat of a police car. Officers Bentley and

Lyons sat on either side of their prisoner. Hill got in the passenger side; officer Carrol put the car in gear and it sped away.

SECOND FLOOR – PARKLAND HOSPITAL

Irony of all ironies, in 1963 there was no Federal statute making it a crime for an individual to kill the President! According to Texas law the murder of John F. Kennedy was just another Dallas County homicide -- and had to be dealt with as such.

Dallas County Coroner Earl Rose and an older police officer sent to assist him stood in the hallway resisting efforts by the Secret Service to pass by with a bronze coffin containing the President's body. Rose and the policeman had the law on their side. The crime occurred in Dallas County. They had jurisdiction.

"Our orders," SAIC Kellerman yelled, *"come from the Attorney General of the United States* to put the President's body aboard Air Force One." Flanking him were Agents Greer, Ready, Meyers and Hill, formidable opposition for an aging police officer and a young, albeit determined Dallas coroner.

Kellerman and the other Agents were all armed. Standing nearby, the President's stunned widow looked on.

Behind them, ambulance driver Aubrey Rike stood next to the bronze casket he had been hired to drive to Love Field.

President Johnson and "his people" were already aboard Air Force One waiting for the late President and Jackie to arrive.

Rose stuck to his argument about jurisdiction -- the body stayed with him. Kellerman drew his .357 Magnum and stuck it in Rose's face. The other Agents drew their weapons, too. The cop didn't know what to do.

"Get out of our way" Kellerman shouted at
Rose, "or we'll run you over!"

DPD HEADQUARTERS

The halls were teaming with newsmen, assorted
police personnel plus people who didn't belong
there. Network television crews hurriedly lay
cables in the hallway so newscasters could get on
the air.

Chief Jesse Curry had recalled Captain Fritz
from the TSBD.

New problems had developed. The murder of a police
officer in Oak Cliff needed his attention and calls
from dozens of state and county officials had to be
answered. Then, too, he wanted to check on an
employee of The Book Depository who hadn't returned
to work.

After a brief conversation with Curry, Fritz put
the phone down. He had inherited another problem --
this one at Parkland Hospital. County Coroner Earl
Rose called to report that the Secret Service had
forcibly removed the President's body and were
headed for Love Field. Rose insisted the Police
recover the body and return it so he could perform
an autopsy.

Fritz called U.S. Attorney Barefoot Sanders for
advice. Sanders told him not to press the issue.

ABOARD AIR FORCE ONE

Federal Judge Sarah Hughes stood in front of
Lyndon Johnson, his wife Ladybird, a group of
Johnson's staff . . . and Jackie Kennedy.

Hughes had been summoned to administer the oath of
office to the new President. "Do you, Lyndon Baines
Johnson swear . . . "

In the basement of the Dallas Courts Building the car carrying Lee Oswald and his captors stopped in front of a hallway leading to an elevator. Photographers were already waiting to photograph "the cop killer."

"You can cover your face with your hands if you want", Sgt. Hill advised Lee. "Why," Oswald replied. "I haven't done anything to be ashamed of." Hill nodded to Bentley and Hawkins, who took the prisoner to the elevator.

When they arrived on the third floor, Oswald was ushered into a small office where Homicide Detective's Guss Rose and James Stovall began questioning him. Rose looked through the suspect's billfold.

"What's your name?" Rose asked.

"Lee Oswald," he replied.

Gus Rose looked further, withdrew a Selective Service card bearing the name Alec J. Hidel and frowned. "This says your name is Alec J. Hidel. Which one are you?"

"Your the cop," Oswald replied. "You figure it out."

Captain Fritz stuck his head inside the office and motioned for Stovall to come outside.

"Get a search warrant and go out to twenty-five-fifty, Fifth Street, in Irving." Pick up a man named Lee Oswald and bring him down here. He left the book depository and never came back."

Stovall was puzzled. "I won't have to go anywhere, Captain. That's him sitting inside."

Bobby Kennedy sped through the nearly empty streets
of the Capitol heading for The Ebbit Hotel where
Harry Williams and other 'Guerrilla' personnel
awaited him. So secret was the information he had to
discuss, the Attorney General would not talk about
it on the telephone. Along the way he called WHD
Chief Jack Behn and demanded that the President's
secret tape recordings be removed from the Oval
Office and delivered to him personally. Next, he
called National Security Advisor McGeorge Bundy and
ordered him to change the combinations on all the
President's safes. On his car radio a news bulletin
informed that the Dallas Police had a suspect in
custody named Lee Harvey Oswald. Although arrested
in connection with the murder of a police officer,
Oswald had now become a suspect in the murder of the
President.

David Phillips' propaganda machine shifted into
high gear:

Oswald, was a *"SHARPSHOOTER*!" Although this
designation had a sinister ring, *"SHARPSHOOTER"* was
the second lowest category of achievement on the
rifle range.

Oswald was identified as a former defector to the
Soviet Union who lived in Minsk for three years,
then returned to Texas with a Russian wife; he was a
Castro sympathizer using the alias Alec J. Hidel; he
was "Secretary" of The New Orleans Chapter of THE
FAIR PLAY FOR CUBA COMMITTEE, (a non-existent
organization that was just another Oswald
"charade.") A New Orleans television station
replayed coverage showing Oswald distributing 'The
Committee's pro-Castro literature in the city's
streets. Also aired was a contentious television
debate with virulent Anti-Castro activist Carlos
Bringuer, during which Oswald acknowledged being "a
Marxist." The coverage of these events was played

and replayed for weeks all over America and
eventually all over the world.

AIR FORCE ONE

Colonel James Swindal pulled back on the stick of
the Boeing 707 which was soon airborne. Air Force
One had begun its two hour journey back to the
nation's capitol. On board was a dead President . .
. a new President . . . and a new widow.

D.C.

At the CIA'S hotel of choice, Bobby Kennedy huddled
with senior members of Second Naval Guerrilla,
including Roberto San Ramon, Harry Williams and a
CIA Agent. Upon hearing the news from Dallas,
Richard Helms returned immediately to Langley.

In a subdued tone Bobby told the gathering that
the operation would almost certainly be postponed.
Harry Williams should inform Manuel Artime
(training the insurgents in Nicaragua)and the
Cuban coup leader, Comandante Augusto hiding in a
safe house near Havana.

"How long will the delay last", Williams asked?" A
couple of weeks, maybe longer," Bobby replied. He
needed time to discuss it with Lyndon Johnson who
wasn't aware the plan existed. As President only
he could make the determination. Williams
mentioned he already had two calls about "Harvey
Oswald" from contacts in New Orleans. They did not
buy his story about being a Castro sympathizer
because the only company he kept was with *Anti-*
Castro types. His FPCC activities were likely a
cover while working *against Fidel.* This only
exacerbated Bobby's concerns. Did Oswald know
about the coming invasion?

Back in his car the air waves were alive with
revealing details about Oswald: He was a former

Marine radar operator who defected to the Soviet Union in 1959, then returned to Texas in June 1962. Using the name Alec J. Hidel, he operated as the Secretary for the New Orleans Chapter of The Fair Play For Cuba Committee and distributed their leaflets around the city. To Bobby this was a red flag. He knew there were many Castro infiltrators in the pro-Castro ranks. If Oswald had knowledge of the impending invasion of Cuba, would he reveal it to his interrogators? Bobby's secretary patched in a call from Lyndon Johnson. "We've got your brother's body with us, Bob. Jackie and some of the others are aft, settin' by the coffin. She's the bravest woman I've ever seen." Bobby's only response was a curt "Yes." "Colonel Swindal", Johnson continued, "says we'll be in D.C. a little after six. We'll transfer the coffin to Walter Reade for them to do an autopsy." This was another red flag.

"I'd prefer it be done at BETHESDA NAVY HOSPITAL, Lyndon." "Fine. We'll call and get that changed right away." "Thank you. Would you ask Admiral Burkley to call me?" "Of course," the new President replied.

When Burkley called, Bobby told the Admiral the autopsy had to address significant National Security concerns. He would explain these further when they met at the hospital. Bobby put the phone down. Thoughts of what life would be like without his brother seeped into his consciousness.

Their weight was so profound he began yelling at God for doing this to them.

Joe Jr. appeared next to him in the passenger seat. Softly, he began reasoning with his younger brother.

"We loved Jack, too, Bobby. But maybe his death coming at this time is God's blessing." "*Blessing*! How can you say something like that,"

Bobby screamed. "Because I believe it. His reckless behavior was bound to force him from office in disgrace and put a stain on our family which could never be erased. This way he has a chance to be a martyr with a heroic image that will live forever. You're in a position to help make that happen." Bobby's concentration shifted from the road to the passenger seat. By then Joe, Jr. had departed. Bobby wondered if he was hallucinating. Joe, Jr. had been dead for twenty years.

RFK got to Andrews Air Force base an hour before the plane was scheduled to arrive. Desperate for quiet and to avoid prying eyes, he climbed into the back of a truck and lay down. His thoughts immediately centered on 'what Joe, Jr. told him. Was it true? Was the task of continuing the public's perception of Jack as a heroic figure now martyred by his death, Bobby's job?' "Yes --*it's your job,*" he heard Joe Jr., say. Was this real? Bobby put two fingers in front of him and forced himself to concentrate on them.

DPD HEADQUARTERS

Seated in a chair at the corner of Capt. Fritz's desk Lee Oswald had already spent the best part of an hour answering or deflecting questions from: Fritz, Detectives Stovall and Rose, FBI Agent's Fain and Hosty, Secret Service Inspector Thomas Kelley, plus several Texas Rangers. With their outsized cowboy hats and six shooters holstered on traditional old western gun belts it was all Lee could do to keep from laughing at the The Rangers. Far from being panicked by the constant stream of questions, Oswald was enjoying them. Before his "defection", Naval Intelligence personnel trained the young Marine in the art of resisting interrogation, a technique he used successfully during questioning by Russian Intelligence when he first arrived in Moscow and announced his intention to defect. Had it not been for his experience as a

radar operator, tracking the progress of U-2 spy
planes, the Russians might well have shipped him
home.

"Are you a communist," Fritz asked. "No, "Lee
replied, "but I am a Marxist." "What's the
difference," Inspector Kelley asked. "That would
take me quite a long time to explain," Lee smiled,
"but basically a Marxist is someone who believes in
the teachings of Karl Marx – and Communism is a
political movement that advocates a classless
society and common ownership of property." "Sounds
like an answer out of a textbook" Agent Hosty
remarked. Oswald just smiled and clasped his hands
behind his head."

Using his patented subdued tone, Fritz asked: "Did
you shoot the President because you're a Marxist?"
"I didn't shoot the President", Lee replied. "Why
did you shoot Officer Tippit, "one of the Rangers
asked. "I didn't shoot anyone." "Do you own a
rifle", Fritz asked. "No." The Captain reached into
the middle drawer of his desk, produced a manila
envelope, extracted a black and white picture and
laid it on the desk in front of the suspect. The
photo depicted Oswald with a holstered pistol,
clutching a copy of the daily worker in one hand, a
Manlicher Carcano rifle in the other. "Then how do
you explain this," Fritz asked. "It's a fake,"
Oswald replied. "I know quite a bit about
photography. That's a composite using my face on
the top of someone else's body."

CHAPTER 19

ANDREWS AFB – 6:04 P.M.

Bobby waited until Air Force One pulled to a stop,
then climbed out of the truck and sprinted for the
stairs just as they were put in place. Inside he
pushed past the crush of people inhabiting the aisle
leading to the back of the aircraft. Some, including

the new President, tried to shake his hand or say something sympathetic. He ignored them, just kept pressing his way past the sea of bodies blocking his way. When finally he reached the knot of Kennedy loyalists surrounding Jackie and the coffin, she literally fell into his arms and sobbed. "It was so terrible, Bobby -- as much as I needed you I'm glad you weren't there to see it." As he clutched his sister in law to him Bobby felt crusty dried blood crumbling in his hands. "I'm sorry I wasn't with you," he murmured.

The bulkhead door slid open, exposing the group to the glare of television lights trained on Air Force One. Preparations to place the casket on the arms of a fork lift began. They were clumsy at first as too many hands tried to take hold. At one point the eight hundred pound bronze casket nearly tipped over. Surer hands righted it.

Descending the steps, Lyndon Johnson watched, nonplussed. He had counted on being at the center of shepherding the casket from the plane to the ambulance that awaited. They didn't call them "photo-ops" in 1963, but for the new President that was exactly what he felt had been missed. And he was angry.

The unrelenting glare of lights created an almost surrealistic atmosphere. Surely it would have more compelling at dusk with a bugle playing taps in the background. But in this light, the scene was stark and unforgiving. Bobby helped Jackie into the backseat of the ambulance then squeezed in beside her. Slowly, the vehicle moved beyond the lights and was swallowed by the darkness.
On the tarmac, Lyndon Johnson stepped up to the hastily prepared assembly of microphones knowing the whole world was waiting to hear what he said. The ungainly Texan knew it should be something both dignified and profound. Aware that he was incapable of profundity the new President would gladly settle

for dignified.

"This is a sad time for all people," he began in his Texas drawl. "We have suffered a loss that cannot be weighed. For me, it is a deep personal tragedy. I know the world shares the sorrow that Missus Kennedy and her family bear. I will do my best. That is all I can do. I ask for your help -- and God's."

The assemblage of Kennedy appointees, staff, military officers and Secret Service Agents listened respectfully. But their respect rapidly vanished, drowned under overpowering waves of insurmountable loss. As renowned journalist Jim Bishop put it:

"It was the wrong voice; the tone was that of a supplicant when America hungered for a leader." Lyndon Johnson was a boss --not a leader.

As the ambulance continued its journey toward Bethesda, the Maryland countryside was coal black and stone silent. There was no echo of the heroics in Whittier's "Barbara Fritchie" for counterpoint while Jackie told Bobby about the bloody carnage that transpired in Dealey Plaza less than five hours earlier.

"I heard a sound like a balloon popping", she said. "Jack grabbed his throat and said: "I'm hit!" Then I heard another "pop", "pop" and he lurched forward. Suddenly Connally lurched forward too and I heard him say: "My God, they're going to kill us all." Jack was leaning against my shoulder making gurgling noises. There was a loud "bang" and Jack's head exploded all around me. I felt something warm and sticky in my hands, looked down and realized I was holding his brains." For Bobby each word of her recitation was like sticking splinters in his eye's -- one at a time.

LBJ

While the helicopter descended toward the White House lawn, Lyndon Johnson held his face in his hands and made a quick inventory of the things which had to be accomplished as soon as they arrived. Notwithstanding the fact that he was unceasingly vulgar, patronizing, oafish, egocentric and crooked, under the prevailing circumstances the fifty-five year old native of Johnson City, was most likely the best prepared person in America to be President.

His genius for passing domestic legislation was legendary. The youngest Majority Leader in the history of the U.S. Senate worked major miracles. In that chamber he was both feared and respected. Foreign policy was a different matter. About this he knew little and cared less. He realized that would have to change.

His first priority would be to keep as many Kennedy people on as possible to help him through the maze of transitory problems which had to be dealt with immediately. The biggest obstacle to this would be Bobby Kennedy. Their animus went back to 1960 and Johnson's selection as Vice President.

In telephone conversations since Johnson became President, the Attorney General was curt to the point of rudeness. When they met in the plane Bobby ignored his attempt to shake hands. He needed the younger Kennedy to help bolster a sense of continuity and solidarity in the government, inspire confidence in its allies, and warn the Soviet Union that their adversary was just as united as it was five hours ago. As for inspiring and reassuring the American people Johnson would quickly make known his intention to continue JFK'S policies. Certainly Bobby would appreciate that.

BETHESDA

The towering **Bethesda Naval Hospital** seemed like it would have been more at home in a German Expressionist movie than the Maryland countryside. Even at half-mast the brightly illuminated stars and stripes provided the only relief from the stark atmosphere shrouding the area where the behemoth medical center was located. It was foreboding. Foreboding was right in character for the grim procedure about to be performed on the lifeless body of John F. Kennedy. After the casket was taken from the ambulance through the front door of the hospital, Jackie and Bobby and their entourage were escorted to a suite on the seventeenth floor where they would stay during the autopsy. Accompanying them was: Dave Powers, Kenny O'Donnell, Larry O'Brien, Clint Hill and five other members of the WHD.

The ceremonial nature of delivering the bronze casket was a sham. Twenty minutes earlier, the body of the dead President had been delivered to the rear entrance of the hospital wrapped in a body bag inside a plain light blue shipping casket, similar to those used to transport dead servicemen returning from Vietnam. How this and certain other anomalies went *undetected* remains a mystery to this day. Even more amazing was contemporaneous notes taken by two FBI agents *before* the autopsy commenced, memorializing that "surgery has been performed to the top of the skull." Outside of the tracheotomy, no surgical procedures were performed at Parkland Hospital. Where did the "surgery to the skull" take place, accomplished by whom and pursuant to whose authority?

Bobby Kennedy had already briefed Admiral Burkley, regarding the necessity for the autopsy report to reflect that all the President's wounds resulted from shots fired from the rear, thus cementing the notion of a lone gunman . . . eliminating conspiracy. The report would be crucial evidence for use in Oswald's trial.

Inhabitants of the seventeenth floor suite followed continuous television coverage from Dallas. This included an impromptu press conference on the steps of the Dallas Courts building depicting the accused assassin's wife and mother being questioned by reporters from a local TV station:

"Why," one of them asked Marguerite Oswald, "do you think your son shot the President?" "My son wouldn't shoot the President," she replied, "He works for the government. He's worked for them for years."

This exchange provoked Bobby Kennedy's worst fears. A subordinate was dispatched to instruct all three networks to excise this coverage from subsequent broadcasts . . . in the interest of National Security. Requests for clarification should be directed to the Attorney General's office.

(NOTE: On the night of Kennedy's murder, the author saw this provocative interview at his home in Los Angeles. Several other viewers, including legendary JFK researcher Mary Elizabeth Ferrell confirmed having seen it too. However, to my knowledge, during the ensuing forty-four years of television programming devoted to re-examining the assassination, this interview has never been shown again. That fact not withstanding, Marguerite Oswald repeated her assertion several times -- but never again on camera.)
By now the population inside the suite included: Toni Bradlee, (wife of future Post editor, Ben Bradlee), Evelyn Lincoln, Jackie's secretary, Pamela Turnure, Jean Kennedy Smith, Jackie's mother, Mrs. Hugh Auchincloss, and later, Robert McNamara. Jackie went on a non-stop talking binge and steadfastly refused to change clothes. Bobby stayed in constant touch with Admiral Burkley who sometimes visited the suite, while the autopsy

dragged on. At other times, Bobby visited the room where the procedure was in progress.

DPD

Lee Harvey Oswald was led into a narrow enclosure for a police lineup. Standing erect in front of a white screen he looked exactly like he did when he was brought to the station over seven hours earlier: Hair tousled, a bruise over one puffy eye, a torn white t-shirt and dirt on his trousers. The others in the line-up were all police officers, much older than the suspect, well dressed and perfectly groomed.

Unseen by the former Marine were two "eyewitnesses" whom the DPD hoped would identify Oswald. The first was forty-five year old Howard L. Brennen, a steam fitter with a family *and a dread fear of communists.* He claimed to have seen the barrel of a rifle poking out from the sixth floor window of the TSBD, *and having caught a momentary glimpse of the shooter leaning out the window after his final shot.*

The second witness, Helen Markham was a waitress who told police she was waiting for a bus on the opposite corner from where officer Tippit's killer fired the fatal shots.

"Well," Detective Hill asked Brennen, "do you see the man you saw in the window?" As Brennen stared at Oswald he realized a positive I.D. might result in communist agents hunting him down. Detective Hill kept staring at the diminutive Brennen, waiting for a reply. After an interminable wait, the steam fitter whispered: "It might be the man in the middle, (LHO) but I can't say for sure." "Does he look like the man you saw?" "I only saw him for a second or two so I don't want to say for sure. I don't know." Hill sighed and turned to Helen Markham. "Can you identify the man you saw shoot the police officer?" "Yes, she replied

-- the one with the torn t-shirt." "Why are you
sure?" "Just looking at him makes my blood run
cold," she croaked. Hill took off his hat and
wiped his brow on his sleeve. With witnesses like
these it would be difficult to convict Oswald of
jay-walking. To add to Hill's troubles the
suspect began making a fuss.

"This isn't *fair*," he shouted. "I'm the only one
here who looks like he's been in a scrape. The
other's are all at least ten years older me. I know
my rights. I demand a lawyer."

It had already been a long day. Hill knew it was
destined to go on for many hours. He put his hat
on and escorted his "witnesses" back to another
detective's office, where they went through their
stories again.

DALLAS

Jack Ruby was always in trouble. But Friday's
circumstances placed his very existence in doubt.
The Tippit fiasco had landed his target in the
hands of the Dallas Police. Ruby had accepted a
"contract" and money to insure that Lee Oswald was
eliminated immediately after 'the fireworks' in
Dealey Plaza. Failure was not an option. His
employers had already been in contact demanding
assurances from the sleazy nightclub owner that
"the problem" would be resolved. To accomplish this
would require help from certain members of the
Dallas police with whom Ruby was well acquainted.

If he couldn't get one of them to off "the patsy"
the only alternative would be for Ruby to kill
Oswald himself. With that in mind, the balding,
pasty faced, overweight, asexual strip club owner
stowed his nickel plated thirty-eight snub nosed
revolver in his coat pocket and headed for the
police station.

He prowled the halls of the police department

attempting to locate where Oswald was being held. He tried to open the door to 'HOMICIDE AND ROBBERY'. A policeman told him: "You can't go in there, Jack."

Later that night he got his opportunity. Ruby leaned against the wall listening while District Attorney Henry Wade held a brief news conference announcing that Lee Harvey Oswald would be arraigned on charges of "murder with malice." Totaling disregarding the defendant's rights to the presumption of innocence the D.A. expressed confidence that Oswald would be convicted of murdering the President. One of several assertions he proclaimed to bolster that conclusion was that "Oswald belonged to "The Free Cuba Committee." "No, Henry," Ruby contradicted, "that's *The Fair Play For Cuba* Committee." How a local strip club owner knew the distinction between these organizations didn't provoke any interest.

Anxious to show that Oswald was not being abused, the police brought him in front of the television cameras for a *fifty second* news conference. "Did you kill the President," reporters shouted. "No, I've not been charged with that. The first time I heard that was from reporters in the hall." The enclave erupted in a fire storm of questions and the event soon ballooned out of control.
The police wisely whisked their suspect away. With so many reporters and cameramen crowded in front of the accused, Ruby didn't have an opportunity to get a shot off.

He set out to find a policeman who would agree to kill his elusive quarry. His first stop was an all-night garage where he talked with Harry Olsen, a Dallas cop accompanied by his girlfriend, one of Jack's stripper's named "Kay". Olsen and the stripper were all over each other. Ruby saw there would be no chance to propose such a proposition. He resolved to try again the next day.

CHAPTER 20

BETHESDA

For Bobby and Jackie the autopsy was taking too long. Much had to be accomplished and time to organize it was short.

Two sets of problems delayed things. First, Commander's Humes and Boswell, the lead doctors were *academic pathologist's*, not competent to perform a *forensic autopsy* as would have been a county coroner -- like Dallas' Dr. Earl Rose. They had never performed an autopsy on an individual who died from gunshot wounds. In short, they were not qualified for the job.

Second, they were Navy **Commanders** whose progress was interrupted by **Admiral** Burkley, directing and correcting their actions. Burkley's purpose was obvious. *Locate and trace wounds that ratified the concept of a lone gunman operating from above and behind his target; short circuit searches for any contradictory evidence.*

JFK'S abdominal cavity and the adrenal glands were *off limits.* This because Bobby was aware that his brother not only suffered from Addison's disease (hotly denied in the 1960 primary) but also "gonococci disease"(gonorrhea) for which he regularly received massive dozes of penicillin. On two occasions Humes and Boswell saw the Attorney General conferring with the Admiral, imploring him to conclude the autopsy, which had only gone on for three hours. (It was not unheard of for such a procedure to last *two days.)*

Emotional considerations also took their toll. Both Jackie and Bobby constantly dwelt on the horror Jack's body was being subjected to -- surgical procedures which were both bloody and ghoulish to non-professionals. They were aware that these activities were being photographed for forensic purposes. What guarantees were there that the pictures would not be purloined and wind up in the tabloids? (Some did.)

DALLAS

In Friday's waning moments, evidence of Oswald's visits to the Russian Embassy in Mexico City suddenly became the basis for the Federal jurisdiction necessary for the FBI to take over investigating the assassination. This was affected by using the two magic words, *NATIONAL SECURITY*.

The Dallas District Attorney's office announced its murder indictment against Oswald would note he had assassinated President Kennedy "in the furtherance of an international Communist conspiracy." Longtime Johnson assistant, Cliff Carter immediately telephoned officials in Dallas and instructed them to excise all mention of "conspiracy".

President Johnson personally telephoned the Dallas Police. He *ordered them to "stop investigating"* and turn over all evidence against Oswald to the FBI.

"You have your man," Johnson told Captain Fritz. *"Now charge him with first degree murder and go for the death penalty."*

In Chicago, the FBI located the receipt for the sale of a 6.5 Manlicher Carcano rifle, Sn2766 sold to A. Hidel with a 4-power scope by Klein's Sporting Goods. It was shipped on March 20th. 1963 to a P.O. Box in Dallas. The box belonged to Lee Harvey Oswald. The need to buy the weapon through the mail was difficult to understand. This and similar rifles were readily available from gun stores in Dallas, no questions asked.

D.C.

Shortly before 4 A.M. (Saturday), Bobby and Jackie accompanied the coffin to the East Room of the White House, where the body was available for viewing by the Kennedy family. There was considerable conflict as to whether or not there should be an open coffin for the public. Jackie was adamant in her opposition. "Do you want Jack to be remembered like some character you would see in Madame Tussaud's wax museum?" Finally, it was decided the coffin would be closed.

The former First Lady embarked on making arrangements for the funeral. She decided it would be fashioned after the grand affair held in 1865 for Abraham Lincoln, with JFK'S body lying in state at the Capitol Rotunda. Seemingly inexhaustible, Jackie sent staff to the Library of Congress to research the century old ceremony.

Barely functioning, Bobby went to the Lincoln bedroom and tried to sleep. He was heard sobbing and crying out for an explanation of how this tragic event was allowed to occur. Sleep came in brief fits, interrupted by recollections of his early life with Jack that brought on more sobbing.

"Why God - why?" "He always has a purpose, Bobby," he heard Joe Jr. say. Opening his bloodshot eyes he saw his eldest brother leaning against the wall. "Believing that will make this easier," he continued. "Use all your years of believing to help you through this." Bobby had a question, but by the time he struggled to a sitting position, Joe Jr. was no longer there.

"Joe! Joe, come back! Tell me how to save Jack from everything that will come out?" After waiting for many minutes he realized Joe wasn't coming. Heartsick he fell back on the bed and was soon sobbing again.

Several hours later Bobby wandered the halls of the
White House -- alone with his memories of happier
times:

Jack's return from his triumph at the Berlin wall;
his euphoria after proposing the Nuclear Test Ban
Treaty during commencement at American University;
the smile which passed between them when Governor
Wallace stood aside and allowed black students to
enter the University Of Alabama; the relief they
shared when Premier Khrushchev backed down during
the Cuban Missile Crisis.

Passing the door to the Oval Office he saw a man
removing his brother's beautiful replica of a
famous American sailing vessel. Poking his head
inside he saw rugs rolled up, items stuffed in
boxes and the President's rocker turned upside
down. "What", he demanded "is going on here?"
Hearing the Attorney General's voice, Evelyn
Lincoln came from her office. Barely able to
suppress tears she confided: "The President -- uh,
I mean Johnson, asked me to be out of here by nine
this morning." Almost on cue, the new President and
his entourage came through the door. In a flash,
Bobby was in his face: "Couldn't you wait until
after the funeral?"

"Bobby, it's very important for us to give the
world a sense of continuity here. Seeing me in the
Oval Office, helps promote that. I'm having a
cabinet meeting at two-thirty today. I want to
discuss many things including investigating what
happened yesterday." Without another word the
Attorney General turned his back on Johnson and
walked out of the office.

In addition to being furious with the Texan for
emptying his brother's office like a landlord might
do to an overdue tenant, the s.o.b. was forcing
Jack's secretary out of her office. Then too,
Lyndon's comment about investigating his brother's

murder sent alarm's clanging through Bobby's brain. A thorough investigation was sure to uncover a litany of White House horrors any one of which would destroy Jack's image:

Encouraging eight attempts on the life of Fidel Castro; backing Cuban exiles for another invasion of Cuba that might well be the catalyst for another nuclear crisis; countless liaisons with women including Sam Giancana's girlfriend, Judith Exner; the suspected East German spy Ellen Rometch's sexual hi-jinx *in the Oval Office,* paying her hush money and arranging a one way trip back to Germany; hiring prostitutes to come to his hotel rooms during campaign visits to various cities; persistent rumors about complicity the demise of Marilyn Monroe; the scandal over awarding General Dynamics an enormous contract to produce the TFX fighter plane that both the Air Force and the Navy vehemently condemned as not the equal of their competitor; the list was endless.

As the highest law enforcement officer in America it was incumbent on Bobby to initiate the very investigation that would ineluctably lead to an inglorious end of Camelot almost before the myth was born. As older brother Joe had pointed out, it would "bring a stain on the Kennedy family which could never be erased."

From that moment forward, the stricken younger brother of the President faced a Shakespearean-like dilemma: To investigate -- or not to investigate -- that was the question.

At that same time J. Edgar Hoover was on the phone telling the new President about a confounding problem in Mexico City. Photos taken of "Oswald" entering and leaving the Russian Embassy, plus tape recordings of his telephone calls from the Cuban Embassy were received by Agents in Dallas a few hours earlier. The photos bore no resemblance to the accused assassin and the voice on the tape recordings was not the voice of Lee Harvey Oswald.

"It appears", the famed G-man said, "there was an impostor operating down there." This was disturbing. The entire premise for federal jurisdiction in the case was based on Oswald's activities in Mexico City creating National Security issues. "Is anyone outside the bureau aware of this?" Johnson asked. "No." "Good. Stamp that information "TOP SECRET" and keep investigating. I'll decide what's National Security and what isn't."

"Edgar" promised to press on with the full force of the Bureau's assets and capabilities. Two hours later he and constant companion, Clyde Tolson, went to Pimlico Racetrack where they spent the entire day.

DALLAS

Lee Oswald slumped in a chair by the corner of Captain Fritz's desk. Inside the smoke drenched interior was a collection of officials from the SECRET SERVICE, THE FBI, THE TEXAS RANGERS, TWO DALLAS DETECTIVES AND CAPTAIN FRITZ, ten, all told. But there was no police stenographer and no tape recording device. Captain Fritz made occasional notes. When he testified before the Warren Commission Fritz was asked why no stenographer was present? "The room," he said, was too small to include a stenographer." D.A. Jim Garrison later quipped: "It was either a very small room or a very large stenographer."

THE WHITE HOUSE - EAST ROOM

At ten a.m. a funeral Mass was said in front of a group including relatives and friends of the slain President. During the reception that followed, Bobby was distant, preferring to stand in the corner while the rest of them put their best face on --except for Joe, Sr. who struggled in silence, because he was unable to recognize Jackie's family and very few of Jack's friends. The stroke that robbed him of speech had not diminished his other faculties. For Bobby, being there was agony. He wanted it to end so he could be alone. Even gentle entreaties from Ethel couldn't bring him out of a deep abyss of pain.

DALLAS

Since announcing that Oswald would be moved to the county jail on Sunday, Chief Curry was bombarded by the media to specify a time for this event. Moving Oswald was a procedural matter. After being "filed on" all suspects were moved to the county jail.

At headquarters, officer Buddy Walther was waiting to be relieved so he could go home and a grab an hour's sleep. The phones rang relentlessly with callers from every part of the globe. Most of them wanted to talk with Captain Fritz or Chief Curry. A few even asked to speak with Oswald. "Please" one of them persisted, "I just want to ask him if his wife has a sister."

The next call was one Walther would remember for the rest of his life. The caller, (a man) asked: "What time are they going to transfer Oswald?" "Last I heard the Chief said eleven tomorrow mornin'." "Well, if you do, we're going to kill him." With that, the caller hung up. Somewhere in the recesses of Walther's memory he was sure he knew the caller's voice but couldn't place it with a name or a face. Sunday night the policeman suddenly recalled --the voice belonged to Jack Ruby.

Ruby put the receiver down and stared out the window of his shabby Oak Cliff apartment. He hoped his warning to headquarters might delay the inevitable. Having exhausted all possibility of getting a Dallas policeman to shoot Oswald, the besieged former errand boy for Al Capone and wannabe gangster now accepted having drawn the short straw. Accomplishing the hit would have to be done alone. Over the years he'd heard stories of what Sam's goons Lenny Patrick and Dave Yaras did to those who failed. The site of choice was a meat packing plant on the south side of Chicago. Victims were strung up on meat hooks next to cattle, their hands and feet were cut off, after which they were castrated and left to bleed to death.

Ruby began orchestrating how to carry out the hit on Oswald in a manner which would provide him an excuse for having done so -- the type of excuse which might keep him out of the electric chair.

At the Western Union office, located a block from Dallas Police Headquarters, Ruby executed the first part of his plan to off Oswald. He gave the clerk twenty-five dollars and seventy cents for a money order destined for Karen Carlin, one of his strippers who couldn't pay her rent.

On the fifth floor of the DPD, Captain Fritz and his detectives were almost ready to take their prisoner down to the basement where an armored car waited to transport him to the county jail. The accused changed into a fresh pair of pants and a black wool sweater and was being manacled to Detectives Jim Leavelle and L.C. Graves, his escorts for the trip.

Officer Vaughn was guarding the auto entrance to the basement checking credentials of those who wanted to view the transfer. Although Ruby would later claim having walked right past Vaughn into the basement, he in fact gained entrance from an open door to the police building on the opposite side of the auto entrance. This he accomplished with the aide of a Dallas policeman who has never been reliably identified.

There was no other way for Ruby to get inside and go down a flight of stairs to the basement unless he took the elevator.

DPD

As the elevator descended, officer Lavelle told Oswald: "If someone shoots you I hope he's as good as shot as you are." Oswald pooh-poohed this saying: "Nobody's going to shoot me." At the basement Captain Fritz went in front of the others, decked out as usual in a spotless pearl grey Stetson. Sixty-five armed detective's were on hand to protect the prisoner.

A bank of television lights blinded those entering the basement where the armored car waited in the background. Broadcasters spoke into their mikes alerting viewers to Oswald's presence.

Near the front of the crowd, shielded by several others, Jack Ruby awaited his prey. Dressed entirely in brown, nobody noticed him or the nickel plated revolver clutched near his thigh. Captain Fritz moved beyond the lights and lingered in a shadowed area, watching as the trio of Lavelle, Graves and Oswald moved into the brightest part of the glare.

Jack Ruby brushed past onlookers, brought his gun belt high, pushed it into Oswald's stomach and pulled the trigger. The report echoed off the walls of the basement like a clap of thunder. Oswald scrunched over into a fetal position, groaned and slumped to the floor. "Oswald's been shot," NBC announcer Tom Pettit shouted. A few of the astounded assemblage of policemen jumped forward, grabbed Oswald's assailant and wrestled him to the ground. "Wait a minute guys," Ruby shouted, "you know me -- I'm Jack Ruby!"

Rushed to Parkland Hospital, Oswald died on an operating table an hour later. The cops had lost the most important prisoner in history to a fourth string hood who just walked out of a crowd and killed him with a single shot. It *was not the Dallas Police Department's finest hour.* They quickly became the laughing stock of every big city homicide bureau in America.

RFK learned about Oswald's demise from a radio broadcast on his way back to the White House. This only added to his conviction (and the public's) that the bizarre happenings since the shots rang out in Dealey Plaza went far beyond appearances. Conspiracy was already on everyone's mind. Ruby offing LHO in such a blatant way only fueled public suspicions.

Bobby knew he had to act quickly to cut off the myriad of plans in the works to investigate his brother's murder. The circumstances of Oswald's demise would greatly accelerate the process. He had already been thinking of using a citizen's commission to augment the FBI'S REPORT and hopefully supplant investigations by both houses of Congress and the State of Texas' proposed "Board of Inquiry." Such probes offered enormous opportunities for publicity which many politicos would find irresistible. A few minutes before the grand reception, following the funeral Bobby telephoned Deputy Attorney General Nicholas Katzenbach.

"Nick," he began, "draft a memo to Johnson's guy, Moyers, for *your signature* -- that points out the advisability of appointing a citizens commission to investigate the assassination. The way Oswald was taken out is sure to exacerbate speculation about conspiracy. It's incumbent on Johnson to cut that off right away." "But," Katzenbach interjected, "shouldn't we be taking the lead in the investigation?" To this obvious inquiry Bobby gave a one word reply: "No. When you've got the draft, call and read it to me." Then he hung up. Katzenbach ascribed Bobby's brevity to his continuing angst over Jack's death.

MONDAY

Every station in America broadcast the President's funeral. Images of the rider less horse leading the flag draped coffin to the mournful sound of The Black Watch's bag pipes, John-John saluting his father as the caisson rolled past him, head's of state walking behind the Kennedy's, marching stoically along Pennsylvania Avenue. It *was* television's finest hour.

ARLINGTON CEMETERY

As the coffin was being lowered into the ground and bugler, Army Sergeant Keith Clark commenced taps, Bobby Kennedy was barely ambulatory. This was truly the end of physical closeness with his brother. Jackie and the others didn't try and hide their tears. Nearing the end of the call, Sergeant Clark mangled one of notes creating a high pitched discordant sound before pressing on to its conclusion. All that was left was watching the perfectly coordinated rapid folding of the flag, followed by its presentation to Jackie. It was more than many could bear, especially Bobby who had just seen a large portion of his life disappear into the ground.

An eternal flame at the head of the grave was impressive, but it did not fill the terrible void left by the crushing finality of President Kennedy's departure.

CHAPTER 21

At the Justice Department, Nick Katzenbach set about drafting the requisite memo. On a piece of yellow foolscap he wrote:

"With Oswald dead, there can be no trial. Something has to be put out to convince the public that Oswald, and Oswald alone, killed the President. The public must be satisfied that Oswald was the assassin; that he did not have confederates who are still at large; and that the evidence was such that he would have been convicted at trial."

The memo went on to suggest the advisability of the President appointing a citizen's commission for a thorough investigation which should identify all the facts and all of the reasons for their conclusions.

Satisfied, Katzenbach phoned RFK and read him the memo. "Fine," Bobby told his Deputy. "Send it to Moyers right away."

Moyers thought it an excellent solution to the President's dilemma with the Congress and the State Of Texas and sent it to him with a strong endorsement.

Notwithstanding the fact that the memo was signed by Katzenbach, Johnson knew who motivated it. As a Washington insider he was well aware of his predecessor's propensity for dalliances with females. Bobby certainly had that in mind. It didn't matter. From a practical political standpoint a "Blue Ribbon Commission" with a limited number of members was far more desirable than putting the case in the hands of politicians, some of whom were bound to use an investigation as an opportunity for self aggrandizement.

The new leader of the free world immediately set about getting reactions to the idea of a citizen's commission from a variety of former Congressional colleagues.

These included: House Speaker John McCormack, Senate Majority Leader Mike Mansfield, Illinois Senator Everett Dirksen, Dean Rusk, House Leader Carl Albert, Gerald Ford and many others. The reactions were uniformly favorable. Both House and Senate leader's agreed not to pursue separate inquiries. To Texas Attorney General Waggoner Carr, Johnson merely *told* his fellow Texan this was what they were going to do. Then he made an appointment for RFK to come in and discuss the makeup of the commission.

So Bobby's gambit worked.

On November 27th he met with Johnson in the Oval Office. Lyndon showed him a roster that included Chief Justice Earl Warren to head the group, plus the following Commissioners: Senators John Sherman Cooper, Richard Russell, James Eastland, Congressmen Hale Boggs and Gerald Ford, Attorney and close friend, Abe Fortas.

Bobby insisted two of them be replaced by choices of his own --Allen Dulles and John J. McCloy. RFK knew Dulles would never reveal the CIA plots with the Mafia to kill Castro, or the plan for a second invasion of Cuba all of which the Agency he formerly headed was deeply involved. He could also be counted on to influence other Agency people who might be called to testify.

As for McCloy, Bobby pointed out that having an international lawyer, businessman and former High Commissioner of Berlin in the mix would make the commission more balanced than having so many Southern politicians. Their animus toward his brother's stand on civil rights was already a problem. Bobby's father had a cordial relationship with McCloy for many years and would look out for Jack's interest. Dulles was fine with Johnson.

He had heard McCloy's name but still wasn't sure who he was. Like the master politician he was the new President acceded to Bobby's wishes.

"It's important," RFK pointed out, "that Warren makes sure not to pursue the Cuba angle." The President put his pen down, leaned back and looked at Bobby over the top of his steel rimmed glasses. "McCone," Johnson said "told me his people believe Castro was behind it." The younger man knew he had to choose his words very carefully. Johnson still didn't know about "Second Naval Guerrilla" and now was not the time to tell him. "McCone told me the same thing a couple hours after my brother died. Can you imagine how the country would react if it turned out to be true?" "Disastrous," Lyndon replied. "They'd demand retaliation." "Yes, and you don't want to be put in that position."

"Who do you think did it," Johnson asked. "I don't know -- Organized Crime, Cuban exiles -- maybe some people at CIA. Finding out who did it won't bring my brother back."

So the deal was struck, and Bobby left.

Johnson phoned Earl Warren and gave him his marching orders. The Chief Justice tried to beg off. "You have to do it, Earl. A war over Cuba could cost the lives of forty million people in an hour. That's more than anyone can pay. You'll be serving your country's highest interest to make sure the public is convinced that Oswald did it."

On November 29th the press published the names of President Johnson's **"Blue Ribbon Commission."** It soon became known as *"THE WARREN COMMISSION."*

Cuban involvement was not pursued; neither was organized crime. Evidence pointing to Jack Ruby's involvement with gangsters was stamped "TOP SECRET" and withheld from the Final Report which was presented to the President on September

24th 1964. Cuba and The Soviet Union, it
declared, were not involved. Although The Commission
was unable to produce a convincing motive that drove
him to murder JFK, Lee Harvey Oswald they concluded,
acted alone.

POST MORTEM

I am not a moralist. But I was not the recipient of
thirty four million, two hundred twenty thousand,
nine hundred and eighty four votes from citizen's
who placed their confidence in John F. Kennedy, to
respect and protect the dignity of the highest
office in the land. "Faithfully executing the
law(s)" does not include suborning murder.

Kennedy's recklessness earned this appraisal from
one of his closest advisors:

"He was a brilliant man -- but he wasn't a good
man."

The devastation wrought on our government's
credibility by those responsible for covering up
his murder is incalculable.

Its deception has been the catalyst for the
continuing erosion of the people's confidence in
their government and the country's mainstream
media. Their handling of Kennedy's assassination
has caused deep mistrust in just about everything
the government tells them.

The justification for the cover-up can still be
traced to those two magic words:

NATIONAL SECURITY.

An old quote, attributed to several people down
through the years, goes: "When fascism comes to
America it will arrive in the guise of National
Security."

The "magic" of National Security has metamorphosed into more and more inventive forms of deception. It has been expanded to excuse the government for every imaginable abuse of power.

What is the legacy of their lies and deceit?

A government that can't trust the people is a government that can't be trusted.

NOTES:

Fearing that Sylvia Duran *might describe* "*the blonde, green-eyed Oswald*" who came to the consulate several times, David Phillips had the Mexican Secret Police arrest and hold her incommunicado. She in fact gave them "the blonde, green-eyed" description of "Oswald." However, when the they submitted their report of her interrogation, Duran's description of the visa applicant's appearance had been excised.

President Kennedy was fond of this quote from Oliver Cromwell:

"You are obliged to tell our story in a truthful way.

Paint us with all our blemishes and warts, all those things about us which may not be so immediately attractive."

In writing this book, *I took Cromwell's advice.*

While there were many attractive things about John Kennedy, the unattractive ones were devastating.

His lack of respect for the sanctity of his office was outrageous and unforgivable. His recklessness was the catalyst for emboldening his enemies to murder him. They knew they would be safe from prosecution because the government -- especially the Attorney General and President Johnson could be relied upon to head off any meaningful investigation.

Texas Attorney General Waggoner Carr came to Washington with evidence of Oswald's employment as an informant for the FBI. This data included his informant number and his salary, ($200 per month). Johnson sent Carr home and Hoover assured the Warren Commission the information was not true. Later, Commissioner Hale Boggs declared: "Hoover lied his eyes out to us."

In Dallas, SA James Hosty showed SAC Gordon Shanklin the threatening note Oswald left with the receptionist sixteen days before Kennedy's arrival. After conferring with Director Hoover, Shanklin gave the note back to Hosty and told him: "I don't ever want to see this again." Hosty promptly flushed it down the toilet, a fact he later admitted to a congressional subcommittee headed by California Congressman, Don Edwards.

On a tape recording of Johnson talking on the telephone with Commission member Richard Russell, President Johnson and Russell concluded that JFK and Governor Connally couldn't have been hit by the same bullet, thus undermining the Commission's claim of a lone gunman.

During a 1970 interview with CBS'S Walter Cronkite, Johnson declared:

"Their might have been international connections. This Oswald was quite a mysterious fellow and he did have the connections that bore examination."

That same year he told ABC newsman, Howard K.

Smith: "Kennedy was out to get Castro, but Castro got him (first)."

The new President ordered an end to "this Murder Incorporated in the Caribbean" and called a halt to raids against Cuba. Transcripts of testimony in front of THE SENTATE RULES COMMITTEE was sequestered for fifty years. Thus we will not learn THE RULES COMMITTEE'S evidence detailing Johnson's misdeeds as a Senator, until 2014.

The two people who benefited most from JFK'S demise were *Lyndon Johnson and Fidel Castro.*

Ironically, the Cuban exiles who hated Kennedy and applauded his murder were the biggest losers. After November 22nd, all efforts to depose Fidel Castro ceased. In poor health now he remains the longest reigning head of state in modern history.

CONFESSIONS:

GANGSTERS:

CARLOS MARCELLO

While serving a prison sentence for bribery in the 1980's, Marcello bragged to various inmates: "I had Kennedy killed."

His conviction was overturned in 1989 and he was released. Marcello died in 1992.

SANTOS TRAFFICANTE

In 1989 when he lay dying, Trafficante summoned his attorney, Frank Ragano to his bedside. Ragano claims Santos told him a mistake had been made which he blamed on Marcello: *"Carlos fucked up. We shouldn't have killed Giovanni (John). We should have killed Bobby."*

SAM GIANCANA

In his book, 'DOUBLE CROSS', Giancana's
son, Chuck, claimed his father told him:

"The hit in Dallas was just like any other
operation we'd worked on in the past. We'd
overthrown other governments in other
countries plenty of times before. This time
we did it in our own backyard."

On the night of June 19th 1975, barely twenty four
hours before he was scheduled to testify in front
of the Senate Intelligence Committee, Giancana was
shot to death in the basement of his Chicago home.

JOHNNIE ROSELLI

Interviewed by The Senate Intelligence Committee in
1975, Roselli claimed a CIA hit team sent to Cuba
to murder Fidel Castro was caught, tortured,
subsequently "turned" and sent back to the U.S.
where they were used to kill President Kennedy.

The following year, The Committee decided to
recall Roselli. They were too late. In September
his body was found hacked to pieces and stuffed
in a 55 gallon drum which surfaced in Miami's
Dumfounding Bay.

Columnist Jack Anderson reported on an interview he
had with Roselli shortly before his demise.

He claimed Roselli, told him:

When Oswald was picked up, the underworld
conspirators feared he would crack and disclose
information that might lead to them. This almost
certainly would have brought a massive
U.S. crackdown on the Mafia. So Jack Ruby was
ordered to eliminate Oswald. (In an earlier
statement, Roselli divulged: "Ruby was one of our

    boys.")

JACK RUBY

After his conviction for murdering Oswald the
Texas Supreme Court overturned Ruby's
conviction.
The lower court was ordered to try him again.
During a short recess while the trial court
was setting the new date, Ruby relaxed in the
gallery and gave reporters a chance to
interview him.

One of them caught this impromptu *on camera
confession:*

*"The only thing I can say is . . . everything
pertaining to what's happened never came to the
surface. The world will never know the true facts
of what occurred . . . my motive, in other words. I
am the only person in the background to know the
truth pertaining to everything related to my
circumstances.*

The truth, he said, would never come out.
*"Because unfortunately, these people, who have so
much to gain and have such an ulterior motive to
put me in the position I'm in, will never let the
true facts come above board to the world.'*

"Do you mean people in high places, Jack," the
reporter asked"

"Yes," Ruby replied. *"People in high places."*

CONFESSIONS BY CIA OFFICERS

DAVID SANCHEZ MORALES ("The Big Indian")

Near the end of the HSCA'S investigation, one of
their fifteen committee investigators, Gaeton
Fonzi, was curious about a reference in Phillips'

autobiography to a large native American whom he referred to as "El Indio". The committee tried without success to locate David Sanchez Morales whom Fonzi suspected might be "El Indio." They had no idea who he was or what he did. Neither, *so they claimed*, did the CIA.

Through a series of complex circumstances the author and an associate were able to locate Morales' lifelong friend, a restaurateur in Phoenix, Arizona named Ruben Carbajal.

Carbajal, and Phoenix attorney, Robert Walton, who represented both Carbajal and Morales, related the following:

In the spring of 1973, in Walton's hotel room at the Dupont Plaza Hotel, Washington D.C., Carbajal, Walton and Morales, were drinking pretty heavily. When Morales learned Walton belonged to an organization at Harvard that was active in supporting JFK, Morales became enraged.

He flew off the bed and railed at Walton for supporting a man who had been responsible for the death of many of Morales' friend's during the Bay Of Pigs. As his rage subsided, Morales said:

"We took care of that sonofabitch." According to Walton, there could be no mistaking what Morales meant. ***He was taking credit for participation in the murder of President Kennedy.***

Morales died of a heart attack in May 1978 at a time when the House Assassinations Committee was trying to locate him. Carbajal is of the opinion that his best friend was killed by his former employers, the CIA.

(A more detailed account of this incident is memorialized in Chapter's forty-two and forty-three of *Gaeton Fonzi's excellent book, THE LAST*

INVESTIGATION. THUNDER'S MOUTH PRESS - 1993)

DAVID ATLEE PHILLIPS

Shortly before he died of lung cancer in July 1988, Phillips told former HSCA investigator, Kevin Walsh:

"My final take on the assassination is there had been a conspiracy, likely including American Intelligence Officers."
Coming from the CIA'S former Chief of Western Hemisphere this statement has profound significance.

CONFESSIONS BY Anti-Castro CUBANS: TONY CUESTA, (HERMINIO DIAZ GARCIA AND ELADIO DEL VALLEE)

In December 1995 at a conference of assassination investigator's held in Nassau, **former head of Cuban Intelligence, General Fabian Escalante** revealed that after his release from a Cuban prison in 1978, **Tony Cuesta** asked to see the General before he left Cuba to rejoin his family in Florida.

He told Escalante he had taken part in the Kennedy assassination. ***Cuesta named two other Cubans who were actual shooters in Dealey Plaza, Herminio Diaz Garcia and Eladio del Vallee.*** As recently as March, 2007, General Escalante personally confirmed Cuesta's admission to the author.

Diaz was killed in September 1966 during a raid in Cuba; del Vallee was hacked to death in his car at a Miami shopping center barely two hours after David Ferrie allegedly took his own life in New Orleans.

Fearing his family would be harmed, Cuesta asked Escalante not to reveal fingering Diaz and del Vallee while he was still alive. Cuesta died in 1993.

ACKNOWLEDGMENTS:

Information for this novel came from a variety of sources, including:

Chicago Independent - November 1975. "the plot to kill JFK in Chicago Nov.2, 1963". By EDWIN BLACK

Tampa Tribune - Various articles written on November 18th 1963, including reports on Kennedy's motorcades during his visits to McDill Air Force Base, Al Lopez Field, and The International Hotel. Also, "Threats On Kennedy Made Here" 11/23/63

"Ultimate Sacrifice" - Lamar Waldron and Thom Hartmann. Additional details regarding JFK's trip to Chicago November 2, 1963, and Tampa, November 18th, 1963.

"Survivor's Guilt", Vince Palamara. Virtually all references to Secret Service's WHD and PRS, including, but not limited to JFK'S visits to Chicago, Tampa and Dallas were derived from Palamara's book.

"Someone Would Have Talked" - Larry Hancock. General references.

"Bloody Treason" - Noel Twyman. General references.

"JFK: THE CUBA FILES" - Gen. Fabian Escalante (Former Head of Cuban Intelligence.) Data about the shooters in Dealey Plaza and identities of two men who spoke with Silvia Odio in Oswald's presence.

"The Lost Prince" - Hank Searls. Details about Joe Jr.'s death and relationship with Jack, Bobby and their father.

"Nemesis" – Peter Evans. Data, relating to an affair between Jackie Kennedy and Rozwell Gilpatrick.

"Not In Your Lifetime" – Anthony Summers. General references.

Houston Chronicle – Various articles, regarding JFK'S visits to Houston, November 21st 1963, and Dallas, November 22nd 1963.

Dallas Morning News – "Wanted For Treason" advertisement November 22nd, 1963, plus other articles in that same edition.

John F. Kennedy Memorial Library – President Kennedy's Appointment's calendar for November 1963, plus General Godfrey McHugh's itinerary for the trip to Texas.

The author wishes to thank Larry Hancock, Vince Palamara, Edwin Black, Gaeton Fonzi, Noel Twyman, and Mary K. Weber for their support in supplying important data required to substantiate various portions of this book.

Special thanks to author Peter Evans for his expertise and guidance which contributed significantly to the outcome.

Finally, thanks to my son, screenwriter Matt Dorff for his valuable input.

SELECTED BIBLIOGRAPHY

"Bloody Treason", Noel Twyman. Laurel Publishing 1997.

"The Death Of A President", William Manchester. Harper & Row 1967

"The Day Kennedy Was Shot", Jim Bishop. Bantam Books 1968

"Double Cross", Sam and Chuck Giancana. Warner Books 1992

"Goddess: The Secret Lives Of Marilyn Monroe", Anthony Summers. Macmillan Publishing Company1986

"Grace & Power", Sally Bidell Smith. Random House 2004

Final Report: The Assassination Records Review Board, September 30, 1998. (U.S. Government Printing Office)

Final Report of the House Select Committee On Assassinations, Feb. 1979. (U.S. Government Printing Office

"Robert Kennedy In His Own Words, The Unpublished Recollections Of The Kennedy Years". Bantam 1988

"The Last Investigation", Gaeton Fonzi. Thunder's Mouth Press 1993.

"Live By The Sword", Gus Russo. Bancroft Press 1998

"Mafia Kingfish", John H. Davis. Signet Books 1989

"Master Of The Senate", Robert A. Caro. Alfred A. Knopf 2002

"Nemesis", Peter Evans. Harper Collins 2004

"Not In Your Lifetime", Anthony Summers. Marlowe & Company, New York 1998

"Official and Confidential", Anthony Summers. Putnam 1993

"Survivor's Guilt", Vince Palamara. (Self Published)

"Someone Would Have Talked", Larry Hancock.(JFK LANCER Productions and Publications, Inc. South Lake, Texas)

"Texas In The Morning", Madeleine D. Brown, Diamondback Pub. 1997

"Ultimate Sacrifice", Lamar Waldron & Thom Hartmann. Carroll & Graf 2005

"With Malice", Dale K. Myers. Oak Cliff Press 1998

THE GIRLFRIENDS

Marilyn Monroe

Angie   Dickinson

Judith Campbell Exner

Ellen Rometsch   Mary Pinchot Meyer

THE CONSPIRATORS

CIA OFFICERS

David Sanchez-Morales   William King Harvey   David Atlee Phillips

ANTI-CASTRO CUBANS

Sylvia Odio

Tony Cuesta

Eladio del Valle

Herminio Diaz Garcia

THE MOB

Johnny Roselli

Carlos Marcello

Santo Trafficante, Jr.

Sam Giancana

CUBANS

Fidel Castro

Raul Castro

Sylvia Duran

Miguel
Casas
Saez

NO known
Pictures

ISBN 978-1-4243-3827-6

About the Author:

As a child Dorff worked at Republic Pictures as an extra and bit player.
At fifteen he became one of the original members of Hollywood's
"Player's Ring Theater".
Following a season of summer stock in McLean, Virginia the actor was
drafted. Dorff completed sixteen months as an infantryman in Korea
and was honorably discharged as a Sergeant in January 1955.
A few months later he was hired as a Story Analyst and assistant to
Producer George Englund at Pennebaker, Inc., **Marlon Brando's**
independent film company, headquartered at Paramount Studios.
Three and a half years later he left the industry for an entirely new
career selling international makes of heavy duty metal working
machinery.
In 1960 he joined the Hollywood Hills Democratic Club and did
precinct work for candidate John F. Kennedy.
Dorff began researching the JFK assassination in 1974. He has hosted
seminars on that topic, one of which, held in San Francisco, was
attended by six former staff investigators for **The House Select
Committee on Assassinations**.
Later he was invited to many similar events in Dallas as a
panelist/moderator and wrote speeches for the legendary JFK
researcher, *Mary Elizabeth Ferrell*.
He hosted **"CONTROVERSY",** a Century Cable television show,
which was shown in Los Angeles, New York, Chicago, San Francisco,
Austin and Miami. Guests included authors Anthony Summers, John
Davis, David Lifton, CIA Agent John Stockwell, etc.
Dorff founded **"The Dorff Report"** an information letter centered on
the JFK investigation and other controversial topics.
He has two children by his first wife, actress and casting director
Beverly Long. Matt Dorff is a highly successful screenwriter. His
sister, Holly has worked as an actress since she was two and a half and
teaches "looping" classes in San Francisco.
This is the author's first novel.